MURDER AT THE ABA

"Again demonstrates the versatility of that master, Isaac Asimov . . . very funny . . . Only a master storyteller would be able to combine murder with comedy . . . The dialogue is good, the clues tantalizing, and the ending superb."

The Jackson Sun

"An A-1 puzzle, one that will fool the sharpest armchair detective."

Newport News Daily Press

"ASIMOV IS ALWAYS GREAT FUN!"

Seattle Post-Intelligencer

Also by Isaac Asimov
Published by Fawcett Books:

BANQUETS OF THE BLACK WIDOWERS
THE BEST MYSTERIES OF ISAAC ASIMOV
CASEBOOK OF THE BLACK WIDOWERS
MORE TALES OF THE BLACK WIDOWERS
TALES OF THE BLACK WIDOWERS
THE UNION CLUB MYSTERIES
A WHIFF OF DEATH

MURDER
AT THE ABA

Isaac Asimov

FAWCETT CREST • NEW YORK

NOTE: Despite my way of writing this book, all of the speaking characters in it (except myself, of course) are fictitious, and any resemblance to actual persons living or dead is purely coincidental, and can only exist despite my best efforts to prevent it. In this connection, please see the note at the end of the book, but only after you've read the book.

TO HARLAN ELLISON,
whose brightness of personality is
exceeded only by his height of talent

Cast of Characters
(in order of appearance)

Darius Just writer and narrator

Martin Walters historian; friend of Darius

Henrietta Corvass in charge of the interview section of the American Booksellers Association (ABA)

Michael Strong hotel security guard

Thomas Valier of Prism Press; Darius' publisher

Giles Devore writer; ex-protege of Darius

Teresa Valier of Prism Press; wife of Thomas Valier

Roseann Bronstein bookseller; friend of Giles Devore

(unnamed) ticket seller at party

Isaac Asimov prolific writer and self-esteemed wit

Sarah Voskovek in charge of public relations for the hotel

Shirley Jennifer writer; good friend of Darius

Mary Ann Lipsky secretary of Teresa Valier

Harold Sayers bookseller from Bangor, Maine

Hilda cloakroom attendant

Anthony Marsogliani chief of security for the hotel

Herman Brown plainclothesman

Joseph Olsen policeman

(unnamed) art director for the hotel

Eunice Devore wife of Giles Devore

Gwyneth Jones woman working in the interview section of the ABA

Ginger receptionist for Sarah Voskovek

Gordon Hammer man working in the interview section of the ABA

Nellie Griswold woman working for Hercules Books

Dorothy another cloakroom attendant

(unnamed) would-be assassin

CONTENTS

Part One

SUNDAY

25 MAY 1975

Trace back the violent death of a friend and see how it happened.

It wouldn't have happened if A hadn't happened first, and that wouldn't have happened if B had not taken place before it. And so on, all the way back to the primordial mists of time.

In the particular case in which I was involved, however, we can limit the direct causes to a specific, limited series of events, all of which had to have happened for violent death to have its chance. If any one of them had not taken place, someone now dead would be alive; or if dead, at least not then, not that way, not murder.

And I was at the center of so many of those events. Unwittingly, of course, but there.

I trace it back to Sunday, May 25, 1975, which was the first day of the 75th annual convention of the American Booksellers Association (ABA) at a scattering of hotels in midtown, and to a woman whose turn it was to push her book at a press conference.

She was scheduled to face the members of the press at 4 P.M. and she had to decide what to wear. There, it seems to me as I try to reconstruct her motives in my own mind, she was faced with a dilemma. On the one hand, she was young and good-looking and had a body in which all parts fell smoothly into place, so that she had the natural desire to display said body to the world. On the other hand, she was a feminist, and the book she was pushing was feminist, and there was the possibility that to use the lure of the body to promote the book would be a non-feminist thing to do.

I don't know whether she hesitated at all; or if she did, how long. I don't know if she tried on different dresses or settled the matter by pure reason in her mind.

The point is that she ended with a white dress which, above the waistline, was made up of generous swatches of open network, and under it she had above the waistline nothing at all but her own gorgeous self. When she remained in repose, her breasts remained safely behind the small, strategically placed opaque sections. When she raised an arm, as she might, the dress hiked up on that side and one nipple went peek-a-boo.

All this, it happens, I pieced together later. I was not there when it happened; I had nothing directly to do with it. That, too, was a link in the chain of events.

When our feminist friend decided to peek-a-boo at the world, she put down the first flagstone of what became a pathway to death. The fact that I was not in the interview room at the time was another flagstone.

Had she chosen to come down in a role of blushing modesty, none of it would have happened (perhaps), whether I was there or not. Had I been there, none of it would have happened (perhaps), even if she had come down in the nude.

But she wore what she wore, and I was not there, and it all came to pass.

And where was I that I was not there?

I was en route. I had left at 1:30 P.M., and I was aiming for the ABA Convention.

My editor felt it would be a good thing for me (a writer, but not particularly a superfluously successful writer) to show up and get a little publicity, and grin a little at the assembled booksellers. I had no objection to this. Everything about it would be deductible as a business expense and it would make an excellent excuse to stay away from the typewriter for a few days.

Originally, I had been aiming for Monday, the 26th, which was Memorial Day, and had decided to let the first day go by. A couple of months before I had agreed to give a morning talk, you see, at some temple on the 25th, at a site some hundred miles from the city. I saw no reason why I shouldn't let them feed me afterward (I have a long-standing love affair with lox and cream cheese on a toasted bagel, especially with a slice of Bermuda onion pushed in when no one is looking) and make a day of it. Time for the convention the next day.

But then a historian friend of mine, Martin Walters, called me a week before and asked me if I could help out in a little bit of public relations at the ABA Convention. He was under the impression that I was a staunch supporter of learned writings and had the even more curious notion that my name meant something to the world of scholarship and could be used to good effect.

Both assumptions seemed to me to be in the highest degree wrong, but he was a friend and you help out friends, and besides it did not seem to me that I was required to tell him the truth—that my knowledge of history was spotty and that the world's knowledge of my attainments was even spottier.

I said, "When would you need me?"

"It's scheduled for four-twenty P.M. on Sunday," he said.

I did some rapid mental calculations, and decided I could eat my bagels and still make it.

"I'll be there," I said, adding cautiously, as I always do out of a spot of irrationality within my rational self, "barring acts of God."

But the act of God had already taken place. It was another flagstone in the path. In fact, since the request for my presence came a week before our feminist friend swirled before her hotel-room mirror and decided she looked too appetizing to be believed, my own statement "I'll be there" might be looked upon as the real beginning.

I gave my talk, explained politely that I would have to eat and run. I then ate, at 1:30 P.M., ran for my car, and drove to the city at a moderate clip, feeling no doubt that I would make it.

Nor did I have any cause to change my mind till I hit the Cross-North Highway. I don't suppose anyone could call a traffic jam on the Cross-North an act of God, however. The Almighty doesn't have to take any measures to insure it.

Yet I thought I had calculated it logically. It was the middle day of a three-day weekend. Everyone who had wanted to go somewhere had already gone. Everyone who

intended to come back had not yet left. I assumed I was
in the eye of the hurricane, so I was perfectly at ease.

The trouble is that there is no time of the day or year
when one or two cars don't manage to stall themselves on
the Cross-North. There must be a million motorists who,
when at a loss for any source of fun, decide to drive their
heaps onto the Cross-North and abandon them there.
Once the word streaks out (telepathically, I presume)
that the lanes on the Cross-North have narrowed, everyone north of the city funnels into them with wild cries of
delight.

That was the beginning of the fatal irritation that filled
me that day. I'm not exactly famous for my equanimity,
but there's no law that says I *have* to be irritated, unless
you want to say that there's a cosmic ukase that states
that the Cross-North would irritate anybody.

So I was irritated. I moved along at a slow crawl, seeing
a long triple line of cars ahead of me, all moving at a
slow crawl, like a heat wave with no relief in sight. I
annoyed myself by wondering why I hadn't taken the
Western Parkway instead, and every once in a while I
threw myself into an absolute fury by glancing at my
wristwatch.

But I made it! I made it!

I managed to get to my apartment, which is only a
trifle over a mile from the hotel I was heading for, park
the car, wash up a bit, change, grab a taxi, reach the hotel,
make my way to the fifth floor, locate the interview room,
and walk into it at exactly 4:20 P.M.

Exactly 4:20 P.M.

2   MARTIN WALTERS   4:20 P.M.

If I had arrived twenty minutes earlier, everything
would have been different, everything would have been
well—and twenty minutes was exactly how much time I
had lost on the Cross-North. The nameless idiot who had
stalled his car somewhere near the Oak Avenue exit was
therefore also a layer of flagstones.

And yet, to be truthful, I was pleased at having arrived at 4:20 on the dot. I was Phileas Fogg making it around the world and back to the club on the second agreed upon. I even breathed hard, as though I had been running, when, except for crossing the crowded lobby at a reasonably brisk walk, engines and motors of various kinds had done all the work.

I waited the usual fifteen seconds for someone to notice me, but nobody did. I wasn't too surprised. The room was a madhouse, with ABA employees trying to herd the reporters and the reporters clearly wondering, more or less out loud, how they were going to manage to put together any kind of wordage at all.

Besides which, although I have avoided saying so till now, I am exactly 158 centimeters tall. It sounds good, put that way, if you're not used to the metric system, but pass your hands over the figure and mutter the magic words "2.54 centimeters to the inch" and it becomes five feet two—plus the eyes of blue that go along with that height, and a fat lot of good that ever did me.

Unless people know me, they tend to look straight over me, so after fifteen seconds, I let them know I was there. I've got a good loud voice and no compunction whatever about using it.

So I said quite loudly and clearly, "I am Darius Just and I'm taking part in the Martin Walters press conference on the 'The Peace Negotiators.'"

It didn't make much impact, since most of the people continued talking as though it affected them not at all whether I was Darius Just, or just Darius, or simply zero —and that didn't exactly overwhelm me with gratitude.

I was about to repeat myself at a rather higher decibel rating when a woman walked up to me in an irritated fashion, as though I had interrupted her at important work (which, from her standpoint, I suppose, I had done), and said, "The Walters' press conference?"

I found out later that she was running the interview department for the ABA. Her name was Henrietta Corvass; she was just a little too plump for her clothes; and she had an annoying air of super-efficiency as though she had twenty fingers with which to pull strings.

"Got it first crack out of the box," I said.

"But *you* don't. It's just finishing."

I goggled at her for a moment and then a horrible suspicion crossed my mind. "What time is it?" I asked and glared at my watch.

"Four twenty-two," she said.

My watch was on the minute. "Well, then, four-twenty is the scheduled time—"

At that point, Martin walked out of the next room. There he was, full size (just over six feet), with his pleasant, grinning face, and with his pince-nez glasses of the kind you wouldn't expect to find outside a museum. Combine that with a tuft of white hair on his chin and a generous growth, equally white, on his upper lip, and he looked like a nineteenth-century literary figure.

He was a gentleman, by which I mean he was someone who never, under any circumstances, alludes to my height. You'd be surprised how few such individuals there are. Perhaps because of his constant preoccupation with the past, he also had a remarkable shyness in connection with the greater liberality of language permitted by modern mores. Or maybe that went along with his gentlemanliness.

For instance, I heard him quote the following limerick which had been constructed by a friend of mine named Asimov, who'll play his part in these events later. It went as follows:

> *There was a young couple from Florida*
> *Whose passion grew steadily torrider.*
> *They were planning to sin*
> *In a room in an inn.*
> *Who can wait? So they screwed in the corridor!*

When he quoted it, he blipped out the sixth word in the last line in a very embarrassed way. He actually said "blip" instead. And mind you, he was addressing an all-

male audience (would you believe a stag organization in
these libbish times?).

Then, too, he said to me once, with a look of good-
humored indignation, "The trouble is that people use
vulgarisms as general intensifiers, without any conception
of the meaning. Like the woman who stepped off the curb
on Park Avenue and said with deep annoyance, 'Oh, *shit!*
I stepped in some doggie poo-poo!' " But before he uttered
the exclamation, he lowered his voice to such a whisper
that I almost lost the point.

But now he was just grinning at me a little uneasily
and said, "Ah, Darius, it was good of you to show up.
You're a pal."

"I'm a patsy, you mean," I said furiously. "You live
so fiercely in the past you're incapable of giving me the
correct time, present tense. You said four-twenty and I
killed myself over crowded highways" (I didn't and they
weren't, but I was going to choose moderate phrases at
this point) "to get here and you never waited for me."

At this point, Martin might have broken the chain of
circumstances by groveling. I wouldn't have asked for
much. He might have beaten his head against the wall,
or licked my hand, or thrown himself on the ground and
asked me to jump up and down on him—any little thing
like that.

He didn't. He decided that what was needed here was
a good laugh. So he gave me the old Santa Claus routine,
put his arm around my shoulder, went ho-ho-ho, and
said, "Here's what happened, Darius. There's this woman
who was up before us, pushing some feminist book she
wrote, and she came down in a practically transparent
dress with practically nothing on underneath, if you know
what I mean."

I knew exactly what he meant. "So?"

"Well, her business manager said that was no way in
which to greet the members of the press."

"Why not?" I asked bitterly. "Are the newspapers re-
cruiting fourteen-year-old boys these days?"

"Well, no," said Martin genially. He was still seeing

the humor of it. "It's just that they'd fill their reports with descriptions of her dress instead of a description of her book. Anyway, he sent her up to change the dress. That meant the press would wander off unless something were thrown at it at once, so since I was there, they asked me to do my bit twenty minutes early. It couldn't be helped, Darius, but" (his voice dropped into confidentiality) "these conferences don't mean a thing anyway."

It wasn't a catastrophe, you understand; nothing terrible had happened to me. I had missed out on a twenty-minute session that meant nothing, did not concern any book of my own, and would have bored me.

But I had been made to look foolish in my own eyes, and I could not relieve my feelings by blaming anyone. A woman had chosen an unsuitable dress, a business manager had objected, an interview secretary had taken the logical action, a friend of mine had cooperated—and as for me, I had been held up by traffic for just the right amount to be made a fool of.

If I had scooted through the Cross-North without delay, I would have been at the hotel by 4 P.M. and would have moved in with Martin, taking full credit for being early. If I had been delayed forty minutes instead of twenty, I would have missed the press conference in any case and the matter of its having been moved up would have been irrelevant.

As it was, though, I was furious, with no satisfactory vent for my fury. No one had deliberately wronged me. I didn't have the heart to be angry with Martin, who had clearly been helpless, so I said, "Well, that's all right," and smiled unconvincingly.

I wandered off angry and sorry for myself—and was all the angrier because I knew in my heart that the hurt had been trivial and that I was being childish. I was wound up and all set to wait for someone against whom I could find some reasonable cause for resentment, and when that person was found, I would strike out, and strike hard.

And in taking that attitude, however justified it might have been in purely subhuman terms, I was laying down the biggest flagstone yet, and was beginning to set up my own responsibility for murder, one which might have been greater than that of anyone else—including that of the actual murderer.

3 MICHAEL STRONG 4:30 P.M.

The die was not yet cast, of course. I might have felt angry enough, or sufficiently humiliated, to go home and forget about the convention altogether.

But I didn't. The fact was that there was always the chance, as at any convention, that I might meet an interesting woman. I had taken no hotel room of my own, living, as I did, close enough to the convention site to commute, or even walk. Still, the woman in question might have one and that would be convenient. I'll admit I wasn't in the mood at the moment, with the press conference fiasco settled darkly about my shoulders, but I knew from a reasonable amount of past experience that I could get into the mood, if necessary, without breaking my back.

And besides, I did want to look over the exhibitors' booths, most of which (not quite all) were on the second floor of this particular hotel. According to the exhibitors' guide, there were 600 booths occupied by about 350 exhibitors—a record. They were catering to an expected convention attendance of 12,000, also a record.

To me, it seemed delightful that there were so many attendees, almost all booksellers. Despite the existence of libraries and book clubs, booksellers remain the backbone of the field, the indispensable bridge between publishers and authors who produce the books and the public who reads them.

And, of course, the publishers compete with each other in catching the eye of the booksellers, who are, in turn, eager to find out what items it might be profitable to stock.

It's hard sell for both publishers and authors. Every publisher crowds his display with garish exhibits of past successes and upcoming (it is to be hoped) sure-fire winners.

Not all the little promotion gimmicks are tasteful and authors are not above cooperating in some exercise of kitsch. There are the sweaters on which the name of some book is stitched and then worn by some young woman who is a full size too large for the garment. The name curves over hill and dale in consequence and the hope is that those observing the scenery will see the name of the book as well.

There was the fellow I had passed on my way to the exhibitors' section who had looked, at a distance, to be wearing chain mail. I had come closer out of astonished curiosity and it turned out that he was wearing a costume made out of the ring openers of beer cans. He was, of course, advertising a book, possibly his own, that was on the subject of the care and feeding of beer-can rings for fun and profit. I thought about it for a moment and then decided that anything that kept beer-can rings (and soft-drink-can rings) off the city streets and out of the greenery and onto the bodies of beer and soft-drink readers couldn't be all bad.

There was also a fellow who wandered stolidly about the convention, from the first day to the last, dressed in an angel's costume to publicize a book whose name I never quite caught. I saw him once or twice in passing but became conscious of him really when he made first page, second section, in the papers. They didn't mention the book he was advertising either.

Then, of course, there were the press conferences, in which I had played so inglorious a part, and the autographing sessions—where favored authors signed books for all comers. (The books, of course, were freebies, since you don't charge a bookseller—you *smile* at a bookseller.)

So why not look at some of the displays, if only to stare hungrily at some of those sure-fire winners I spoke of and wish uselessly that one's own book could be one of them.

My fifth book was coming out with Prism Press and I was hoping, quite earnestly, that it would do better than the first four and relieve me of some of the necessity of a too strictly hand-to-mouth existence.

To be sure, each of the four previous novels was a *succès d'estime*, which means each appealed to a level of critical acclaim that met the approval of a rarefied region inhabited by too few people to supply enough sales overall.

It's a comfort, I suppose, knowing that my books would outlive all those trashy best sellers ("trashy" is the standard adjective used by authors who don't make this list) and that I will be appreciated after my death, but I hate having that death hasten my starvation.

With all of this, or some of it anyway, more or less in my mind, I was about to walk into the exhibitors' room when I was brought up by the apologetic sound of a voice saying, "Do you have a badge, sir?"

My hand went automatically to my left breast and there was nothing there. My editor had sent me a badge in advance along with other paraphernalia and I knew I had brought them with me. I groped about in my various pockets and looked at the person who had spoken.

He was obviously a member of the hotel security staff. At least he was wearing a kind of uniform in tan; pants, shirt, and light jacket all the same color, plus a visored cap. The name of the hotel was over the left outer jacket pocket and the word "security" was under it. How much evidence does one need?

I judged him to be quite tall, about six feet, and his upper arms were well muscled. He had thin, light hair and I couldn't see his eyelashes or eyebrows at all, they were so light. It gave his eyes a pink-rimmed, unprotected look. His chin was receding and the dimple in its center seemed to be for the purpose of marking its place. His face was somewhat freckled and he looked anxious.

I said, "Here it is." I held the badge out to show it to him and then I pinned it carefully to my jacket.

"Darius Just," he said thoughtfully. "Aren't you a writer?"

I owned the soft impeachment. "Yes, I'm a writer."

"I know you," he said. "I know you." He snapped his fingers two or three times rapidly. "Wasn't Giles Devore your protégé?" He pronounced the last word with an English soft "g" and with a long "e" at the end.

"I helped him get started some years ago," I admitted.

"He's a great writer. You must be proud of him. I loved his books."

"He'll be glad to know that," I said, without enthusiasm of my own. It was clear that to this honest but stupid employee my claim to fame lay in the fact that Giles was my protégé and that was not exactly the way in which I hoped to go down in literary history.

I raised my arm partway to signify a fond farewell and said, "Well, take care."

But he said, "Hold on just a bit." He was scrabbling about in his pockets, then gave that up and snatched a sheet of paper from a nearby desk that was loaded with throwaways. "Could I have your autograph?"

I paused in resignation. I have not yet reached the point where I receive so many requests that I have any unbearable desire to refuse to sign. I said, "Sure."

I took the paper and was about to reach for my pen but he beat me to it. He pulled open the left side of his jacket and chose carefully among no less than three pens, taking out, I presumed, the most honorable. As he handed it to me, he said eagerly, "My name is Michael Strong. Middle initial P. Would you say, 'To Michael P. Strong'? Just 'Mike' would be all right, too."

I wrote "To Mike" since that would take less effort, and refrained from asking if the P stood for Patrick, but I bet myself ten to three that it did.

I said, trying not to be too damned sarcastic, "Shall I sign it, 'Sponsor of Giles Devore'?"

"No, just your name," he said innocently. "I'll get Mr. Devore's signature later on one of his books."

No scrap of paper for Giles; there are hierarchies to

these things. "Will it be all right if I go in now?"

"Sure! Thanks a lot, Mr. Just," and he waved me in cheerfully.

Guards are essential at exhibitions of this sort to prevent theft. Even with their presence at each door, books and other items are stolen in surprising numbers. Who knows how many undesirables, criminally unbadged, passed by unchallenged by Michael Strong, for instance, while he was busy making the best of the fact that I wasn't Giles Devore.

But it wasn't my place to worry about rip-offs, and the efficiency, or lack of it, of security. Or it didn't seem to be. I walked in. And what the guard had managed to do, with his bumbling, was to turn my smoldering undirected anger just a little in the direction of my old friend Giles Devore.

4   THOMAS VALIER   4:40 P.M.

I could have looked up the location of Prism Press in in the thickish exhibitors' guide I had picked up in the interview room, but I was in no mood to do that. Grimly, I set about tracking it down by guess, making bets with myself as to how poor a position the Valiers had managed to find—and therefore how poor a position there would be for the display of my books.

What I didn't realize at the time—and couldn't—was that a life was hanging in the balance and it all depended on the level of my irritation. Let anything happen that would lighten the load of peevishness and all might be well. Let Prism Press be in an advantageous position— let there be a good display of my new book, *Tomorrow Is for the Birds*—and the scythe might not swing.

Let there be even something milder, more general— such as just what was happening—the walk I was taking between rows and rows of placards and letterings in blocks and banks of color—and I would cool. Hard sell, blatancy, commercialism, or whatever—no matter how I disapproved of it all in principle—it was books they were selling, and I love books. I love the jackets and the titles and the samples and everything about them.

And as the tension slowly began to leak away, I got stepped on!

It could have been my fault; I wasn't exactly watching my steps. Besides, it was crowded, and bumping was a way of life.

It's what being stepped on means to me, though. It's that disbelieving look downward. It's that oh-there-you-are sort of bemusement.

I've been stepped on all my life and there are two ways in which you can react. One is to learn to slither and fade into the woodwork. You can cultivate unnoticeability and a trick of sliding your foot out from the downfall of another.

But that's not my way. It takes too long and it requires a spirit resilient enough to be crushed for long periods of time without losing shape. I don't have that. I have to choose the other way of fighting back, on the spot and at once.

Which means that I spent a good portion of my early years being beaten up, sometimes in anger, and often in amusement, which is worse. It doesn't happen so often now. I have had to invest precious time at the gym in order to learn how to counter superior brawn in a variety of ways. What it amounts to is that I had to learn to unstep the steppers by force.

And since word gets around, I am rarely stepped on, except by accident.

As in this case. And because the press conference fiasco still rankled, I welcomed a chance for physical action. I elbowed the stepper in the side with considerable force and said, "On your own feet, buster."

Whoever it was staggered to one side, managed to regain his balance, focused on me after some confusion, and said, "Sorry, kid," and moved on.

Kid!

I'm forty-two. Granted I look younger than that, but

no one would guess me at anything younger than thirty-two. *Kid!*

He was playing his automatic tribute to my height and the soothing effect of my surroundings was suddenly gone. I was frowning once more and annoyed at the world.

I eventually came across Prism Press. It was between a dictionary display and a booth belonging to a publishing house that put out devotional literature. Thomas Valier was there himself, nattily dressed, just above average height, with not a speck of gray in his black hair, which had its every wave neatly in place. He was the very picture of the talented and stalwart young executive. No charge for pictures.

At that, he was an honest-to-God executive. Prism Press is privately owned and Tom Valier and his wife are the private owners. That has its advantage. Prism Press is small enough so that you can speak to the head man—Tom in this case—and know that he *is* the head man and that he knows every corner of the house business. With Prism Press you never find yourself dealing with helpless editors bound by the faceless decisions of a board meeting or of a decision from distant Olympus.

And that's not all good either. In the large firms, when you *do* attract the beneficent attention of Olympus, there is money and power to play with. Tom of Prism Press could give you all the personal attention you need, and from his favorable decisions there was no chance of adverse appeal—but the financial push behind his personal attention was sharply limited.

Still he was amiable enough and I liked him—but not now. In fact, at this moment, I disliked him intensely, for there were no advance copies of *Tomorrow Is for the Birds* on display, only a small placard announcing it was forthcoming. Not so Giles's new book, *Evergone*. There it was, a nice pile of about twenty—*Evergone* by Giles Devore. No doubt they would be handed out to strategically placed booksellers.

I said abruptly, "How's it doing, Tom?"

"Darius!" Tom saw me at the last minute. It's a way

people have. It's as though it takes them time to bother with anything not at eye level. "Fine. Fine. Lots of inquiries about *Evergone*."

He didn't look happy. In fact, he looked strained, but I wasn't worried about that. I wasn't exactly happy myself. I said, "What in hell do I care about *Evergone*? How's *my* book doing?"

I could swear that Tom had to think before he remembered having a new book of mine on his list. "It's hard to say," he ventured at last, "without actual copies to show around. We'll have those in time for the American Library Association Convention. That's where your sales are, anyway."

"That's where they'll stay, I guess. Wasn't my manuscript in your hands before Giles's was?"

"Yes, but remember, there was some question about revising the—"

"I remember, I remember," and I waved him quiet. I didn't want to go through it again.

5 GILES DEVORE (in retrospect) 4:45 P.M.

How the devil had Giles Devore done it? I didn't understand it even when I was helping to make it possible. I don't understand it now. What he writes is *not* well written; it is clumsily constructed. Yet it has a kind of rough-hewn vigor about it that seizes you at once and won't let you put down anything he writes. You keep meaning to, but only after turning one more page, and then one more page, and then one more—

I met him in 1967, when he was twenty-one. I was thirty-four, with two books under my belt (and very little else). Still, that meant I was an established author, if not a successful one, so young Giles felt it made sense to come to me with a manuscript.

Like all authors I know, I suffer from the arrival of unsolicited manuscripts and from the eagerness of budding practitioners to get those one or two hints ("Start all sentences with a capital letter and place a space after every comma") that will suffice to convert their fledgling works into absolute masterpieces.

Generally, I return such manuscripts unread, but Giles was too innocent to send me one in the mail. He arrived in person, without as much as phoning to make an appointment first. He told me, when I asked, that if I had not been in, he would have called again, and then again, until I *was* in. This was a level of unsophistication which wrung out of me a kind of shamefaced pity.

I daresay I could have knifed the literary throat of the young man without remorse if I hadn't had to see it so trustingly exposed to the knife.

He was six feet three inches tall, appropriately wide, but in those days he was very thin. (He has filled out considerably since then.) He walked with an apologetic stoop as though he were sorry he was six feet three inches tall. He was, and still is, the only man I ever met who managed to get across, convincingly, the embarrassment of height. Had I never met him, I wouldn't have thought such a thing existed, or could exist.

So there he was, in 1967, standing before me with a manuscript in his hands—an honest-to-God manuscript of a novel in a typewriter-paper box, wordlessly apologizing for being tall, and looking down on me in such a way that it seemed he was looking up to me. No, I don't know how that can be possible, but he made me feel taller than he was and it may be that which worked on me to the point where, to my own surprise, I heard myself saying, "Well, sit down and let's take a look at this thing."

Three hours later, he was still sitting there, and I was still reading, and it was seven in the evening. I invited him to the diner across the street, where we both had sandwiches, and then I went back to the reading.

No, I wasn't under the impression I had discovered a genius. To tell you the truth, the book was awful, simply awful—unbearably overwritten with abominable dialogue.

But I kept reading. That was the surprising thing about it. I kept reading. He had the trick of making it impossible for you to guess what was coming—and of somehow making you want to know.

For the first and last time in my life—never again, I swear to you—I took personal charge of a human being and his book. He rewrote it twice under my direction, and it took two years.

It wasn't exactly a pleasant two years. Except for an allowance he had from his father, Giles was without perceptible income, and my own suffered because of the time I was spending on *him*, damn it. Toward the end, when I was determined to hold him face down at the typewriter till he was done, I even had him move in with me for two months and five days.

I remember the length of the period to the very day, because he was unbearable.

He wasn't loud. He didn't drink or smoke. He stayed carefully out of my way. He was unfailingly polite and humble. He was meticulously clean.

That was the thing, the "meticulously clean" part. I don't mind cleanliness, of course; I make efforts in that direction myself.

But carefully washing your hands every time you stand up from the typewriter? Carefully folding your clothes at any time they are not actually on you? Carefully dusting and mopping and cleaning a little area about yourself till it seems like a jewel set in the rusty metal that was the rest of my apartment?

The only messy habit he had involved pens. Almost every writer I know has a thing about pens—they hoard them, bite them, favor them, and who knows what else. As for Giles, he unscrewed them. Whenever he was off in the limbo where all good writers go to hear their dialogue and arrange their plot sequences, he unscrewed his ball-points.

And quite frequently, perhaps three times out of ten, the little spring inside would fall out and land on the floor. I must have helped him find them a dozen times at least. I had to. He wouldn't return to his writing without it. Later, he took to using throwaway ball-points that couldn't be unscrewed and that had no springs.

But never mind the cleanliness and the unscrewing of
ball-points. He finished at last and I brought the manuscript down to Prism Press myself. I would have taken
it to Doubleday, but I felt it only fair to give Tom the
first chance. Besides, I felt I could talk Tom into doing
it even if he didn't want to, and I couldn't do that to
anyone at Doubleday (and even if I could, it would go
up before a board meeting and be turned down).

Tom agreed, with some hesitation, to publish it. He
now denies he felt any and would have it be recognized
that he was aware of its merits at once, but I have every
faith in the accuracy of my powers of recall.

The book was published in 1969 and didn't really go
anywhere particularly at first. It sold a little over four
thousand in hard cover—which, at that, isn't bad for a
first novel that came out just when the Nixon admini-
stration was cutting the heart out of any federal support
for libraries.

This may surprise you when I tell you that the book
I'm speaking of is *Crossover*, which is now virtually a
cult object.

It wasn't until 1972 that Prism Press managed to find
a paperback publisher for it and that was when the book
hit its stride. It suddenly found its public in the colleges
and it became an overnight sensation. Perhaps it was
the kind of semi-fantasy that appealed to people who
were living in the semi-fantasy of Watergate. In the book
the crossover point (the title, you see) between fantasy
and reality is reached half a dozen times and crossed now
in this direction, now in that. By the time it ends, as you
know if you have read the book, it is doubtful whether
the over-all decision is for fantasy or reality.

Even though it is not well written it is beautifully done,
almost as though the flaws in the writing are an essential
part of the flaws in the Crossover universe—the flaws
that make it possible to slip back and forth.

The final success caught Giles as much by surprise as
it did anyone else. As soon as Tom had taken the book

and Giles had received his two thousand dollars' advance (no more than that and it had been Tom's first notion to offer him five hundred) I kicked him out of my place. Giles tried to give me half the advance, but of course I didn't take it. Still it's rather grimly pleasant now to recall the strength and reality of his gratitude—then.

He went off to New Jersey somewhere, got married in 1973 to an older woman, and got to work on a new novel. I'd see him now and then, when he was in the city, and he was always unfailingly polite, even humble, but he never offered to show me the new novel while he was working on it and you can bet I never asked.

And now he was almost thirty and his second novel was there before me, bound and ready for the reading— and I had not yet read it.

6 THOMAS VALIER 4:45 P.M.

I picked up a copy of *Evergone* resenting that it was there, resenting that it looked as good as it did, resenting that it would do as well as I knew it would.

"Is one of these for me?" I said with an attempt at lightness.

"No," said Tom, "not just yet, Darius. These are autographed door prizes. Tomorrow, Giles will be autographing a new printing of hardbacks of *Crossover*. Each one will be numbered—"

"And there'll be a drawing and the lucky winners will get autographed copies of *Evergone*. I understand."

I looked at the volume again, opened the cover, and glanced at the front-flap matter. It was clear at once (as I had suspected from the title) that it was a sequel to *Crossover* or, at the very least, an independent book set in the Crossover universe. I couldn't blame Giles for trying to ride the wave but I bet myself four to one that it was a poorer book than the first and four to three that it would flop. I wasn't so foolish as not to recognize a strong component of envy there; I was tilting the odds in my own favor egregiously.

Giles's picture filled the back of the jacket. He was caught by the photographer in a look of particularly cow-like dejection and it must have been taken at least a year earlier, for his mustache (which he had begun to grow after he became a published writer) was still relatively thin and it had not yet reached the state of tangled undergrowth that now spread over the upper lip and into either cheek.

I next opened the book to the dedication page. *Crossover* had not been dedicated at all—Giles said he didn't feel the book was worthy and that a dedication would amount to an insult to the person thus honored. I couldn't argue the point, lest it seem that I was pushing for the dedication myself.

The new book did have a dedication: To my Wife.

I resented that, too. What the hell had *she* done for him? Literarily, I mean.

I placed the book back on the pile and said grudgingly, "I suppose it can't help selling."

"It had better," said Tom, looking despondent. "The advance was ten thousand."

"What?" I had never heard figures like that from Tom. I didn't know Prism Press could count into five figures left of the decimal point. I had had a three-thousand advance for my own forthcoming book and Tom had acted as though he were cutting his heart out and placing it, still palpitating, in my greedy claws.

"It was either that," Tom said, "or forfeit the paper-back rights."

"In that case," I said, "you have a bargain. The paper-back ought to net you at least a hundred-thousand advance and you get half of that."

"Well, maybe. You can never tell when the bubble will burst. The paperback houses have been overpaying drastically for some books that haven't made it, and for all I know they'll draw the line at this book. As a matter of fact"—he dropped his voice—"this book isn't as good as *Crossover*."

I said, "You didn't think *Crossover* was all that good

either, when I first gave it to you."

"Whatever I thought, this one isn't as good."

Naturally! I thought to myself, with a kind of grim smugness, that the new one didn't have *me* plugging away at it.

"What do you care?" I said. "It will sell anyway."

"So much the worse," said Tom, in what seemed like downright despair, "because in that case the third book doesn't go to me."

"He didn't cross out the option clause in the *Evergone* contract, did he?"

"No, but he is going to ask, in writing, for a fifty-thousand advance toward his third novel and when I can't meet that—and I can't—he'll be free to go to one of the big houses. Harper's perhaps. An option clause, my friend," he said bitterly, "only holds authors who have nowhere else to go to."

"Like me, Tom?"

"I didn't say that."

I shrugged it off. Tom's estimate that *Evergone* wasn't as good as *Crossover* made it possible for me to sit inside the Prism Press booth and sample the book. It was in what was clearly Giles's choppy style and I came across a forceful and roughly eloquent passage at first opening. It petered out, though, into a sinuous trail of trash, twice as long—something I would never have allowed to stand if I had had anything to do with the book.

I spent twenty or thirty minutes at it (Giles could still keep you reading, even without my help) while Tom began to close down the booth for the day. I was actually cheering up a little and then a new voice distracted me.

"Darius!" The breathy catch-in-the-throat quality was instantly recognizable. I didn't have to look up to know it was Teresa Valier, the other half of Prism Press.

"Darling!" I said dutifully, as I rose, put the book back on the pile a second time, and embraced her.

Teresa wasn't a bad object for embracing. She was a large, plump, cheerful woman with brown hair combed straight back and a loud laugh that sounded as though it were attached to a spigot that could turn on full but in no other way.

She wasn't laughing now; nor was she cheerful. She linked arms with me and began walking, so that for a moment I nearly lost my balance. She was a forceful woman, who gave the impression of enveloping you in a way that had nothing to do with her size.

She said, "Come on and let's have a drink while Tom's closing up."

I half trotted to keep pace with her. "How come Tom is handling the booth himself?"

"It's Sunday," she said, "and I don't want the girls working on Sunday."

"Tomorrow's Memorial Day," I said, "will they be working then?"

"No. It's us again. I'll be handling Giles's autographing session and Tom will be at the booth. Then I'll relieve him and he'll be seeing some booksellers. Actually, Darius, I want to keep him occupied. He's not exactly a happy man right now."

"I noticed," I said. "I even notice that you're not happy, either."

We went down by escalator, which was always full, up and down, throughout all the sessions. At the foot of the escalator was a bar, which was apparently a good place, for it was always full, too.

Teresa found us a pair of seats at one end. "Have a drink," she said.

"You know I don't drink," I said, and helped myself to a pretzel.

"Ginger ale," she said, "on Prism Press. How's that?" And she ordered a vodka sour for herself.

I said, "What's this? Generosity? How come?"

"I have my reasons. Are you going to the party to-night?"

"At seventeen-fifty a ticket?" I said, "I considered it and rejected it. The fact that I even considered it is itself laughable."

"Come on, go," she said, "and charge it to us."

"Good God, still more generous. Why?"

"Because you're a good and loyal author of ours."

"Thanks, but I've always been that. Why now?"

"Because I know that Giles Devore will be there and I want you to talk to him. You know what's happening, I suppose. Tom must have told you."

"He told me," I admitted. "Giles is pushing for the big money. Obviously he's found himself a hard-nosed agent."

I've never had an agent myself. Maybe I'm wrong in this, and maybe that's why I haven't advanced any farther than I have, but I value doing my own dickering even if I take a loss. Besides, it means that I can take on small jobs on my own terms and consider something other than money in the process. Considering anything other than money is something agents never do.

She said, "Of course he has an agent, but that's not the trouble. You writers make me laugh. To hear you talk every publisher is a bastard, every agent is a son of a bitch, but every writer is a saint. I tell you it's not the agent, it's *Giles* who wants the pelf. The agent is a friend of mine and he says so, too; he can't do anything with him."

"Of course the agent says that. It's a common ploy."

"It's true in this case. We have to reach Giles some-how and convince him not to turn his back on us. That's where you come in."

"Why, what can I do? If he's determined to get himself the whole apple pie, what arguments can I raise against it? The great wealth and fame that I have achieved by not going for it?"

"Don't talk like that, Darius," she said earnestly. "He respects you." She took my hand in hers and looked into my eyes as though she were trying to hypnotize me. "He respects you."

I took my hand away and made the kind of sound that is sometimes spelled "Tchah," when you encounter it in writing. "He has so much respect for me that he never consulted me on his new book."

"And it shows it, Darius."

I shrugged. "I can't do any good, Teresa. If he respects me, it doesn't show. It's not as though he dedicated the book to me." I was trying to be flip.

Funny thing. I didn't really mind the ten-thousand advance, the demand for fifty, the drive for the big time, all that fame and fortune. I had discounted it for myself a dozen times over in the dozen years past and I was hardened. I was aware of the sting, but it was on the other side of a thick skin, and though I felt the touch of it, I did not feel the pain.

I despise envy on principle and I feel only contempt for those who fall prey to it; so I never let myself feel it, you see, unless I can call it something else. If I can call it resentment at lack of just and proper appreciation, then that is much more noble and the matter of dedication supplied that.

Teresa seemed to be on my side. Perhaps she thought I was more likely to help her out if she was (she's bright enough, or calculating enough, if you prefer, to see it that way). She said, "We suggested he dedicate *Evergone* to you, you know."

On the outside I had to be stoical. "What the hell," I said. "A wife comes first. Flesh of your flesh; bone of your bone; beneficiary of your will. I never had a wife, however, so I'm just guessing."

Teresa seemed to huddle over her drink. My own ginger ale was gone and I kept sucking at the ice and cracking pieces between my teeth.

Teresa said, "You know it's not proper of Giles to leave us. We made him; Prism Press and you. If we hadn't published the book where would he be? Or if you hadn't coached him?"

My resentment against Giles wasn't great enough to allow me to succumb to the sophistry. I had to protect the honor of writers in the abstract. I said, "Not so, Teresa. He'd be nowhere if *he* hadn't put the work into it *himself*. If he were someone else, I could have never beaten him into success, nor could you have published him into it."

"All right, but he's made money and he's going to make more money. Why does he have to grab for it all? Why can't Prism Press make a little money, too? We're a small house and this is big time for *us*. It's the first chance we've had to do something on the grand scale. Haven't we earned the right to go up, and won't he go up with us? It's not so much me, either; it's poor Tom. If you knew how many *years*—"

"Granted," I said, hastily, to cut her off. "Let's say you have the moral right to capitalize on having been his first publisher and the ethical right to share in his good fortune. I'm not a great philosopher on questions of morals and ethics, but let's suppose you have. One thing I know is that you don't have the *legal* right to share in it. If you can't meet his financial terms and he wants to leave you, you can't stop him."

"But it's not even to his benefit, Darius. You know that. We're a small firm and he's our big writer. *The* star. *No* competition." She must have understood my feelings then, for she added, "I mean as far as *he's* concerned, Darius. You know that we'll always love and appreciate *you*, but your books don't quite have the kind of trashiness that would make them—"

"It's all right, Teresa. Don't try to plaster up the cracks. You're selling Giles on staying with Prism and for that reason you must convince him that he's the big star without competition. I can take it. Go on."

"You understand, Darius. I know." And she patted my hand. "We can concentrate on Giles, because we go up with him and we can't go up without him. If he's with any of the large houses, however, he's just one of a dozen or more and not the largest. He'll be lost in the shuffle.

In the long run, he'll do much better with us. Can't you explain that to him, Darius? He'd listen to you."

I said, "I can't guarantee that Prism Press will make him rich, you know. He'll tell me that I'm a better writer than he is; that I've taught him all he knows; that I brought him to Prism Press in the first place—and what is Prism Press doing for me, with all my good writing and enormous loyalty? And what do I say to him?"

"Now, Darius, you know we've always done what we can. There's no accounting for the way the lightning of public fancy strikes."

Well, that was true, too. I said, "If I see him, I'll talk to him."

"That's all I ask," she said, and stood up. "I've got to join Tom. I'll tell him you'll talk to him and maybe that will keep him from killing himself. Thanks, Darius. We won't forget it."

I didn't gather much comfort from her promise of eternal gratitude. Eternity lasts five minutes in the world of publishing. So I just said, "Of course, if he doesn't show up—"

"I'm sure he will."

She left and I was alone—to brood over my new role as errand boy to the literary eagle. I had fed and warmed him when he was nothing but beak and feathers—seventy-five inches of them—and now he was in his aerie and I had to climb the heights to face him and plead with him.

I felt myself sliding deeper into frustrated resentment and the feeling was unpleasant. I had half an hour before the doors would open for the party and I tried to shake the feeling by watching and listening to others in the bar.

8 ROSEANN BRONSTEIN 6:05 P.M.

Booksellers' conventions are like any others, I suppose. Most of the action is in the bars.

The booksellers set up formal discussions and panels, of course. There are some aimed at the beginner, the fellow with the store who has just opened a line of books, or the other fellow who just bought into a bookstore. There are panels on the special problems of occult books (a big line—showing you can be literate and stupid, too) and of religious books and of large paperbacks and of children's books and of questions of promotion and production and sales and so on.

I didn't attend any of them, so I can't give you the details.

Lots of the booksellers don't attend them, either, or, if they do, they let their minds wander. The formal business isn't the important part of the convention, I suppose; just as so many of my classmates at college used to think the lectures weren't the important part of their education. It's not what you know, it's whom you get drunk with.

If I sound bitter, it's because I don't drink. I have no moral objections, you understand, but it is by my keen, incisive brain—or whatever adjectives you prefer—that I make my living; and I have never quite seen that banging it with a hammer called alcohol (or dope) can improve its functioning.

So I sat in the bar, feeling out of place, killing time before the party was to start, and lacking any desire to attend even if Prism Press was to pick up the tab. There'd be more drinking there, and no Giles. If Giles were there, what would that be but an invitation to humiliation. There was no way in which I could bring myself to attempt to plead effectively; or to succeed if I made the attempt.

I had the impulse to leave and go home despite my useless promise to Teresa, and if I had all would have been well; at least the world would have been short one murder and long one life. In fact, I think I would have done so if I had not found myself listening to the talk at the next table.

It was not, at first, for any reason; not even out of idle curiosity. It was just that the sounds were there and my ears were in the neighborhood and that it was too much trouble to tune out.

But then the conversation grew to have a grisly fascination for me. From internal evidence, the people at the next table were minor editors—second lieutenants in the world of publishing—and they were talking about their jobs.

The situation was not good. Books sold as well as ever, or better, and the number of books published continued to rise; the inflation that had followed the oil embargo of 1973, however, had raised the prices of everything so that expenses outpaced profits.

And how does one make up for lagging profit? The easiest way is to cut down on staff, either by outright firing or by not replacing those who, for one reason or another, leave.

I was sorry for them, and yet the rottenness of their situation illuminated my own immunity to their lot.

Odd! When I began writing and trying to sell, editors were like demigods to me. They walked in power, and bestrode the world. Their heads were cloud-high and their voice was thunder-loud and their glance lightning-sharp. Actually, I don't know about the last. I couldn't meet the eyes of editors; I was afraid to.

They had the power of life and death, and at their lightest breath, success (or failure) wafted your way. If their lordly whims were offended by anything in the manuscript, a negligent checkoff on a form meant that a secretary would return your material with a rejection slip. Could a god do more?

But an editor can be fired, I eventually learned. And when he is fired, he is no longer an editor, merely an item in the statistics of the unemployed.

Not so a writer. He cannot be fired. He might be rejected, he might fail, he might starve, he might be forced to keep body and soul together by taking some menial (i.e., non-writing) employment, he might be ignored by the critics and denounced by the public—but he was a writer, a failed writer, an unsuccessful writer, a starving writer, a *writer*. No editor could change that fact.

Listening, and musing, pinned me to the spot long enough to keep me from being aware of the presence of Roseann Bronstein until it was entirely too late. In fact, it was not until she had taken the place vacated by Teresa Valier and had said, "Hi there, little fella," that I knew what had come to pass.

A friend of mine, who had been brought up totally immersed in the Yiddish language, and who was fond of lacing his speech with Yiddish idioms literally translated into English, would often say, "It became dark before my eyes," when he wanted to express a dramatic extremity of anguish. The only times when it seemed to me that this might be more than a mere metaphoric turn of phrases was whenever Roseann saw me before I saw her. She would, on those occasions, invariably greet me in those precise words, "Hi there, little fella."

How do I describe Roseann? She is not exactly ugly or grotesque, but I think they invented the word "unattractive" for her. She does not attract! I have never met anyone who was willing to talk about Roseann who did not acknowledge a desire to retreat when she approached.

She was short and round, had a wide face and a loud, cheerful voice. Her skin was rough and when her arms were bare they gave the impression of being slightly, but permanently, goosefleshed. Her face was always innocent of makeup and there was a perpetual smell of old clothes about her. There was something utterly sexless about her appearance, as though she dated back from a time before the two sexes were invented and differentiated.

And yet hidden beneath all this was a woman. Her breasts were prominent enough, though probably flabby (I wouldn't know), and, if half the stories were correct, she was fascinated by men.

"What can I do for you, Roseann?" I asked tonelessly.

"I met Teresa Valier in the lobby and she said you were in here."

"I must remember to do Teresa a favor sometime in return. Trip her at the top of the down escalator, maybe."

Roseann laughed heartily enough to attract attention from nearby tables. I have never known her to register anything but amusement at remarks concerning herself.

It's the reason why, however repelled I am by her, I never find myself actually disliking her. Laugh at yourself and the world laughs with you.

Roseann said with a fine, and futile, attitude of carelessness, "Teresa said you're going to the party."

I looked at my watch. "I have twenty-five minutes to make a decision."

"She said you'll be talking to Giles Devore."

"If I see him," I said, pronouncing my words precisely. "I don't intend to look for him."

"I hope you see him. I know you've got influence with him."

My God, I thought pettishly, an instant replay. I have become a pipeline to Giles—with everyone in the world at one end of the pipe, but no Giles at the other.

"I don't," I said. "None at all."

"Oh, come on." She grinned broadly, revealing large teeth with one of the upper incisors clearly capped, hitched her chair closer to the table, and leaned over to knead my arm. I suspect that she was merely performing what she considered an erotic rite designed to rouse my libido and urge me into greater cooperation. Or perhaps she just enjoyed the feel of a masculine arm.

Whatever her intent, my skin crawled at her touch, and I was embarrassed by that. I've lost count of the number of girls against parts of whose bodies I've allowed my hand to rest, and always with a cool, slow stroking motion that I liked and that I always assumed they liked, too, even when nothing further came of it or was intended to come of it. It is only when I react to Roseann that I wonder how many girls have skins that crawl at *my* touch, and I am embarrassed retroactively for having annoyed every one of them.

"Talk him into coming to my place for an autograph session for his new book," she said, with a voice that gave me the impression of a crow trying to coo.

"Why me?" I said. "Ask him yourself."

A vague embarrassment passed over her face and her arm dropped back to her own side of the table. "I can't, little fella." Then she said in her own natural voice, held low and controlled, "You know, I made him, Darius. His book went nowhere in hard cover and would have gone nowhere in soft cover, if I hadn't pushed it."

We all made him, I thought sardonically. I made him. The Valiers and Prism Press made him. Roseann Bronstein made him. Yet somehow he was standing there on his own now, and could spit at us all.

Of course, there was something to what Roseann was saying. There is a large public that reads only fashionable books (and only enough of them to be able to talk about them fashionably). A book needn't be good, or readable, to be fashionable, though it could be both, of course. And the way you can tell that a book is fashionable is to have it on the best-seller list. That means best sellers sell by virtue of being best sellers and therefore tend to remain on the best-seller list. For that matter, if a bad seller were put on the best-seller list by mistake it is very likely to become a best seller in truth merely because it was tabbed with the name.

There are ways of putting books on the best-seller lists by means of a good, hard (sometimes expensive) push and then letting them stay there and earn back the investment.

A strategically placed bookstore could do it. It might push a book over the line. And that meant Roseann Bronstein.

She is the owner and major force behind the Oriole, a downtown bookstore. It is a large barn of a place whose stock can't possibly be known in full by any human being, including Roseann, but she says that, given time, she could find any book in the world—within reason.

I wouldn't in the least consider it impossible that, growing interested in *Crossover*, she could push it effectively not only in her store but in other stores where her opinion in such matters was valued—and that meant places as far away as San Francisco. She was well placed to push the book in the downtown university area, and that was where, as a matter of fact, it had caught on first.

There was no question, for instance, of the great success of the autographing party at the Oriole in December 1973, because I was there. Giles was signing paperback after paperback in a never-ending stream while Roseann hovered over him in proprietorish fashion. That was the first time, I remember, that I had ever seen him sign books with those inscribed throwaway ball-points.

I remember he tried to get me to use similar pens, pointing out their triangular cross section and how easy that made the grip, but I demurred. I don't sign books that often (though I signed about a dozen the day of that party—get a reader excited enough and he will find even a minor-league signature acceptable) and any pen will do for me. In fact, it's a good idea not to carry a pen sometimes, since then when the inevitable youngster pushes a torn piece of paper at you, you can smile and say you have no pen, and of course, he'll have none, either.

After that, Giles got to the point where he would use no pen but his own—monogrammed and triangular. How could he tell the fatality of it?

With that autographing party in mind, I said to Roseann, "I know you pushed the book, Roseann. Too bad you don't push mine the same way. I take it Giles is ungrateful?"

"We were friends," she said. "I did it for him out of friendship. We were very good friends." She paused a little as though to recall the goodness of it and get it straight in her memory, and I got the very unpleasant feeling that by "very good" she meant that they had been lovers. I had the grotesque vision of Giles selling his body in return for Roseann selling his book. (I hoped earnestly that Roseann hadn't heard my just expressed hope that she would push mine the same way.)

She was kneading my arm again. "You know, times are hard, and the Oriole is a relic. I've got to remodel, or move, or something—make it last my time—"

"Come on," I said. "The Oriole is as permanent as the university is. It's a historic monument."

"The pigeons shit on it, if that's what you mean, and the university isn't all that permanent, either. It would help if Giles were to hold another autographing party, maybe identify himself with the place in some way. I did it for him when he needed it. He can do it for me now."

"Well, ask him."

"*You* ask him. I haven't even managed to talk to him in over a year. In fact, it's six-thirty now. Go, will you? I don't want you to miss him."

"I might not see him."

"You'll see him," she said in desperate confidence, and heaved herself to her feet, puffing and stirring up the old-clothes smell.

"I'll do what I can," I said.

"Thanks, little fella," she said, and slammed my shoulder in what was meant to be a rough, man-to-man, gesture of affection and sent me staggering sideways.

My first reaction was one of intense annoyance, but then I caught a glimpse of her face in a moment when her self-protective shield had failed her—anxious, pitiful, knowing herself unloved and unlovable.

I was sorry for her. Whatever there was inside that hulk, the inside Roseann, it was nothing at all like the body that imprisoned it, and it was helpless ever to express itself.

I said, "I'll go to the party, Roseann."

And that was the moment of decision. The conversation at the next table had held me for Roseann, and Roseann, by allowing me to catch her in all her vulnerability, made it impossible for me to refuse to make at least the effort.

So I went up the escalator to the third floor and to the ballroom where the party was to be held, and I had lost the chance of escaping, the chance I had all but taken.

9 **MARTIN WALTERS 6:35 P.M.**

The party was clearly beginning, for there was something unmistakably partyish about the women. They wore long dresses in black and exposed skin in white (a few blacks, too, but I didn't see many) and carried purses, stoles, and a variety of other accouterments that had to be checked. Since the hotel carefully did not put a checkroom on that particular floor, it meant that the menfolks had to perform their time-honored male chauvinist task of scurrying up and down the escalator to find checkrooms.

I keep waiting for the liberated woman who will say, right after "Equal pay for equal work," something like, "I'll take care of checking the coats this time, kid." I haven't found her yet.

There was a long table at which last-minute tickets were being sold, so I adjusted my nameplate and stood in line. There were only two or three ahead of me. I had two ten-dollar bills ready when it was my turn.

The young lady behind the desk was filling out forms. I suppose they wanted some record of attendees. She made her side vision do the work as she reached for the bills without looking up from the form.

"Name, please," she said.

"Darius Just," I said.

"How do you spell the last name?" she said.

"You guess," I said, and she looked up to stare at my nameplate. Then she carefully spelled it out.

"How else can you spell it?" I asked.

She didn't seem put out. She had dark hair and a skinny face and had probably spent her whole young life countering wise guys. She said, "It could have two 's's' or a final 'e' or it could begin with a 'd.' We have all kinds of queer foreign names now."

"But it's just Just," I said.

"That's it," she said, and handed me my ticket and two-fifty in change.

I stepped away glumly. I suspect that I made that small fuss in order to give her a chance to study the name and recognize me. She hadn't, and it was a booksellers' convention, too. How quickly they forget! Except that I had no reason to think she knew anything about me to forget in the first place.

But then, how come she didn't ask me how to spell my first name? Perhaps it was only the easy names that roused her dark suspicions.

I took the opportunity of stepping into the men's room before starting the round of happy festivity. The Duke of Wellington is supposed to have said that he never ignored an opportunity to piss, since a convenient time might not arrive very quickly thereafter, and I have always tried to follow the same principle.

I was washing my hands when someone moved up to the sink beside me and it was Martin Walters.

It was only a little over two hours since the embarrassment over the press conference that I had come on time for and still been too late for, and I scowled at him.

Martin had no difficulty reading the scowl. He dried his hands and said with an uncomfortable smirk (perhaps it was intended to be an ingratiating smile), "Listen, Darius, I'm sorry about this afternoon. I really am."

"It's all right," I said, but it wasn't, so I changed the subject. "Do you know Giles Devore?"

"Yes. Why?"

"You haven't seen him up here by any chance?"

"I just got up here. And even if I saw him, I wouldn't see him."

"Oh? What's the matter."

"He stood me up."

"Receiving end doesn't taste as good?"

He smiled uncomfortably again. "Come on, Darius. It was different. In our case, it was the force of circumstances, you know that. In the case of Giles, it was just a matter of forgetting or not caring. I'm in charge of the entertainment for a dining club and I arranged with him to come down and give a little talk on the significance of fantasy or something like that. It wasn't much, but I thought it would start some good conversation, you know—only he never showed. It was very embarrassing and when I called him the next day he said, coolly, he

had forgotten. No sign of contrition; seemed totally unmoved. It was the most unprofessional thing I've come
across in a long time. I've wiped him out of *my* book."

"Too bad," I said, not managing to be as sympathetic
as I ought to have been.

Once out of the men's room, I gave up my ticket and
moved into the outer of the two rooms into which the
ballroom was divided. That one was the bar, and I paused
just long enough to make sure that Giles Devore wasn't
there. Then I moved on.

10 ISAAC ASIMOV 6:45 P.M.

In the inner room, there were four large buffet tables,
one against each wall. I presume they were all the same,
but I visited only the nearest. Free dinner, I said to myself, and had myself some fried chicken, two kinds of
sausage, a few slices of tongue, a glob of potato salad,
some five or six olives, plus a roll and butter on a
separate plate.

I found myself a table that had not yet collected anyone at any of its four chairs and sat down with a little
sigh. If I were left alone, if I were allowed to eat in peace,
I might yet brush away all the implacably humiliating
events of the day. Some people dissolve their woes in
wine; I'm quite likely to assuage my sadness in spiced
sausage.

It wasn't to be. Nothing broke right that Sunday. I
hadn't completed my first mouthful when a cheerful voice
boomed out, "Good old Darius Dust. Mind if I join you?"

I've got to explain about the name Darius. It was
wished upon me by a self-educated father. You can't
trust self-education, it goes too far, gets too bloated,
knows no moderation. My father's name was Alexander
and he knew that Alexander the Great had defeated
Darius III of Persia, and that was it. Perhaps he had the
feeling that even though he would see to it I had a
thorough education (he did) I would never be able to

surpass *him*. Since he was five feet ten, I guess I never did.

My mother, a very little woman whose genes, in that respect, I inherited, went along with it. She had no choice. No one ever had a choice within hearing distance of my father.

To be the smallest kid in class is not exactly a passport to happiness. To be any kid named Darius, surrounded by Jims, Toms, and Bills, produces little joy. To be the smallest kid in class, and named Darius, too, is something like sitting under a neon sign that flashes on and off with the message, "Kick me!"

It wasn't until I was in college before my name stopped serving as an insult to everyone my age I ever met; an insult to be personally avenged at once.

I hated that name at first, but held on to it with a wretched obstinacy. No one was going to force me out of it. By the time I reached a coterie of friends old enough and sophisticated enough to be able to pronounce it and feel at home with it, I began to like it.

Correct pronunciation helps. Even among relatively sophisticated adults, it isn't a familiar name. Outside Herodotus, one is only likely to come across it in an old chestnut of a poem called "Darius Green and His Flying Machine" by John Townsend Trowbridge, written a little over a hundred years ago. I hated that poem. Naturally the only Darius in popular literature was served up as comic relief.

I'm not sure what proportion of the general population knows how to pronounce the name, but even in the rarefied circles within which I have my being (God help me) I hear it more often mispronounced than pronounced. The first impulse is to pronounce the name so as to rhyme it was "various," but that's not right. The accent is on the second syllable, with a long "i," so that in rhymes with "pious" and "bias."

That has its disadvantages, too, for once you learn to say Darius properly, you are bound to notice that it sounds something like "dry as." Then, if you have a par-

ticularly feeble mind, it occurs to you that if you change
Just to Dust, the name becomes "Dry as Dust," which
is not exactly ideal for a writer.

Actually, only one person I know has the kind of per-
verted sense of humor that thinks this is funny. When
I heard someone say "Good old Dry as Dust. Mind if I
join you?" I knew, without looking up, that it was Isaac
Asimov. Word play is his idea of the empyrean heights
of wisdom.

I didn't let it bother me. I just said, "Hello, Ikey. Of
course I mind having you join me, but sit down anyway."

As it happens, there's nothing that Asimov can possibly call me that I would hate as much as he hates being
called Ikey. So one of these times, when it finally dawns
on him that every "Dry as Dust" will elicit an "Ikey"
without fail, he will quit. Anyone else would quit after
two tries. I give Asimov twenty years.

Since this book is rather in the nature of a collabora-
tion, with his name on it as sole author, however, I had
better be particular about describing him.

He's five feet nine inches tall, rather fat and more
than rather grinning. He wears his hair long, and it's
clear he does it out of laziness, rather than out of any
desire for a splendid leonine effect (which is how I've
heard him describe it), because it never seems more than
sketchily combed. The hair is somewhat gray and the
sideburns, which run down to the angle of his jaw and
which have been aptly described as looking like Brillo,
are nearly white. He's got a bulbous nose, blue eyes, a
bolo tie, and glasses with black frames. He has to remove
his glasses to read or eat because he won't admit his
age long enough to get bifocals.

He's like me in some respects. He doesn't smoke or
drink any more than I do. Like me, he also likes to eat,
but I don't get fat on it and he does. He thinks the difference is metabolism, which is funny for a guy who
claims to be a biochemist. I know the difference is exercise. I work out in a gym nearly every day—but once
Asimov has managed to lift himself out of bed in the

morning, that is his exercise for the day. Except for typing, of course. His fingers are in good shape.

He had his plate heaped much higher than mine was, but he couldn't stop himself from glancing anxiously at what I had retrieved as though I might, perhaps, have found a goodie he had overlooked.

"What's the score now, Isaac?" No use calling him Ikey except under provocation.

He knew what I meant. "A hundred sixty-three at the moment," he said, with his mouth full, "but who's counting?"

"You are," I said.

He swallowed, and said in an aggrieved tone, "I *have* to. That's my shtick. Everyone wants to know how many books I've published and if I don't tell them they're disappointed. What's more, if they ask me the question in two successive months and the figure doesn't go up by at least one, they feel cheated. Look, there's no need for you to be resentful. You've had a movie made out of one of your books. I haven't."

I winced. The matter had been profitable, but it was easily the worst movie ever made by the worst set of idiots you could find even in Hollywood. I kept hoping no one would see it.

A hundred sixty-three books is no record, of course, but I never met anyone for whom writing is as painless as it is for Asimov. And he's aware of it and his pleasure over it can be rather disgusting to see.

He crossed the room once, at a book-and-author luncheon, and someone muttered in my ear, "There goes Asimov pushing his self-assurance ahead of him like a wheelbarrow." (The same might be said of his abdomen, of course.) Someone else once said that Asimov walked as though he expected the air to part in front of him.

Actually, my own theory is that he lives so much of the time inside his own head that he is unaware of the outside world, so that when he seems to be utterly self-possessed, it's just that he's unaware that there's anything to be disturbed about.

I said to him, "What are you doing here, Isaac? Why aren't you home writing a book?"

He groaned. "In a way that's what I'm doing here. Doubleday wants me to write a mystery novel entitled *Murder at the ABA*. I don't know what I was thinking of when I signed up."

"Why did you sign?"

"What did you expect me to do? I've signed so many contracts, it's a reflex action with me. And they want a completed manuscript by August. I've got three months on the outside."

"That's all right. It will only take you a weekend, won't it?"

Asimov made himself a cold-cut sandwich on a giant scale and demolished half of it at a bite. With most of the bite gone, he said, "The worst of all my literary troubles is the fact that I'm not allowed to have any literary troubles. If you said you had to do a book faster than you could do it, everyone would soak your jacket with sympathetic tears. When I say it, I get cheap jokes. The same cheap joke every time, I might add."

This from a man who thinks Darius Dust is epigrammatic wit.

I didn't break down in tears. "Just the same you'll do it. You've done mysteries before, haven't you?"

It was a pretty safe assumption. The man has written on every subject imaginable and if ever anyone didn't look it, it's Asimov. He looks stupid at first sight. And when you hear him tell endless jokes, hug every girl in reach, and never by any chance say anything thoughtful, you're convinced of it. It takes considerable time before you find out that the man is so secure in his intelligence that he never troubles to display it.

Which annoys the hell out of me, actually.

"Of course I've done mysteries before," he said indignantly. "I've written straight mysteries and science fiction mysteries; novels and short stories; for adults, for teen-agers, and for grade-schoolers.

"Then what's the trouble?"

"I've got to give this local color. I've got to hang around here for four days and see what's happening."

"You're doing it, aren't you?"

"But I *can't* see what's happening. In my whole life, I've never seen anything that goes on around me."

"Then how have you written a hundred sixty-three books?"

"*Published*," he said. "I have eleven in press. . . . Because my books are without description. I have an unornamented style."

"In that case, get someone to help you."

It was odd that I should say that, for at that moment, I couldn't possibly have supposed that matters would end up in such a way that *I* would help him.

After all, he *did* manage to do the book in time. You're reading it—*Murder at the ABA* by Isaac Asimov.

It's just that it's *my* story and *I* am first-person while he is third-person. And since I've left the writing entirely in his hands and don't entirely trust him, the agreement is that I am to be allowed to add any comments of my own (within reason) in the form of footnotes where I consider him too far off base.*

He had finished his platter and by that time the room was considerably more crowded than it had been when we had entered. It was quite hopeless to expect to see Giles in that mess. The noise level had become uncomfortable and the filth of cigarette smoke hung in the air.

---

* For instance, I can point out that while Asimov is sticking to the outline, he's dramatizing me into total distortion. I am five feet five and not five feet two. The subtle (or not so subtle) saturation of the story with my supposed pygmy complex is just designed to make him shine by contrast.

        —DARIUS JUST

Just is five feet five if you count his elevator shoes! I'm not supposed to be literal here anyway. This is a work of fiction and I will take any liberties I choose with the facts. And as for making myself shine, I ask anyone who knows me to read these last few pages in which I figure and testify that I am sticking to Just's ridiculous attitudes vis-à-vis myself at some considerable cost to my self-respect.

        —ISAAC ASIMOV

There was still time to leave, and then Asimov would have had to make up his own story—but I didn't budge because I hadn't had my coffee yet. There was always something to prevent the evasion of Fate.

I said, "Do you want some coffee, Isaac?"

"Sure, but let me go get it. I need the exercise."

That wasn't it at all, of course. He came back with coffee for both of us and five assorted cookies for himself. At least he didn't offer me any of them.

He dipped the chocolate-covered one in the coffee, transferred it expertly to his mouth without losing a drop, and said, "And what are you doing here, Darius? You don't look particularly ecstatic."

"I've no reason to look ecstatic," I said. "I've had a hell of a day and I don't intend to go into details."

"Considering that you have no family responsibilities at all and write only one book every three years, what can possibly give you a hell of a day?"

I could almost believe he was serious in that question, but I ignored it anyway and said, "You haven't by any chance seen Giles Devore at the convention?"

"Yes, I have."

I was astonished. I was not expecting that answer. "In here?"

"No, at the registration booth. He's autographing books tomorrow morning. At the same time with me, in fact."

"I know he's autographing books," I said. I swear I said it in the flattest possible way, without any hint of hidden meanings. In fact, I was cooling down and—who knows?—everything might have come to nothing, when Asimov stirred up my resentment against Giles for no reason I could see except to amuse himself, and laid *his* flagstone.

His blue eyes glittered and his eyebrows lifted and fell rapidly. (For someone who claims to see nothing of the world outside himself, he can have an unerring touch for the sore spot on the soul.)

He said, "I'm glad he's your protégé and not mine. I don't know about you, but I would find it sickening to have a protégé zoom past me."

"He's not my protégé," I said.

"Listen, that first book of his was written out of your vest pocket. Everyone knows it—and the more fool, you."

"Why? For helping?"

"No, of course not. For expecting gratitude."

I shrugged but, inside, where he couldn't see, I burned. Damn it, I *had* expected gratitude, and whether that made me a fool or not, the lack of it made me furious.

I said, lying in my teeth, "I never expected anything."

But Asimov's eyes were no longer on me. They were straining across the room and I didn't have to follow them to know he was looking at a girl. I forgot to say that in among his general inability to see anything in the outside world, there is an odd capacity to see every girl within two hundred feet.

11 SARAH VOSKOVEK 7:20 P.M.

She was not my type. Five feet nothing at the most. I like my girls five feet seven or eight. The average American girl is five feet four, breasts average, hips average. If you imagine taking her by neck and ankle and giving a quick outward jerk in both directions, you will have a girl who is sixty-eight inches tall, with small firm breasts and narrow hips. That's what I like.

This one was just the reverse. An average girl had been taken by neck and ankle and had been compressed. Result: sixty inches, with breasts like pouter pigeons and a rear end like a bustle. She was very pretty; I'll give her that. Her hair, almost black, was raised into a beehive (to add height, I suppose). She also had a pair of eyes that were just as dark, and that were large and with bluish whites. She had a slightly curved nose and her cheekbones were high and pink. Her white dress reached to her ankles but fell far short of her collarbone at the other end.

She was walking in our direction and Asimov's eyes never wavered from her. I watched, too, with less delight, and made little bets to myself as to when her trajectory would veer and carry her off into the night, never, perhaps, to be seen again. I didn't particularly care when that might take place, but it didn't.

Her trajectory never veered. She ended up at our table and, ignoring me completely, said, "Pardon me. Aren't you Dr. Isaac Asimov?" She had a trace of an accent, Slavic, perhaps.

"Hot dog," said Asimov, with a wide and jovial gesture of his arms. "My fame precedes me. I'm all yours, dear. Just tell me where, when, and how many times."

"Yes," she said, "your fame does precede you. You have been described to me and you *are* Dr. Isaac Asimov."

It didn't faze him, nothing of the sort does. He kept on smiling and said, "To repeat myself, what can I do for you?"

"May I join you for a moment?"

"As many moments as there are in eternity," said Asimov, still hewing to the line.

"Five or six will suffice."

The combination of accent and meticulous English was enticing. I found myself wishing it came out of a more attractive body.

She sat down, and said, "My name is Sarah Voskovek and I handle public relations for the hotel."

Why I should have chosen to interfere at this moment, I can't exactly say. Perhaps I resented being ignored. Perhaps Asimov's recent dig concerning Giles had left me anxious to strike back at anyone, however meaninglessly.

So I said, "What are you doing here on Sunday night? These aren't working hours?"

She looked at me coldly as though she were preventing the glance of her eyes from actually touching me. She said, "I am here as a guest of the ABA, and I work when I please."

And she was looking at Asimov again as though I had existed only for the moment it took to despise me. I took a deep breath and bet myself a grim five to three I'd get a chance at the little bitch before she left.

She said, "I understand, Dr. Asimov, that you are planning to write a murder mystery about this hotel."

Asimov looked dashed at this sudden descent into business. He said, "Boy, the news spreads fast. Not about the hotel, Miss—Miss—"

"Voskovek."

"Well, not about the hotel. *Murder at the ABA* is the suggested title. My publishers have asked me to do it."

"But the ABA Convention is taking place at this hotel. How realistic do you intend being?"

"As realistic as necessary," said Asimov, suddenly the writer. "The whole point is to include local color."

She said, "Nevertheless, it should not be necessary to mention the name of the hotel."

"It might not be," admitted Asimov.

That's when I won my five-to-three bet—or, for a moment, thought I did.

I leaned across the table to her and said, "Look here, little sister. This man is going to write a book. It's none of your business what's going to be in the book. If, after he has published the book, you conceive your privacy to have been invaded, or the hotel to have been libeled, you can sue. Until then, you can have nothing to say, and this attempt at prior restraint is disgusting. Why don't you go off now and indulge in your public relations, for which you seem to have no talent."

She looked at me as if she were studying a specimen of uncertain genus, but one that didn't interest her. It was a long, leisurely look, a quite calm look, and then she said, with no sign of an expression on her face, "It must be quite rare for you to find someone shorter than yourself on whom you can exert your fancied masculinity."

"Wow!" said Asimov.

I had to catch my breath. It was not what she said, of course; I've lived on comments of that sort for a generation. It was just the utter unexpected irrelevance of it. When I could speak, I was stuttering.

"Lady," I said, "your inches and m-mine——"

But she said, "I will speak to you at some more suitable time, Dr. Asimov." She turned away and walked off, not hastily.

12 GILES DEVORE 7:35 P.M.

I had an overwhelming urge to run after her and land my shoe right on the tempting target of her buttocks, but I was just barely master of myself to the point of avoiding it. What a hell of a dustup that would have given rise to. So I held on and felt the palms of my hands grow damp and sweaty with frustration.

Of all the humiliations I had suffered that day, this one was the worst.

Asimov didn't help by saying, "What do you care, Darius? You know your effect on women. Turn on the charm next time you see her and when she crumples into your arms, step away and let her hit the ground."

He thought it was funny. I didn't. What could I do but ignore him and confine myself to inner fuming.

I just wish I could remember what it was I was going to say just as she left. It was going to be devastating. It would have absolutely crushed her if I could have gotten it out. But I can't remember. I tell myself that it's just as well, under the circumstances, that I can't——but I wish I did.

Then Asimov said, "Hello, Giles. How's the celebrity?"

"Hello, Isaac," said the familiar mincing voice.

I had forgotten about him. I wasn't searching for him. I had reached the point where I no longer intended to search for him. If he had kept to any other part of the large room, I would never have seen him. If he had arrived ten minutes before——ahead of Little Miss Big-Mouth——I might, just possibly, have felt calm enough to avoid what the whole day had been building up to. If he had arrived ten minutes later than he did, I might well have been absent, for in those few moments after that woman had left, I knew there was nothing further to keep me at the convention. Enough was enough.

And Giles was there at the precise spot and at the precise time.

I looked up in surprise. He was standing there, stooped a little, his arms dangling, his face hangdog. He was distinctly plumper than the last time I had seen him; prosperity continued to go to his waist as it so often does. His glasses were black-rimmed and remarkably like those of Asimov, whom he might have resembled distantly if he were not half a head taller and if it weren't for his shaggy black mustache. His lower lip, visible by itself, gave him a monstrous-little-boy-pouting look. Combine the mustache and glasses and make his nose more curved and prominent than it was and he would look as though he were wearing one of those Groucho Marx masks.

He said, "I met Teresa Valier downstairs and she said you were looking for me, Darius."

Teresa didn't quite trust me, then. She'd been searching on her own.

"Then sit down," I said savagely.

At this point, Asimov, apparently deciding that the role of innocent bystander was notoriously too dangerous to play, rose and said, "If you don't mind, there are some people over there I have to see." He waved vaguely and was gone. His departure didn't bother me.

Giles sat down and placed his big hands flat on the table, palms down, before him. He looked as though he were waiting for me to toss him a dog biscuit.

I said, "Congratulations on the new book."

He shrugged. "Thanks, but it won't go anywhere much with Prism Press."

"You're leaving them, I understand."

"Yes. Writers have to find their level," he added in his sissy tenor voice (which constantly gave rise to assumptions that he was gay—which he was not), "and Prism Press is not my level."

"But it is mine, is it?" I asked.

"You are free to leave too, Darius—unless it is."

Insufferable bastard!

"And what about Roseann Bronstein? I understand that you're refusing to do an autographing session for her."

"Has she been talking to you, too, Darius? No, I won't. I can't stand her."

"You don't have to stand her to sign some books in her store. Look, Giles, would you like some advice?" I was still holding my temper.

"Not really, Darius."

"Then don't like it, but you'll have it just the same, Giles. Prism Press, even if it's a small house, did your first book and did pretty well with it. Someone else might have done it better, but you don't know that. You might at least stick with them long enough to see how this one goes. You owe them that much surely. And Roseann pushed your book when she didn't have to and when it counted. Surely you owe her a favor in return."

"Favors? There are no favors in this world, Darius. Prism Press did my first book, but what of that? They made money out of it, too. In fact, they made more than I did and they'll make still more money out of my new book. They've had their return. And Roseann had her return, too. And what is it they want now? I'll tell you. They want to ride my coattails for their own financial benefit. Is that high-minded of them? I want them off my coattails for *my* financial benefit. Why isn't that equally high-minded of me? We're all after the loot. Why is that noble for them and evil for me?"

I kept calm even then. Amazing that I did so, as I look back at it now. "And what was I after, Giles?" I asked.

He reddened distinctly. Then he said, "That's different, Darius. I'm aware that I owe you something. And once I'm set with a better house, you can count on a good word from me. Anything that I can do, Darius, I will."

Who the hell wanted his good word? I felt myself beginning to come to a boil. All the humiliations of the day were coming to a head, not the least the newly rankling remark of that pygmy public relations woman.

He was waiting for an answer, some sign I could give him to the effect that he was a kind, loyal person and would go to heaven when he died for this good deed he was offering me. I was trying to choose the words that would send him to hell, when there was a thin clatter of high heels and the distinct feel of a breeze as a woman rushed past.

"Mr. Devore," she panted. "If we don't leave now, we'll be late."

Giles's pouting underlip seemed to tighten, a sign that his familiar mulishness was overtaking him. Perhaps the reminder of his debt to me worked upon him as his own damnable condescension worked on me.

And that was his manner of facing the world when he was angry. He never fought. He never struck out. He would merely become stubborn and refuse to budge. It might be over something world-shaking or something petty; it didn't matter. The degree of stubbornness was the same and I never knew him to shake. Why Teresa Valier and Roseann Bronstein didn't know that as well as I did, why they thought a word from me would make a difference, I couldn't say.

"Can't you get someone else?" he squeaked, and I bet myself a somber ten to one that whatever it was he was supposed to do, he wouldn't do it.

And by then I had recognized the woman. She was the interview secretary of the convention—Henrietta Corvass. She had been unperturbed when I had arrived too late to participate in the penny-ante press conference I was scheduled for, but she seemed a lot more concerned over Giles Devore. He was worth more than I was, obviously.

She said, "It's a major taping, a network show, and they don't want anyone else. We're committed on this."

"I'm not committed on anything," he said, beginning to frown. "They'll keep me up all hours and I've got to be doing an autographing session tomorrow morning."

"It won't take more than a couple of hours. I promise.

I'll see to it that they're through as soon as possible. It's only two miles away and a taxi will take us there in no time."

I could have told her it was no use. No amount of reasoning would sway him. And for once in his life, he should have remained stubborn. Death was waiting in the wings and it might have vanished, if his wrongheadedness had remained true to him.

But he said, "Take Darius here. He'll go."

And that touch exploded me. All the spleen, and all the anger and all the suppressed rage that had been flooding and ebbing within me all day rose and overflowed and blew my head off. In one gigantic moment, I was going to strike back at everyone that had contributed to the failure at the press conference and at everyone who had helped irritate me that day from the man who stepped on my toe to the runtess who stepped on my ego.

I rose to my feet, and at the top of my voice said, "I *won't* go you tower of flab. You poor half-grown novelist, don't you know what your responsibilities are? One half-good book and a second that's not so good, and you think that the shoulders you have been lifted on and the free lifts you have received will go on forever. They won't. Even if they seem to, they won't. You're making enemies, you small man, and your soul is shriveling faster than your head is swelling and that's damned fast. Do you think you've reached the point where you can ignore the world and coast along the Milky Way on the well-greased wheels of your own fatted ego. My God, you'll come down with a crash that will deafen the world with the sound of its own laughter. Go!"

No, that's not *exactly* what I said. It is certainly the essence of it, but I know I put it much more strongly and with a considerably more peppery admixture of expletives.

The exact words don't matter. It was all scarcely what I would have said or done in return for the small provocation Giles had offered me—were it not for all that had been done to me that long afternoon.

Giles had gone dead white and Henrietta had turned

red. I was, after all, shouting at the top of my voice and I was surely heard through most of the room—a room in which almost every other sound had died away. Even through my red haze of rage, I realized I was shouting into a sonic vacuum, but it didn't stop me.

And what I did was to unseat Giles completely. I ripped him bodily out of the stubborn bog into which he had set his will and turned him about. I wouldn't have thought anything could have, short of a gun, but nothing had ever made me release the full range of my fury at him in a public place. It was enough, and I had talked events back into the path to murder. The flagstones were shaping up well.

Giles was suddenly twenty-one again, and managed to look up at me from a point a head and a neck above me with the same suffering-canine look he had had when we first met.

He said, "No need to be angry, Darius. I'd go, except that I've got to do something first."

"Oh, but, Mr. Devore," said Henrietta with a mixture of desperate cajolery and clear impatience, "we'll be late."

I felt myself beginning to return to the real world. I felt a thousand pairs of eyes more or less on me. The hum of conversation was beginning to rise again as the onlookers realized that the noise had not been a preparation for fisticuffs, but a lot of conversation had to be about us.

I felt ashamed and guilty and couldn't fail to realize that though Giles had received it all, he had contributed only the final push. But *every* emotion I felt that afternoon, whether petty or decent, pushed in the same direction. If I believed in a vengeful God and thought we were worth this notice, I'd have said he was pulling strings. As it is, I have no explanation but the endless cussedness of everything.

I said testily, "What is it? *I'll* do it for you." I fell into the role I had filled nearly nine years before, of doing for Giles what he could not do for himself, and that pushed everything a notch further.

Giles fumbled in his left pants pocket and brought out a small transparent change purse. He studied it for a second, then brought out a red check ticket. He said, "I checked a little package in the second-floor cloakroom, the one near the—"

"I'll find it, I'll find it," I said, and took the ticket from him.

"The cloakroom is liable to be closed after I get back and I'll need the thing for tomorrow morning. Please get it up to my room tonight, Darius. It's room 1511. Here's the key."

"How will *you* get in?" I demanded.

"You can take it back down to the desk. Or you can leave it right there by the package. I have another. I always ask for two keys." (Cautious! Cautious! That's our Giles!)

He said, "Just leave the package on the bureau, in the center, and put the key on top of it." He was following the pressing urgency of Henrietta's arm upon his elbow and shouted back over his shoulder, "Don't forget."

I heard Henrietta say, "Now I won't leave you out of my sight, Mr. Devore, and I'll see to it that you get safely back to your room quite early. I'll see you to your room myself."

She was using a tone she would have used to a child, and I think she was doing the right thing. Then they were gone.

13 SHIRLEY JENNIFER 7:50 P.M.

"Don't forget!" Those had been Giles's last words to me.

It was unnecessary advice. I had no intention of forgetting. It didn't occur to me I could possibly forget.

Mind you, I knew Giles. In my heart, I was convinced that it didn't matter if I did forget, and that could have played a part in what followed, too. There wasn't a chance in hell, I was certain, that there was anything important about the package. It was all his own compulsive need for super-security—like this business of always having two keys to his room; two keys which he kept, I'm sure, in two different pockets of two different items of clothing.

And even if, at that moment, I had known just what was in the package he wanted me to get, there would still be no way in which I could have considered the mission to be in the least vital. Except, of course, that it was, and it had been a bitter chain of circumstances that had ended by putting the responsibility for it in my hands.

The question was: What do I do now?

On the one hand, there was no necessity of rushing for the package at once, even if I could conceive it to be a matter of great urgency. The cloakroom would remain open till eleven at least and at this time of year there were not likely to be long lines, and it was just about ten to eight.

For that matter, Giles would be back in plenty of time to get it himself, even if I didn't budge, but, of course, he would worry and wouldn't be able to relax for peeking unobtrusively at his watch. For that matter, he would probably remain unrelaxed wondering if I would forget. The super-secure are never secure.

But on the other hand, quite apart from Giles's package, what I really wanted to do, as I had wanted to do on two or three earlier occasions that day, was to cut my losses, call it quits, go home, and forget the convention. I had Giles's ticket and key in my right jacket pocket, so I could get the package, take it to 1511, leave it and the key there, and be home by eight-thirty and maybe watch television or do a little hard thinking about my next novel.

Earlier something had always happened to keep me from going home and breaking the chain of circumstances, and it happened now again. To be exact, nothing happened this time; something *was*. That something was a matter of stupid pride.

I could feel the wall of silence about me. I could feel

eyes around me, staring at me. I could feel myself the subject of remark. And it all roused the worst in me.

I suppose that I, too, have my share of stubbornness. The kids, when I was young, were not going to beat me into abandoning my name. And this bunch of sniggering whisperers were not going to drive me out of the ballroom because they had been titillated by my outburst of temper—not until I was ready to go.

God, I was ready to go right then, but they could never possibly believe that. There had to be some wait. So I walked to the coffee urn as calmly and indifferently as I could, poured myself another cup of coffee, added cream very deliberately, and walked back to the table. Everyone made way for me. No one said a word to me.

I sat down. I'd drink the coffee, slowly, and *then* I'd go. I half expected some friend or acquaintance, Asimov perhaps, to join me. (Hi, Darius. What happened back there? Heard you yelling at Giles.) No one came. I was truly Pariah for a Day.

I looked about as I drank, trying to make the glance stony and calm.

I didn't know anyone near me. They were worthy booksellers and their ladies, I imagine, but I found none attractive. For some reason or other the women repelled me in particular, at least those I saw. As far as I was concerned, Sarah Vostavosta, or whatever her name was, had given the entire sex a bad name. I tried to imagine the bulging pipsqueak in bed and failed completely. She probably arranged every movement in advance and didn't begin until you had recited every projected movement in the correct order. Then, if you slipped, it was the knee in the groin and out you went into the hall, with your clothes following you in a heap.

When I was through with the coffee, when I had drained the last drop and had looked about me just to show everyone I was perfectly at ease, I stood up. With an inner thankfulness so intense I could almost feel my knees buckle under the pressure of it, I began the procedure that would take me home within the half hour.

It wasn't to be. The cup of coffee had delayed me a crucial five minutes and just before I reached the head of the escalator I saw Shirley Jennifer. Five minutes earlier, *two* minutes earlier, and I would have missed her.

I hadn't seen her for at least half a year, but that was perfectly normal. We could see each other every day for two weeks and then not again for a year. That was the arrangement between us. It wasn't an "affair." We just saw each other now and then, never as a result of planning, and we enjoyed each other's company, and sex was usually part of the enjoyment, though not always, and neither one of us had a hang-up about it.

I said, "Shirley!" with honest enjoyment, and she said, "Darius!" and there we were, hugging happily.

She said, "I knew I was coming here for *some* reason, but I didn't think I would walk right into the arms of the handsomest competitor I have."

Some competitor I was! Her books do far better than mine. She writes family epics—traces the generations. I've tried reading them, since I felt that when you know the body of an author really intimately the least you can do is try to probe her soul, too. Unfortunately—true's true—her books left me cold. They're for women—pre-liberation women, and I'm a man who is rather partial to feminism, actually.

Well, maybe that's what made Shirley so pleasant. She had this notion that women's true happiness lay in pleasing a man, and while I'm feminist enough in principle to think this is entirely wrong, why, when it happens, it's hard not to enjoy it.

Actually, I've never known anyone to enjoy every part of sex as much as Shirley does. She'll lie on the bed, next to you, and just manage to touch hips, and wriggle and make little orgastic sounds even when it's all over for a while—and smoke.

Well, she has bad points, too. She has to smoke afterward, and that means my undershirts pick up the odor. Maybe if she didn't smoke, I wouldn't ever allow six months to go between meetings.

"Did you just get here?" I asked.

"Just came! I was at my agent's." She had a way of dragging out the final syllable of each sentence and giving it a little singing sound that had put me off when I first met her—but it wasn't affectation. She didn't ever speak any other way, and after a while, I found it rather cute. It meant I could recognize her on the phone anytime without fail, however long it had been since I had heard her voice, and that pleased her. I could also tell if she were in a room even if I couldn't see her. I could then walk right to her, and that pleased me.

She went on, "And then, when I came here, I didn't have any cash, not seventeen and a half dollars cash, so I signed a personal check and before they would accept it I had to fill out a form that asked the details of every fragment of my autobiography."

"Have you eaten, Shirley?"

"No-o-o, just some drinks and a few pretzels. Is there anything left to eat?"

There were still a few people lined up at the buffet tables, so I said there was, and offered to get it for her.

She said, "Oh, you wait here. You won't know what I like."

I'd be willing to take bets at any odds that I did, but I always believe in letting women have their way in the things that don't count. It gives them a great deal of pleasure and makes them more amenable in the direction of the things that do count.

Shirley came back, looking good all the way. She was five feet eight inches tall and, in fact, when I described the kind of girl I liked some time back, I was thinking of Shirley. She's just right, every part of her, even the reddish hair, which I think isn't quite her color, because elsewhere it isn't. She's the kind of girl who—Well, I'll tell you. She's the kind of girl who doesn't use perfume and smells good anyway, except her breath after she smokes.

I said, "No pastrami?" I knew she was big on pastrami (and that sometimes affected her breath, too).

"Was there pastrami?" Her brown eyes grew big and for a minute I thought she would allow her lower lip to tremble, but she didn't. She just looked chagrined. "I guess it must be all gone."

"Maybe not at the other buffets. Hold on and I'll be right back."

I managed to get some slices of pastrami and a few of corned beef, the last in the room, I think, and came back with them—which made me a hero in direct proportion to her love of the stuff, which was great.

"You're a doll, Darius," she said.

"If you play with this doll, honey, you know what will happen."

"If *anyone* plays with that doll, honey."

"Not at all," I said, making the ritualistic protest neither believed nor meant to be believed. "No one, Shirley, except you. I padlock my zipper when you're not around."

"And it's not padlocked now?"

"You better believe it isn't."

I let her eat undisturbed for a while. One of her good points is that she never bothers to pretend she doesn't enjoy eating, and why should she? It's my feeling that anyone who doesn't enjoy something as intrinsically enjoyable as food isn't going to enjoy any of the other good things of life—like sex. Or else, such a person would try to make sex replace food and then things would get too high-strung for me. I like sex to be relaxed and playful and I don't want it to be a kind of horizontal fist fight.

After a while, I said, "Are you going to be autographing?"

"No-o-o-o," she said. "Not in any big way. But my paperback people have asked me to stay in their booth for about an hour tomorrow afternoon and sign little cards announcing a boxed set of the Roswell Family series, and so of course I will. And then I thought I would come down tonight and get into the mood, you know. It was a good thing I did, because look what's happened. You-u-u-u."

"You're not staying at the hotel, are you, Shirley?"

"At these prices? When I have a perfectly good apartment on the river?"

"Same place?"

"Of course, the same place."

"Shirley?" We never asked after each other's private lives. What we did, when, and with whom, was out of bounds, but you had to make sure you weren't on a collision course. I just had to say, "Shirley?" and she knew what I meant and she could easily say, "Too tired tonight."

She might really be, or she might be at the wrong stage of her menstrual cycle, or she might be busy at her writing, or in the idealistic stage of a love affair. Who could tell? Someone might be living with her.

But none of these things was true. She smiled her special sunshine smile (the effect on me was sunshine, anyhow) and said, "You're welcome at the Jennifer suite."

After a while she finished eating, and we walked about together, and she introduced me to some friends and then engaged them in animated conversation while I waited patiently.

14 SHIRLEY JENNIFER 9:00 P.M.

By nine o'clock we were ready to leave and, as far as I was concerned, I was not going to return.

Shirley was the first good thing that had happened all day and, in fact, she made up for the whole damned shooting match. I was in a wonderful humor when I left; all set to kiss the world, including the cigar-chewing taxi driver who drove us east (well, I would have asked him to remove the cigar first).

And yet, good thing or bad thing, everything pushed in the wrong direction that day—even Shirley. You wouldn't think that Shirley, who packed more genuine desire to please people in her delicious skinny body than any two saints in the hagiology, should have laid down a big, flat flagstone of her own.

The fact was that, from the moment Shirley had walked into my field of view and arms, in that order, I had completely forgotten the ticket and key in my jacket pocket. Giles and his errand ceased to exist for me.

I didn't think of it during the taxi ride. I didn't think of it when Shirley locked and double-locked the door, or when she prepared a little "drinkey-poo." (I never said she was perfect. In addition to smoking after sex, she talks about drinkey-poos.) I had a little Bristol cream sherry, which I rather like on rare occasions—as when there's a girl in view whose bra I know will be removed within fifteen minutes with the most delightful results.

I didn't think of it when we sat on the couch with the lights low and no damned record-player going. (I don't know who it was who decided that it's romantic to keep music going at such times, but how can it help but get in the way? I remember once when a girl insisted on playing the "Camelot" album during our little romantic interlude, Richard Burton began to sing "How to Handle a Woman" at such an appropriate moment that we both burst out laughing. We had fun, but as sex it was second-rate.)

I didn't think of it when we were kissing on the sofa (kissing while standing I find a little clumsy—and once when I tried it standing on a phone book, I found it even clumsier) or undressing or getting into bed or lying next to her well over an hour later while she was smoking.

I went to sleep peacefully and as far as I know I slept dreamlessly the good sleep of the Just—this particular Just.

In fact, there was not one moment during the entire night, from the moment I met Shirley, when I as much as wrinkled my forehead and thought: Isn't there something I've forgotten?

Not once.

If Shirley hadn't arrived in time to cross my path with all the careful timing of a trapeze act— But she had and it would have been too much to ask of humanity (of me, anyway) to remember something as stupid as Giles's package, when all my attention—every bit of it, both sensory and hormonal—was on Shirley.

So I slept well and peacefully. It's just that since then, there have been nights when I haven't slept at all well, through thinking how well I slept that night.

Part Two

MONDAY

26 MAY 1975

(MEMORIAL DAY)

1 SHIRLEY JENNIFER 8:55 A.M.

I woke up at nearly nine with the smell of broiling bacon in my nose. That's the best way to wake up—second best—and it doesn't happen when you live in a bachelor pad, however well appointed, and mine wasn't particularly.

I said, "Come on, Shirley. Bathroom first and then instant replay." I patted her side of the bed.

But she said, "No-o-o-o. You start that and there's no telling how long it will take, and I've got my signing to do."

"That's not till this afternoon."

"Yes, but there's the book-and-author luncheon first and Douglas Fairbanks, Jr., will be speaking and I *love* him."

"How quickly they forget," I said.

"I love him spiritually," said Shirley, "and if you want to go to the bathroom, go right now, because I'm going to add the eggs."

So I scooted. When I came out, she added the eggs and said, "I fell in love with him when he played Rupert of Hentsau in *The Prisoner of Zenda*." She paused to light a cigarette while the eggs fried slowly, and I edged a bit further away.

"You aren't old enough to remember *The Prisoner of Zenda*," I said.

"I'm mysteriously older than I look," she said, shaking her hair at me, "and I saw it three times on television. Besides, I fell in love with Rupert of Hentsau when I read the book at the age of ten. I was so afraid they'd spoil him in the movie, but they didn't. Douglas Fairbanks, Jr., was just right. No morals at all."

"That's the secret," I said, sighing. "Women love men with no morals."

"That's no secret," said Shirley. "It's not safe to marry a man with no morals, but a man who has them is no good in bed."

72

"I've got morals," I said.

"Not a one," she said, and I decided it was a compliment and helped her dish out the eggs and bacon.

She put out her cigarette and we moved into the little dinette.

"Are you going to the convention today?" she asked.

"I don't particularly want to," I said, "except that I would like to join you at lunch."

"Well, you can't. I'm going to be with my publisher, and I don't want anyone absently stroking my fanny at the table. It doesn't go with my image."

"It goes with *my* image."

"Then stroke your publisher's fanny and impress him. You leave my rear end alone in public."

"All right, but I won't go with you on those terms. Hands that don't touch fannies shall never be mine. Except that—"

For the first time since I had hugged Shirley the evening before, something stirred within me. That is, something that wasn't hooked up to an endocrine gland. I didn't know what it was; not the faintest idea. I just had a feeling of uneasiness.

"Except what?" said Shirley.

"Except that maybe I ought to go in and cheer for poor Giles at his autographing session."

Funny. I could even mention Giles and remember yelling at him and being shamefaced about it now that I was feeling fulfilled and calm, and yet not think of the errand I had failed to run—at least, not consciously.

I went over to the end table near the bed to look at my watch. "I can do it," I said. "I can guzzle down my coffee, take a quick shower, and not be more than a few minutes late, and then I'll see you after lunch, and I get the first chance at instant replay."

I could have done it, too. I think it was my last chance. If I had gotten there and if Giles had seen me, I would have remembered what I had forgotten because he would have left the platform and charged me even with a thousand people waiting for a signature. And then—

But what's the use? My heart wasn't in it. It was just my vague unanalyzed anxiety pushing me, and I probably wouldn't have gone—well, maybe I wouldn't—even if Shirley hadn't put in an objection.

She said, "Oh, going to one of those autographing sessions is cre-e-epy. They just line up. *You've* autographed books."

Not as often as all that. There were two times when I signed books after a book-and-author luncheon, and three or four times after I had given a talk on those few occasions when Prism Press had supplied books the day before I gave the talk instead of the day after. (Other publishing houses are as bad, even the best of them.)

Autographing books is nice in a way. Every book is a sale, and every sale is six bits or more in your private till (before taxes, of course). On the other hand, there's the strain of it. The same thing. The same thing. Best wishes. Best wishes. Best wi—

And you smile and smile. Thank you. Thank you. I'm so glad you like my books. I'm so glad. Thank you. The pleasure's mine. Thank you.

When it's done, you go out and bite the nearest bystander to get the sickly-sweet goo out of your mouth.

Some are better at it than others. I know one author who will sign nothing but hardbacks, and then only his name in a wavy scrawl that means nothing.

Asimov goes to the other extreme, the incredible ham. He's the only writer I know who actually enjoys it. I watched him at a signing session once, and there are no limits to the lengths he will go. He scrawls out "with love" and "with passion" and "with ravished ecstasy" at random, asking only that the person before him be at least vaguely feminine. Once he asked a young woman's first name and then wrote: "To Sheila, in memory of that night on the beach when we, as you so charmingly put it, went all the way." He'd never seen her before, of course, but she went off giggling and clutching the precious souvenir to her ample breasts—and probably lied about it later.

And he'll sign anything, hardbacks, softbacks, other people's books, scraps of paper. Inevitably someone handed him a blank check on the occasion when I was there, and he signed that without as much as a waver to his smile—except that he signed: "Harlan Ellison."

"Who's Harlan Ellison?" I asked afterward.

"Friend of mine," he said. Then he added irrelevantly, "About your height."*

I thought of all that in connection with autographing, yawned, and said, "Guess you're right."

Goodbye, last chance.

"But I'll still go," I said. It was the uneasiness talking, but it seemed to make more sense to blame it on my passion for Shirley. "I still want to see you after lunch. In fact, maybe I'll go to the lunch, find you, sneak over to you when you're not expecting it, and stroke your fanny, and yell, 'Lookit, everybody! Lookit, everybody!' "

"You do that, and I'll tell everyone you're impotent."

"I'll say only with you."

"I'll say you never tried anyone else."

"I'll say that's because you believe everything I tell you."

"I'll say—"

It was a game of ours. First one who couldn't get past the "I'll say—" got a punch on the shoulder, which usually developed into all sorts of other things. In this case it was Shirley who failed, so I kissed her shoulder and she said, "No-o-o-o, you idiot, I've got to get ready."

So I took a quick shower, dressed and went back home to change underwear and shirt, shave, and make myself look as beautiful as a late-spring morning. Then I went down to the hotel on that beautiful spring morning of Memorial Day.

My conscience was still clear.

---

* I think Asimov dedicated this book to Harlan Ellison because of all the checks he signed with that name.

—DARIUS JUST

Quite the contrary; out of sincere admiration.

—ISAAC ASIMOV

I got to the hotel at about ten forty-five. Giles Devore and Isaac Asimov were scheduled to keep on signing books till eleven, so they were still at it, but that didn't bother me any. I wasn't going to catch the last few minutes.

I found out afterward what the autographing arrangements were. A big room was used and it was the only room that might officially be used at the convention for the autographing of books, though lesser objects such as book announcements could be signed at the booths. At one end of the room was a stage at which both signers sat, and the line moved up to the first signer, then to the second signer, with each person guaranteed two free books.

I don't suppose any of the twelve thousand people who attended the convention walked off without *something* free. If not a signed book, then an unsigned one, a gizmo, a promotion device. There wasn't a booth that didn't have someone pushing something on somebody. Some booths were giving out shopping bags into which you could put the stuff that the other booths were emitting.

I made my way to the Prism Press booth, but neither Tom nor Teresa was there. I recognized the bored young lady who was in charge as Mary Ann Lipsky, who was Teresa's secretary. Apparently they were making at least one underling work on Memorial Day.

Mary Ann was a pleasant girl, not very pretty, with a complexion that tended to the mottle and a voice that tended to the lisp, but pretty is as pretty does sometimes, and I could always count on her to be helpful when I was having some sort of hassle with the Valiers. It is always good to have a spy in the enemy camp. So I said, "And how is my lovely princess of Prism?"

She cheered up at once and said, "Hello, Mr. Just."

"No business at the booth?"

She wrinkled her nose." Not very much."

I said, "Where is the Tsar and the Tsarina?"

She said, "The Tsarina is with Mr. Devore at the autographing."

"Oh yes, she said she would be."

"And the Tsar is off in conference somewhere."

"And you don't know when they'll be back?"

"The Tsarina might be back after the autographing, but I don't think so, and I don't know about the Tsar at all."

"Oh well, I won't wait, unless you and I—underneath the chair—"

"Everyone will see us, Mr. Just."

"That's the best part," I said gravely.

She laughed, and I felt good at having spread the cheer about.

I said, "May I leave a note for them?"

"Sure," she said.

I scrawled: "Tried to talk to Giles, but absolutely no go!"

I folded the paper and gave it to Mary Ann, who put it half under a book. She smiled at me affectionately and then turned to talk, with animation, to someone inquiring about someone.

I bet myself a resigned nine to five that the Valiers would decide either that I hadn't talked to Giles at all or that I had yelled at him (as they would undoubtedly hear) and had ruined everything just as he was about to become compliance itself.

Well, I was armored in truth and in the memory of a successful night, so I didn't give a damn.

I asked after Roseann at a few logical places, but couldn't find her or, for that matter, anyone I knew. Then I wandered past a booth where a cookbook was being pushed and where slivers of cake were being handed out in consequence. I kept passing and repassing and had five slivers, each with a kind of vanilla icing that wasn't bad. I like sweet things; cake, too.

I went on a deliberate scouting expedition to see what

else was being given out in the form of comestibles and
had a free cola drink. It was a pity I had made up my
mind to attend the lunch and listen to Douglas of Hentsau, Jr., because I could have made a great meal on the
freebies without ever insulting my uninsultable digestion.

3 MARTIN WALTERS 12:10 P.M.

It was somewhat after noon when I wandered up to
the banquet room and found the doors closed and a sign
that said it would open at twelve-thirty. That was when
it was scheduled to begin, so I don't know why I was
surprised. Every ten seconds a party of two or three tried
moving in, promptly got shooed out by some waiter, and
walked out looking annoyed and embarrassed.

A young man of about twenty-two (I should judge)
standing near me and, I suppose, impressed by my distantly superior attitude, as though I knew far too much
to try to get into a door I couldn't get into, asked if I
were a writer.

I confessed my guilt and he wanted to know my name.
"Darius Just," I said.

He looked uncertain and I knew what was going on
behind his face. He was wondering what he could say
that would be polite and would not give away the fact
that he hadn't the foggiest notion of who I was and what
I wrote. I sighed inaudibly.

It was Martin Walters who rescued me and for that I
forgave him, finally, for the day before.

He called, "Darius!" and motioned strenuously for
me to join him.

I did so, and he said, "What are you doing standing
there in the ranks with the privates? Come join us officers
at the cocktail party."

"What cocktail party?"

"This cocktail party."

I had followed him to a small room just off the banquet hall and there it was—and Martin had a drink before I could draw two breaths.

About a hundred people were talking to each other in clumps, the biggest group maintaining itself at a respectful distance from Douglas Fairbanks, Jr., himself. I looked to see if Shirley were there, and when I saw she wasn't, I knew she could be nowhere in the room. She'd probably arrive too late to do anything but get into the luncheon and I decided I had better not tell her that she missed a chance to touch her hero or she'd be too miserable later to touch me.

Anita Loos of *Gentlemen Prefer Blondes* and Cathleen Nesbit, who played dowager duchesses in at least fifty movies, were there, too; both small and aged and looking happy.

Asimov was there, being introduced. He held out his hand to Anita Loos with a fatuous smile and said, "I've always wanted to play cards with you and Howard Fast, Miss Loos, for then I'd be playing Fast and Loos."

She looked at him in puzzlement and I stepped away quickly. I didn't want to be introduced after that since I despaired of being able to top that remark for sheer imbecility.*

Then it occurred to me that since Asimov was there, Giles Devore ought to be there also. At least he ought to have been finished autographing over an hour ago.

I looked about again, and Martin Walters, remembering my question of the evening before, I suppose (the only other alternative is telepathy), put his head on one side, focused his glance on me through his pince-nez, and said, "Looking for Devore again?"

"I thought he might be around," I said.

"I don't think so. He's probably off somewhere sulking. That man is not a professional. He proved it again this morning."

---

* Darius insisted this passage be included, but what the devil is there about the remark that should be sneered at? It was spontaneous and clever.

—ISAAC ASIMOV

He still thinks it's clever. I rest my case.

—DARIUS JUST

"What did he do, Martin?"

"He made some kind of fuss during the autographing session. I don't know what it was. I was in the room talking to the Hercules Books people and all I know was that the autographing was stopped cold. Nellie— Do you know Nellie Griswold of Hercules?"

I thought a moment. "Maybe by sight. The name doesn't ring a bell."

"If you know her by sight, you're well off. Tall and very—" His hands waved appropriate curves in the air, which was easier to do now that he had reduced his drink to its icy skeleton. Then he looked about to see if anyone had seen him make those terribly obscene gestures. "Don't get me wrong," he said. "She's a nice girl."

"I believe you. I know lots of shapely girls who manage to be nice, too. But what did she do?"

"Oh, you mean about that nut, Devore. She had to run and bring him something. It was awful. It just put a damper on the show. The damn fool had better not sign at all than put on a display like that. He didn't seem to have been drinking, but *something* was wrong with him."

I made a routine deprecating noise. I must admit I wasn't terribly surprised, or even interested. Devore was clearly developing temperament and had already become unbearable. So much the worse for those who had to deal with him, among whom would never again be me (I silently swore).

Martin put down his empty glass on a convenient table and said, "I understand you chewed him out last night, Darius. I was glad to hear it. Do you suppose that had something to do with his being upset today?"

If he wanted some retailable gossip, he wasn't going to have it. "Not a thing," I said quickly. "We're on perfectly good terms."

It is unbelievable to me, as I look back on it now, that I could listen to Martin's reference to a fearfully upset Giles, talk to him briefly concerning the night before, and *still* not have anything register. By then, of course, it was some forty-five to fifty minutes too late.

the picture they made out of the book? It was called *Come the Evening*."

"Yes, I did. I hope you don't mind, but it was a poor interpretation of the book. It fell far short."

I didn't mind at all, since that was exactly how I felt. I melted a bit more at this evidence of good judgment. We weren't far from the wall, and I drifted in that direction. She moved with me, still looking anxious.

I said, "Now that you know who I am, do you wish to rephrase anything you said last night?" I was a little stiff about it but repressed the impulse to add "dearie" or "toots" at the end of the question.

"More than rephrase, Mr. Just. I want to erase it all, and to apologize. It was inexcusable of me to strike out at you like that."

"Because I'm Darius Just, author of *Beware the Evening Star*?*"

I wasn't making it easy for her, and she took a deep breath. I couldn't help but notice the interesting things that did to her cleavage. She was wearing a low-cut gown again and this time I was standing up. I found it rather pleasant to be able to look down at a pair of breasts. There was an easy comfort about it.

"Well," I said, urging her on a bit roughly.

She held her temper and said, "No, Mr. Just. That's not it. You were right to tell me that attempts at prior restraint were out of order. I was officious and unpleasant. I have already apologized to Dr. Asimov shortly before his autographing session and he assured me that he never had any intention of naming the hotel or identifying it in any way. It was only after that that I asked your name that I might apologize to you as well, and when he told me you were Darius Just, well—"

By now I was melted into a mush and had decided she wasn't such a bad little kid if you like them squashed down. "Forget it," I said, "I think I would like to modify some of the things I said last night."

"Such as telling me that I ought to indulge in my public relations? Did that have an improper meaning?"

I felt myself flushing. "I didn't mean it that way," I lied, "but it could sound as if it was improper. I'm sorry."

"No offense taken," she said gravely. It was quite a love feast and I was actually wondering, in a detached sort of way, if I ought to put my arm around her waist as a gesture of friendship, when she said, "But that's not the only reason I have come to seek you out, Mr. Just."

"If we're going to be friendly," I said, grinning, "call me Darius, because I've got to call you Sarah. I can't pronounce your last name."

"Voskovek," she said, pronouncing it distinctly. The accent was on the second syllable, which had a long "o," like this: "Vos-KOH-vek." "Still, you can call me Sarah." She had a dimple on the left side when she smiled; not on the right.

"Okay, then. What's the other thing you wanted to talk about?"

"It's Mr. Giles Devore. Is he a friend of yours?"

"In a way," I said dryly. And then I said, "Why? Why do you ask?"

"There was a queer incident at the autographing session this morning. I had decided to come to the session since I knew Dr. Asimov would be there and I did wish to make up for last night. I lingered on for a while out of—of curiosity and there was a—a rumpus. Mr. Devore was very unhappy. It disturbed me, for it's rather important to the hotel that there be nothing that would make unnecessarily unpleasant headlines—"

"I understand," I said.

"It was over, however. He had been brought something and he had settled down. Later, though, I heard him mutter, 'That Darius! That Darius Just!' And he said it with such *hate*. I had to find you—I hoped you would be at the luncheon, for I didn't know how to locate you otherwise—so that I could both apologize to you and warn you as well. Mr. Devore is a large man and you are—not large—and—"

I said contemptuously, "He's as soft as a pin cushion, Sarah, without the pins. Don't give it a single thought.

With one hand, open-palm, I could slap him silly and make him thank me for the favor. I could—"

I think it was the word "favor" in this connection that did it. At any rate, at just about 1:15 P.M. on Monday, May 26, 1975, I remembered, all at once, and in one big piece, exactly what I had forgotten some eighteen hours before.

"Oh, my God," I said, half strangling. "Oh, my God." I slapped hard at my jacket pockets in an agony of embarrassment. I had changed shirt, socks, and underwear that morning, but I had the same pants and jacket I had worn the night before. The room key was in my jacket pocket; I could feel it. The ticket had to be there, too.

I said, in a gasping sort of way. "Pardon me. Got to do something."

She said, in a frightened voice, "But what is it?"

Harold Sayers, my companion at the table, must have been watching me from a distance of some twenty feet. He rose in consternation and there were eyes at me from other directions. I had even attracted the attention of the head table, but I didn't care. I didn't even care that an ice-cream parfait was being served as dessert and that I might miss it—to say nothing of coffee.

I was off at a run, fumbling for the ticket.

6   HILDA   1:20 P.M.

What the devil was I so panicked about?

Done or not done, the matter couldn't possibly be important except in Giles's own nit-picking mind. I knew that at the start. I *knew* that as I trotted down an escalator moving too slowly for me, ducking past people who were irritated at being shoved and who showed it.

Forgetting is human. What could he do to me?

Besides, he would have come back last night, seen that the stuff wasn't on the bureau, and gone down to the checkroom. He would have demanded it, ticket or not, and gotten the manager or the nearest official available at that time of night and made enough fuss either to force the disgorgement of the package or to make the entire hotel aware of the problem.

Since nobody seemed aware anything had happened late last night, he had his package and the checkroom didn't. He had been muttering against me to Sarah because some small inconvenience at the autographing table had put him in mind of a series of inconveniences that had been plaguing him, and I was included. (Hadn't I gone through the same sort of thing yesterday?)

The trouble was, I didn't believe it.

I ran across the hall to the checkroom indicated on the ticket. How could I help it when in common with a hundred million others I had been beaten into conditioned reflex by the age of ten. Did you ever forget an errand you had been sent on by your mother? Did you ever forget to bring your homework to school? There were physical assaults (what else do you call a spanking?) and writings of "I shall not forget my homework" a hundred times. Endless humiliations.

I was going through it again. My head told me, quite calmly, that the matter was of no importance. My heart thudded, "Golly, I forgot—golly, I forgot—"

I was panting fairly noticeably by the time I got to the checkroom counter. There was no one else there at 1:20 P.M. on a warm Memorial Day and this, fortunately, eliminated one ground for delay.

I whistled to attract the attention of an elderly woman in a shapeless green dress. She seemed indignant at being hailed in that fashion and walked toward me with the attitude of having been a queen in a past reincarnation— in the recent past, at that. She had a little nameplate that said she was Hilda, and wore tinted glasses and hair of a somewhat tarnished chemical yellow.

I presented the ticket and said, "Is this still here?" I couldn't tell her what I meant by "this" because I didn't know.

She looked at the ticket with an expert eye as though there were a trick to reading a large black number that only a checkroom attendant knew. She gave it back at last and said, "If you've got the ticket, it's still here."

"Would you get it, then?"

"That will be another fifty cents."

"What?"

"That's a yesterday's ticket. You paid fifty cents in advance but that was only for yesterday. Fifty cents more for today."

I brought out two quarters. "Here you are."

She walked leisurely to one side of the room while I bet myself a breathless five to two that she'd come back with the news that it was gone, and I rooted hard for the five.

I lost. She showed up in twenty seconds with a package about nine inches long, two inches across, and two inches deep. It weighed perhaps four ounces.

I said, "Is that what the ticket's for?"

She said, "It's your ticket, mister." She was very indifferent to it all.

It couldn't be right. Who the devil would pay fifty cents to check something this size? I said, "Listen, did someone come down last night to pick up something without having a ticket?"

She said, "How late last night? If it was after four in the afternoon, I wasn't on."

I turned away.

She said, "Someone tried this morning."

I turned back. "When this morning?"

"Just before ten, I think. I said he couldn't have anything without a ticket and she dragged him away, Little Pepper; said he was late for something."

I was scarcely listening. He had come to his senses too late and he was being dragged to the autographing by Henrietta as she had dragged him to the television taping the night before. I was almost sorry for the silly bastard.

I said, "You didn't give it to him, then?"

"Of course I didn't. Not without a ticket."

I was about to leave, when I thought of one more thing to check. After all, had it been Giles? I said, "Big man? Mustache? Thick black mustache?"

She nodded her head. "Yes. That's right."

"Was it this package he wanted?"

"How do I know what he wanted? He had no ticket and I don't listen to anyone without a ticket."

I turned away for the last time and made for the elevators. For some reason Giles hadn't noticed last night that I hadn't delivered the material. For some reason he hadn't done anything about it till so late this morning that it was too late. He'd been rushed off to the autographing session. No wonder he had been muttering against me. It was fresh in his mind.

What room was he in? I checked the key I had as I approached the elevator banks. It was 1511, so I got into the correct elevator and pushed the "15" button. I had perhaps twenty seconds to think up an excuse and avoid—well, minimize—recriminations.

Nothing came. I would have to say, "Something came up, Giles, and I didn't have a chance till now." It was almost true, and what the hell could he do about it? My mind said: Nothing. My heart said: Write a hundred times: "I shall not forget to deliver packages for a friend."

7 GILES DEVORE 1:30 P.M.

I stood before the door marked 1511, and since there was no one visible in the corridor either way, and therefore no one before whom I had to put on a meaningless display of courage and resolution, I listened at the door for a few seconds. I might hear him talking to someone and then, of course, he wouldn't throw any real fit before witnesses (wishful thinking, perhaps) and I could be out and away quickly. Or he might be walking about and I could tell from the sound of the footsteps whether he was calm or not.

Actually, I heard nothing at all, so I knocked, and there was no response; no sound of footsteps moving toward the door; no sound of anything, in fact.

I knocked again. Nothing.

I wasted a few more moments trying to gather the

significance of that—just to delay a confrontation I didn't want.

Maybe he had gone to the luncheon, in which case I could use the key, place the package and the key on the bureau, and swear myself blue that I had left them there the night before. I could tell him that if he hadn't seen them, he had either been blind, drunk, or crazy. What could he do to me?

No! He couldn't have gone to the luncheon, for if he had, he would have tracked me down and stood there looming over my seat at the table with a face of doom and a hard-breathed "What did you do with my package, Darius?" in a kind of controlled rage of self-pity. (I knew him so well that I could hear the precise intonation of each syllable ringing in my ear.) That little girl, Sarah Vostovek—ah, I remembered her name—had found me and so could he.

Of course, he could be anywhere else in the hotel, or out of it, for that matter. He might have been reduced to a perfect snit at whatever it was that had annoyed him during the autographing, so that he had flounced up to his room, grabbed his belongings, checked out of the hotel, and gone back to New Jersey.

In that case, when I opened the door, I would find nothing in the room but an unmade bed and damp towels in the bathroom. In that case, I would go somewhere where I could write a note and make a package. I would wrap, address, and mail the object I had in my hand and make the note a manly one of contrition, and then I would go down to the exhibition room and watch Shirley sign her name. With luck, I wouldn't see Giles again for months and by then he would have cooled down to nothing more than snubbing me when we met—which snubbing I looked forward to with delight.

So I used my key and opened the door, stopped on the threshold, and found myself astonished. The room was not empty; it was clearly occupied. There was a shirt draped tipsily over the back of a chair and a pair of pants over the arm, with the pants belt trailing off on the floor.

Two socks were on the floor, near but not on two shoes, as though someone had thrown the socks at the shoes and missed. An undershirt and shorts were over the other arm of the chair and now I could see a bit of a tie peeping out from under the shirt.

It couldn't be Giles's room, and I looked at the key. But that was silly. The key had opened the door, hadn't it? Could Giles have had two different keys, the non-mate having been given him by an erring room clerk, and had he handed me the wrong one by mistake?

No, that was ridiculous. The thin briefcase on the bureau was his. I would have recognized it even without the G.D. on it. Beside it was one of his monogrammed throwaway pens.

I closed the door behind me, double-locked it, walked into the middle of the room, and stood there uncertain. It was all a real puzzler to me, an incongruity. The room was Giles's since it had his briefcase, his pen, and therefore presumably his clothes in it. Yet it couldn't be his in some ways.

The thing to do was to leave the key and package, shrug off the incongruity, and go away. I did put them down on the bureau and then found myself staring at the pen that was lying there. Near it was a thin film of talcum powder with something that looked like finger marks near one end as though someone had tried to brush it away. Automatically and without thinking, I drew my finger through it. I regretted it almost at once and lifted my finger to my nose to see if I had placed any undesirable smell on it.

I hadn't, at least not since I had gnawed at the chicken bone. Absently, I licked at the finger with its taste of chicken and stiffened at once.

Good God! Impossible!

I sat down in one of the chairs—not the one with the clothes draped over it—and stared at those clothes, and then at my finger. To my right was the bureau with the pen, the briefcase, the key, and the package on it, and I reached for the pen automatically, even rising from the chair to do so. A writer reaches for a pen to aid the process of thinking as a non-writer might scratch his head —even if the pen is no more than twiddled. I was careful not to touch the talcum powder, however.

I didn't intend to do more than twiddle the pen, but the hotel pad was lying on the bureau, too, and I reached for it as automatically as for the pen. With both pen and paper in my hand, I had to produce something and I drew a large, firm question mark and then drew short lines from it in every direction. At about the third or fourth mark, the ink gave out. It was a dry pen with just a trace of ink having trickled down to the ball-point while it had been on the bureau.

What the question mark meant was just this: How did Giles's clothes—assuming they belong to Giles—come to be strewn about so? I couldn't imagine the urgency that would make such strewing necessary, not even the pangs of oncoming diarrhea. In that case, you run for the bathroom and drop your pants and shorts; you don't get undressed.

Which reminded me that I hadn't looked in the bathroom. Surely, if he were in the bathroom, he'd have heard me come in, or if the noise of the shower or of flushing had drowned me out, I would have heard that.

I listened carefully, ear canted toward the bathroom, but I heard nothing. I heard city traffic and I heard footsteps in the corridor—not very loud—that seemed to stop at the door, or near it. For a moment, I expected to hear a key scrape against the lock and see Giles walk in, but it didn't happen, and then the footsteps, or maybe other footsteps, sounded again and faded. There was nothing to hear in the room itself.

But having thought of the bathroom, it seemed logical to look inside. There might be something there to explain the incongruity of the room. I walked to the bathroom door, which was slightly ajar, and pushed it inward.

And Giles was there, grinning at me silently, stretched out in the bathtub with one leg over the side, his head cradled against the metal of the faucets, apparently quite,

quite nude, and, apparently, quite, quite dead.

Although I've spent a long time trying to describe what I saw and what I thought since entering the room, it didn't take as long to see and to think as to describe. I doubt that I had been puzzling in the room for as long as three minutes before I walked into the bathroom.

It was 1:33 P.M. of Memorial Day, May 26, 1975, when I discovered Giles's body. I didn't look at my watch at that precise moment, for there was no room in my mind for anything but the absorption of the sight, but I did a couple of minutes afterward. I couldn't be more than a minute off.

How did I know he was dead? From a medical standpoint, I didn't. I didn't feel for his pulse or check for traces of breathing. I didn't even find out whether the body was cold or not. Perhaps someone else might have had the presence of mind to do such a thing, but I hadn't. It was the first body I had ever seen unexpectedly and it blasted me into immobility and non-thought. For a minute, it seemed to me my heart had stopped beating. I don't think I screamed or made any sound at all, because my vocal cords were paralyzed, and by the time I took my first, shuddering breath, seconds after the sight, I was in control again—very shakily.

But there was no doubt in my mind, not a shred, not an atom, that he was dead. The fixed immobility of the body, the open eyes staring right at me with glassy and fixed non-recognition, the lips stretched in an unchanging grimace that was not really a smile. If I had never seen or heard of a dead human before, I'd have known this was an object from which life had departed.

Additional details flooded into my brain over what seemed a long stretch of time that surely must have been a matter of seconds in actual fact. The leg—left leg— draped over the side of the tub was very hairy and the individual hairs were in part plastered to the skin as though the leg had recently been wet. The tub itself had traces of wetness in it.

The shower curtain was partially torn down but no

dead hand was clutching at it. One of Giles's arms lolled its full length along the floor of the bathroom, the other was across his chest. The curtain itself dangled over his groin as though protecting the modesty of the corpse. The one clear thought I can remember during that long, stricken moment was one of wild relief at having Giles's genitals covered.

Then I finally drew that breath, felt my heart take up its duties, and I staggered shakily out of the bathroom. I should, in theory, have reported the matter at once, but I couldn't. I had to sit down—or fall down. I made it to the chair from which I had, just a few minutes before, listened for noise from the bathroom.

For half a minute, I continued to struggle for control. I looked at my watch and it was 1:35. It was an Accutron and I knew it was within ten seconds of the official time. I thought, incongruously, that Douglas Fairbanks, Jr., was about to get up to talk and that I would miss it. In the disorientation of the moment, it didn't occur to me that I might miss Shirley, too.

Finally, I walked over to the bed, sat down on it, and reached for the phone. It was one of those phones with every hole in the dial marked for something and with combinations for this and that. I had no time and certainly no inclination to study the code. I dialed "Operator" and there was the usual maddening wait before the tinny feminine voice said, "Operator. Can I help you?"

I said, as flatly as I could manage, "Operator, I'm calling to report a dead man in this room."

I'll give her credit. There was no scream, no gasp, just a calm "What is your room number, please?"

"Room 1511," I said.

"One moment," she said. It really was a moment, too. She must have sent out a signal that precluded fooling around.

A male voice in my ear said, "Jonathan Turbeville, Assistant Manager, here. What is the problem, please?"

I said, "This is Room 1511 and the problem is that there is a dead man in the bathroom."

The name of the person registered to that room must have been passed to him by then, for he said, "Is this Giles Devore speaking?"

"No, sir," I said. "Giles Devore will never speak again. He's the dead man."

He didn't ask any more questions. He said, "Please stay right where you are, sir. There'll be a man with you in less than five minutes."

I hung up and waited. I was back to thinking hard.

8 MICHAEL STRONG 1:40 P.M.

It was indeed less than five minutes before someone answered. It was less than twenty seconds.

When there came a knock on the door, I didn't for one moment believe it had any connection with my call. I assumed it was someone for Giles. If a voice other than that of Giles, my own voice, had called out for identification through a closed door, the owner of that knock might have departed.

I wanted to see who it was, so I just threw the door open as quickly as I could get to it.

A man stepped through and said in accents of purest astonishment, "Mr. Just!"

I stared at him, nonplussed, and then remembered. It was the guard at the door of the exhibitors' room. We had talked yesterday afternoon and I remembered his name, Michael Strong. I even remembered his middle initial was P.

I said ungraciously, "How did you get here so quickly?" I didn't bother identifying myself. He knew me and I was still wearing my badge.

"Walkie-talkie," he said, indicating something suspended from his belt. "I was closest. You say there's a dead man here?"

"In the bathroom," I said, and followed him.

Strong might have been a member of Hotel Security, but that did not mean he was used to bodies. Petty pilfering by the maids and guests who had locked themselves out of their rooms were much more his speed, no doubt.

He staggered a bit when he opened the bathroom door and looked inside. I was rather glad. I was conscious of the fact that I had not handled myself too well on seeing the body and I didn't want him to shame me by doing better. He didn't. Considering that he had been warned there was a dead body in the bathroom, he did poorly indeed.

He came out, pale, his face contorted, and said, "He's still a little warm, but he's dead all right." He swallowed with an audible noise. "I guess he won't write—" And he ran down.

I remembered. He was a fan of Giles's; he had been planning for his autograph. Perhaps he had obtained it. I removed some of the self-serving scorn I had pumped up for him. If I had remembered, I would have broken the news to him.

Strong cleared his throat and tried to regain his professional aplomb. He said, "It looks to me like he finished his shower, then he slipped and fell. He grabbed the curtain, tore it down, hit his head against the faucets, and was killed. Right?"

I shrugged. I didn't for a minute believe that had happened, but I just said, "I wasn't here."

"You mean you came after he was dead?"

"That's right."

Strong looked at me in puzzlement. "How did you get in, then? Did he leave the door open while he was taking a shower?"

"I had a key," I said. "There it is." And I pointed to it on the bureau.

"How did you get a key?"

"Mr. Devore gave it to me. We're friends. After all, you told me yourself he was my protégé." I pronounced it correctly without thinking and hoped, too late, that he would understand.

I suppose he did, but he went off on a new tangent. He said, "How do you mean, friends?"

My lips twitched and I tried to hold down the anger.

I suppose it was a legitimate thought. "Friends," I said, "in the dictionary definition. I'm heterosexual."

"What?"

"I'm straight," I said, raising my voice. "I like girls. Understand?"

"Yes. But how come you got a key?"

"I had to get something for him and I just brought it up. It's there on the bureau next to the key."

There was another knock at this point, a good loud one. I started for the door, but Strong motioned me away. He opened the door a bit, looked through, and said, "Hello, Mr. Marsogliani," as he opened it wide.

9 ANTHONY MARSOGLIANI 1:50 P.M.

A large, stout man entered. He was a little taller than Strong and a little wider. He had a considerable paunch, a large nose, and a dark stubble against his red face. He carried a half-gone cigar which wasn't lit but which smelled very bad anyway.

He said, in a rolling bass-baritone, "Where's the body, Strong?"

Strong jerked his thumb over his shoulder. "In the bathroom, boss."

Marsogliani (I eventually got to know how his name was spelled) vanished into the bathroom, emerged after half a minute, and said to me, "You the guy who reported the body?"

"I'm the guy," I said.

He looked about the room with what seemed to me to be a practiced eye. His glance fell on the armchair with the clothes on it and it seemed to me he was going to walk in that direction.

"Don't touch anything," I said hastily.

He turned his head slowly and put his cold eye on me. "I'm not going to touch anything. I'm going to call the police." Having taken the cigar out of his mouth to say that, he now put it back.

I said, "Good. Call the police. Tell them there's a murdered man here."

I'd been thinking murder from the minute I had found the body and I had wondered if I could bring myself to say the word. Now I had said it, and without any trouble.

"Murdered?" Marsogliani, who had edged toward the phone, stopped, turned, and looked at me dispassionately. His appearance, his undistinguished brown suit, complete with vest, his dead cigar, had all served to give rise in my mind to the stereotype of the "dumb lawman." His eyes didn't fit the stereotype.

He said, unperturbed, "You killed him?"

"No. I found him exactly the way you see him now. But he didn't die in the tub. He died with his clothes on. It's a frame."

Strong looked as though he were going to jump out of his skin in surprise when I said that, but his boss never turned a hair. "How do you figure that out?"

I said, "I knew the murdered man, Giles Devore, well. I roomed with him for a period of time. I've been in the rooms when he was taking a shower or getting undressed maybe fifty times. He folds his clothes. He hangs them up. He blows into his socks and flattens them out. He *never* throws them around like this. When I came in and saw this I thought I was in the wrong room."

"But the clothes are messed up. How do you account for it?"

"He was killed. I don't know why. The murderer stripped him, then threw the clothes around, thinking that would make it look as though Giles were taking a shower—"

"The murderer wasn't somebody who knew the man's habits, then?"

"No, he wasn't," I said. "Then he dragged him into the bathroom—"

Marsogliani took up the reconstruction: "—draped him carefully with his head against the faucets, soaped him a bit, rinsed him off, pulled down the curtain, and left."

"Yes," I said.

"And all because his clothes are scattered."

"Yes," I said again.

Marsogliani looked at me from either side of that big nose of his. "The dead man is a writer, I understand. You a writer, too?"

"Yes," I said a third time.

"You write murder stories?" (He pronounced it "moider" but I'm not going to try to reproduce linguistic peculiarities.)

I was relieved to be able to say, "No," and I said it forcefully.

"But you read them, don't you?"

"Sometimes."

"Well, then, look here. Life is not like a murder mystery. In mysteries people always do the same thing. Then when some little thing is out of line, some wise-guy amateur detective makes big deductions. In real life, people don't do the same things all the time. They do different things at different times. In real life, people are crazy."

He moved toward the phone again. "I'm calling the police now. As far as I'm concerned that's an accident in there, but whether it's an accident or a murder is not really my business. I just call the police and they'll decide. You want to tell them it's murder, you go ahead, but if you do, mister, just remember that you discovered the body, you had the key, Strong says, and you maybe had a motive. Think it over.

His hand was on the phone and I put my hand over his. Mine was half the size and I don't think he was the least worried about me, but he said, "Well?"

"You don't want it to be a murder, do you?" I said. "Bad publicity?"

"If it's a murder, it's a murder," he said. "But I don't want anyone yelling murder if it isn't a murder. That has nothing to do with publicity. The police don't like it either."

And he lifted the phone as though my hand weren't

weighing his down, waited a moment, and said, "Dial 911, Myrtle."

I waited till he was finished and said, "There's heroin in this room."

I meant it to have impact because I was sore at the guy and, for a minute, I thought I had scored because his eyelids lifted and his eyes seemed to quiver. But when he spoke, it was with heavy indifference. "Where?"

"On the bureau. Right next to where I put the key. It looks like talcum powder, but one of my books involved itself with the drug culture and I know something about heroin. What I thought was talcum powder has a bitter, gritty taste and I'm betting eight to five it's heroin."

"Eight to five, hey?" He walked to the bureau and said, "I don't even see talcum powder. Come here and point it out."

I half ran to the bureau. It was clear.

Marsogliani said, "Are you telling me the dead man was an addict?"

"Not as far as I know," I muttered.

"He has no needle marks on him; at least not on any exposed part of his body. The police may be able to tell better when they run an autopsy. Still, mister, if you tell them you saw heroin and there isn't any, there's no way of describing how much trouble you could find yourself in. I'm not going to tell them anything about heroin because I don't see any; and I'm not going to tell them you said anything about heroin because I don't take anything you say seriously. But you'll be here and if *you* want to tell them anything, that's your business. It's up to you."

10   HERMAN BROWN   2:05 P.M.

The police arrived in about ten minutes, which gave me time to think.

I had made a mistake. I had shot off my mouth with nothing to back up my statements but trivia. I should have pointed to the powder before I said anything about it.

Marsogliani was right. If I yelled murder and couldn't prove it, they'd turn on me and rip me apart. I *did* have the key, I *was* first man on the scene. There might even be people who would be willing to suggest I was jealous of Giles—that I was the tooth-gnashing teacher who hated the smart-ass pupil who had outdistanced him. It didn't seem likely on the face of it that a man my size would lug a two-hundred-pound-plus dead weight into the bathroom and tip him into the tub, but it was no secret that I was stronger than I looked.

So by the time the police came, I was a different guy. If Marsogliani and Strong volunteered nothing, neither would I. Not until I had learned something of value. (Would I? Would I ever? I didn't ask myself that question at this time.)

The police came by way of the basement and the service elevator, I guess, avoiding and bypassing the convention. There were two of them. The young man in uniform had longish hair and a mustache, items almost required for the new generation of police. The older man, round-faced and snub-nosed, was in plainclothes.

They identified themselves. The policeman was Joseph Olsen and the plainclothesman was Lieutenant Herman Brown. The lieutenant looked bored. I suppose dead bodies were an old story to him.

He walked about the room silently, looked in the closet, knelt to look under the beds, walked into the bathroom, then came out just as though it had been empty. He asked Marsogliani and Strong how they came to be there and they laid it upon me very nicely, told their stories briefly, and left. Strong gave me a furtive glance out of the corner of his eye as though wondering what I was going to say and hoping I would make no trouble. Marsogliani left with no sign of concern at all. No skin off his nose.

If Strong had stayed behind, he would have heard me deliver the minimum and make no trouble at all.

Brown took my name, address, occupation, then said, "When did you find the body?"

"One thirty-three. I looked at my watch a minute or so after."

"How did you get in?"

"I had a key. Giles Devore, the dead man, gave it to me last night so that I could deliver a package. I delivered it a little over half an hour ago. There it is on the bureau and there's the key."

"What's in the package?"

"I don't know."

"Why did he ask you to deliver it and not someone else?"

"We were good friends," I said.

He didn't give me the oh-are-you-a-queer? look. Just scribbled in his notebook. He said, "Did you touch anything, move anything, when you came in?"

"Yes," I said. "I didn't know he was dead in the bathroom. I came in, wondered where he was, picked up that pen on the bureau, sat in the chair—like that. Then I looked in the bathroom and found him."

"Why did you look in the bathroom?"

"I wanted to piss."

"Did you?"

"Not yet."

"Go ahead."

That was nice of him. I felt a little less tense when I came out.

He said, "Did you draw that question mark on the pad there, or was it on the pad when you came?"

"I drew it."

"What for?"

"I was wondering where Giles was. I had expected him to be up here but he wasn't. It put a question mark in my mind, I suppose."

He didn't delve very deeply. I suppose with a clear case of accidental death, who needs more? He said, "Do you know if the dead man had a family?"

"He has a wife, Eunice."

"Know her address?"

I gave it to him and he said, "All right. Are you planning any out-of-town trips?"

"No."

"Okay. Hang around just in case there are more questions. I doubt that there will be, but hang around. You can go."

"What's going to happen to my—friend?" I pointed to the bathroom.

Brown said, "We'll call the Medical Examiner, who will send the body to the morgue for an autopsy. After that it will be released to his widow."

I said, "What do I do if people ask—"

For a minute, I thought he was going to smile, but he wasn't in a smiling business. "You mean, is all this a state secret? No. Talk all you want. Is the dead man part of the convention that's going on here?"

"Yes, the American Booksellers Association."

"He's a writer and you're a writer. What are you doing at a booksellers' convention?"

"Writers attend to push their books, you know. Giles was just autographing books this morning."

The lieutenant pulled out his little book again. "When this morning?"

"From ten to eleven."

"Were you there?"

"No, but there must have been a thousand witnesses."

Brown put away his book and shrugged. "Well, he won't be doing anything else at this convention. You had better tell the convention people that he's dead. Is he well known?"

"At this convention, he certainly is."

"Too bad, but what can you do? Get someone to make some announcement." He held the door open for me. "So long. We'll be in touch if anything comes up."

I left.

11   HENRIETTA CORVASS   2:30 P.M.

I went through the corridor and down the elevator in

a fog of unreality. People moved about unconcerned, wearing their badges, attending the convention—which was still going on, of course. You don't stop for individual tragedies. There must have been conventions going on, here and there, the day President Kennedy was assassinated and they went on. Eleven athletes were murdered at the 1972 Olympics and the games went on.

It was hard for *me* to go on, though. Everything had turned unreal. I went to the fifth floor to find the interview room and it was far different from what it had been the day before. Same crowd, same noise, different me.

I pulled Henrietta aside, out of the room altogether. She objected. "What's the matter with you? What's going on?"

I said in a low voice. "Emergency. *Real* emergency. You want me to shout it out?"

It made her nervous and she didn't try to pull her arm out of my grip any more. Maybe she remembered it had been I who had made it possible for her to take Giles to his interview the night before. We were out in the hall on the far side of the elevator bank and I said, "Look. Giles Devore is dead."

She said, "What?" and her mouth stayed open.

I said, "Dead. In the bathtub—dead. I found him an hour ago and the police are there now."

She said, "I was with him only—"

"What difference does that make? Practically everyone who ever died was seen by somebody a few hours before."

"How did it happen?"

"I wasn't there. All I can say is he's lying dead in the bathtub with his head against the faucets. The police say it's an accident. Look, you're the only ABA official I know and I want this off my back. If he's got any other commitments for the convention, cancel them. If there are any announcements to make, you make them, or have them made. If there has to be a minute of silence for mourning, or a cocktail party for celebration, or whatever, you take over."

That was it. I pulled away, kept my eyes on the floor

because I didn't want to see anybody I knew. *Anybody*.
Not for a while. Not till I had some things sorted out.

12   MICHAEL STRONG   3:00 P.M.

I couldn't go home. I had to stay in the hotel. I *had*
to stay at the scene of the crime until I got over at least
some of my confusion.

He *was* killed. Nothing had happened to change my
mind. The skies would fall before Giles would have
thrown his clothes about like that, and how would the
killer have known that?

I couldn't let it go. Damn it, I owed it to Giles to
straighten it out. It wasn't that we had a David and Jonathan friendship, or that I even liked him very much. It's
that I felt *guilty*.

I had been asked to do a little errand for him and I
had forgotten. He had asked me one last favor and I had
flubbed it. How could I tell that my failure to deliver
the package had not contributed to his murder?

I had to make it up to him.

I wandered about aimlessly for a while and then, at
3 P.M., found myself in the bar—in one of the bars, that
is. There are a number of them in the hotel and, as a
non-drinking man, none of them meant anything to me.
This was one of the times, though, that I wished I *were*
a drinking man, if only to have something to do and
something to soften the edges of the hard lump inside me.

At that time of day, the bar wasn't full. I took a corner
table and when the pretty waitress approached, in a little
frilly crotch-high skirt, I mumbled the only combination
of sounds that I can produce that seem appropriate to
the surroundings.

"Virgin Mary, straight up," I said. I'm not sure what
"straight up" means; I think it means without ice, because
if I ever say just "Virgin Mary" the waiter invariably
says, "On the rocks, sir" and I know that means ice.

It did occur to me that Shirley Jennifer was three
floors up, signing something or other in one of the booths.

I could go up there and wait for her with a sick and concerned face and she would ask me what's up and I would tell her and she would get very motherly and take me home and I—couldn't!

By God, I couldn't!

I can't explain it easily, but if I hadn't met her I would have been off the hook. I would have gotten that damned package and delivered it last night. I would not have delivered it at midday today; I would not have discovered the body; I would not be groveling in the humiliation of having failed a friend's last request, and maybe, in that way, having brought on the catastrophe.

Had I delivered the package last night, Giles could have broken his neck, or had it broken for him, and it would have been none of my affair. I could have felt the same perfunctory sorrow that all the rest of the thousands at the convention would feel.

I didn't have to sit there hopelessly involved—if it weren't for Shirley.

Of course, I could see the flagstones which had been laid. If that woman hadn't decided to wear a dress with holes in it, if I hadn't been made to feel like a fool when I arrived (less than twenty-four hours ago), if everyone hadn't combined to fan my anger and turn it against Giles—then I would never have yelled like a madman at him, humiliated him utterly (God, my last conversation with him), and forced him to leave the hotel so that he laid the errand on me in the first place—

But put it all together and I would still have done my bit if I hadn't met Shirley. But because I met her just when I did, I was sitting in the bar, closer to wanting to be drunk than ever in my life and not knowing how to do it.

It wasn't Shirley's fault; she didn't know. But I couldn't see her without thinking—So I made no attempt to see her.

I had to sit there and work it out.

If Giles was killed, who killed him?

Giles had finished autographing at 11 A.M. He would have gotten to his room by, say, 11:15. I found him at

1:33 P.M. He was dead for some time, say, since 1 P.M. That means whoever had killed him had to have done it between 11:15 A.M. and 1 P.M. How many people at the convention could account for their time fully between those limits? Probably a great many, but that would leave a large number who couldn't.

Who would have a motive?

Lots of people would have the motive to do him a bad turn, say a nasty word about him, refuse a helping hand at crucial moments. Martin Walters was annoyed with him for standing him up in connection with a talk; Tom and Teresa Valier were sick over his apparent abandonment of them; Roseann Bronstein perhaps felt spurned in a more intimate way. Even Henrietta might have been irritated with his lack of cooperation. As for Asimov, he was bound to be jealous of Giles's success. Why shouldn't a guy with 163 books turn a little green over someone shooting past him on his second book? (And why should he harp on *my* jealousy if he were not feeling the bite himself?)

But not one of these motives was possibly deep enough for murder.

Or was I wrong? Did I know all the ins and outs of emotions? Did I know exactly how deeply something Giles had done had cut into someone's heart? Did I know exactly how some small deed might fester in a particular type of personality? Was I aware of how unconnected factors might have contributed? Look at all the different things that had combined to reduce me to the kind of rage from which I usually do not suffer, and made me scream at Giles for what could have seemed, on the face of it, no reason at all.

And who could get into Giles's locked room if he did not, like Giles or myself, have a key. Actually, anyone.

If a writer is at a convention in some field allied to writing, he is particularly vulnerable. Anyone, *anyone*, can knock on the door and in response to "Who's there?" say through the locked barrier, "I'm a fan, sir. Could you sign a book of yours that I have here?"

Theoretically, the writer could answer, "Beat it, you punk! I'm busy," but I'd bet myself a hundred to one anytime that there isn't a writer, certainly not a young writer, who can resist the implied flattery.

And how could it be done? It would have to be a blunt instrument at the base of the skull, something the supposed slam against the bathtub faucets could have caused. What was it? A karate chop?

But then what would it take to drag Giles into the bathroom? Roseann Bronstein might have been able to do it, but I'll bet Teresa Valier couldn't. But might it not have been two people working together?

And what of the heroin? I was convinced the heroin *had* been there and *was* heroin but how on earth could I prove it, and if I could, what connection did it have with the murder? Some connection, I'm sure, but what?

In whatever direction my mind turned, I came up with nothing. I could in no way limit the possibilities or work up a reasonable list of suspects. The matter needed investigation but I lacked the talent and the facilities for that and I didn't see how I could persuade the police to do it for me.

And then I heard the sound of someone clearing his throat. I looked up and it was Michael Strong, the security man, looking uneasy and unhappy.

He said, "May I talk to you, Mr. Just?"

I said dully, "Aren't you supposed to be on duty?"

"Someone is covering. Just a few minutes, sir."

"Well, then, sit down. If you're allowed to drink on duty, have one on me."

"No, thanks," he said, and then for a while he just sat there.

"Well?" I said.

"I'm glad I found you, sir," he said. "I thought you might be in one of the bars. It seemed natural."

"I don't drink," I said, "but you found me, so three cheers for your reasoning powers. What can I do for you?"

"I—I want you to know," he said, "that I'm sorry for what happened." He kept rubbing his hands against his thin tan jacket as though to wipe off the perspiration. His rather comical face (or it would have been comical if I had been in the mood to smile) was twisted into a distress that did not make it less comical.

I was pinching my upper lip and I withdrew my hand long enough to give it a what-can-you-do? wave and said, "Do you think he was murdered?"

"Me? No. Did you tell the police—?"

"No. I told the police nothing. They wouldn't believe it. *You* don't."

Just because the clothes were thrown around? That's not much."

"And the heroin?"

"There wasn't any."

"No, not after you two came in. There was heroin before that. I'm not crazy. You or your boss or both of you got rid of it."

He shook his head. Then said, "Why would we?"

"You wouldn't want murder, would you? Bad for the hotel. You wouldn't want a drug scandal. Even worse for the hotel."

Strong thought about it. His brows furrowed together and he made a visible effort. He said, "Suppose there *were* drugs there. That works *against* murder."

"Really?"

"Sure. If Mr. Devore were an addict, he might have been high and then you can't argue what he would do or how he would handle his clothes. Maybe he might be very careful about them when he was normal, but he might throw them around when he was high. He might also be unsteady on his feet and fall in the bathtub, see? That's what probably happened if there really was heroin in the room."

It was my turn to think. What Strong said didn't exactly sound stupid. And really, how stupid could he be if he enjoyed *Crossover?* That was not a stupid man's book. Could he be right? Was I stubbornly tying myself, emotionally, to the theory that Giles had been killed only in order to intensify my feeling of guilt over my failure in connection with the package?

I said, "When's the autopsy?"

"Not before tomorrow. The Medical Examiner isn't even here yet. Probably won't get here till dinnertime."

"Why the delay?"

"It's always that way. It takes time. There's lots of bodies in the city at any given time and the M.E. has to see them in order."

I said, "I don't think Giles was a hophead; I don't think he was high; I think he would have taken care of his clothes neatly and because they were not taken care of, he's not the one who put the clothes there. And the heroin had to have something to do with it; I won't let you talk me out of its being there."

"If it were there," said Strong, "and if Mr. Devore did not take drugs, then the heroin could have nothing to do with him at all. It could be there from the previous occupant. It could have been there for weeks. The maids don't always do things so carefully as all that. You see what I mean?"

I saw what he meant. It seemed entirely unlikely, but it could be so. I knew even less about the whole mess than I thought I had known and my thoughts shrank inward and built a wall of silence about me.

Then Strong said, "Mr. Just, if you don't mind, I'll have to be getting back soon. Could I explain something?"

"Go ahead," I said.

"This is not just part of the job for me. I read fantasy; as I told you yesterday, I admired Mr. Devore's book. I got his signature on my copy of *Crossover* this morning, not the ones they were giving away. I just want you to know my personal feelings."

He brought out a dog-eared paperback edition of *Crossover* and passed it to me. I opened it to the title page and there was Giles's signature all right, with "Best wishes" above it and "26 May 75" under it. The "Best wishes" looked faint and the final "s" almost wasn't there, but the signature was considerably darker as though Giles had put his heart into that. It's a phenomenon I've often noticed with writers. No matter what they write in addition to their signature, it's their own name into which they put their muscles and their heart.

Strong said, "Would you sign your name to it, too, and date it?"

"It's not my book," I said.

"I know that, sir, but I've read two of your books and I've seen your movie."

He didn't exactly move me. I'm not *that* amenable to flattery; and if I were, I was at an unamenable moment. It seemed quite clear to me that a signature by Giles, dated the day of his death, accompanied by a signature of the discoverer of the body, dated the same day, could make the book quite valuable—

But then I thought, hell, we were neither of us Abe Lincoln. At best our signatures would make the book worth five dollars to some collector and I had a notion that Strong wouldn't sell it. So let him have something that he valued greatly and that cost me nothing.

I signed. No "Best wishes," which seemed inappropriate. Just my name and the date, under those Giles had written. Absently, I admired my signature, small, neat, clear, each letter perfectly formed, and, to add character, the upper loop of the capital J large and roundly triangular, so that the rest of the name seemed to be suspended from a J balloon.

I handed it back. "There you are."

He put it into his jacket pocket and said, "I just want to show you how I admire Mr. Devore and why I was hoping you wouldn't say anything about murder and drugs without any better evidence. It would make a terrible impression and could ruin his reputation. Even if everything showed it was an accident and he didn't take drugs, if something like your theory gets to the public, there'd always be people saying he died of an overdose, or that he was killed, and that's what he would be remembered for instead of his books. That wouldn't be right."

Damn it, it wouldn't. "I know," I said, and went back

to pinching my upper lip. One way or another, he was making it very hard for me to insist on murder.

Then I said, "Hey, you had that book signed this morning?"

"Yes, Mr. Just."

"Well, then, you were there. Didn't Mr. Devore make a fuss while he was on the platform? What was that about?"

"Fuss?" Strong looked confused.

"I heard he made a fuss," I said.

He shook his head slowly. "I don't know anything about that. I came early and I was at the head of the line, third or fourth maybe. Then I had to go back to my post outside the exhibit room. Maybe there was trouble after I left. I wouldn't know. It couldn't have amounted to much or I would have heard about it, it seems to me."

He got up and ducked his head as though to say goodbye, and then he said suddenly, "Do you know Mrs. Devore?"

"I met her once or twice," I said.

"I think she would like to see you."

"You mean she's *here?* You've seen her?"

"We tried to call her at her home, but there was no answer, and we gave up. And then at just about that time, she came in and tried to get Mr. Devore on the house phone. Naturally the operator asked her to identify herself and——" He spread out his hands.

"Where is she?"

"I'm not sure. Last I heard she was in Public Relations. She may not be there any more."

"Where is that?"

"It's on the sixth floor; 622. Only thing is, Mr. Just——" And then he hesitated.

"Yes?"

"I don't think it would be such a good idea to talk to her about your theories. Poor woman must be in a pretty bad way; left a widow so young."

I said, "Don't worry about it. I haven't told the police and I won't tell her. Okay?"

"Okay." He grinned with relief. "And, Mr. Just, you keep up the good work. *Your* books, I mean. You should write more."

"I will," I said, "if I manage not to slip in the bathroom."

He looked a little shocked at the gallows humor and left.

13 SARAH VOSKOVEK 3:30 P.M.

A few minutes later, I got up and left, too.

I'd met Eunice Devore oftener than the once or twice I'd admitted to, but I had never taken to her. She was of only slightly more than average height for a woman; five feet five would be my guess; but she managed to look down from that height. She didn't give me the "little fella" treatment Roseann did, and I suppose I could count that on the side of virtue, but she managed to tilt her head just slightly back when she spoke to me, so that her eyes glanced unmistakably downward.

A little thing, but I found it irritating.

She was also a proto-liberationist. That is, long before Women's Liberation had become a force in the land, she was fighting her way through the world of men with long fingernails and a reinforced brassiere. She was a lawyer, wore no makeup of any kind, kept her brown hair short, her business suits mannish, her voice harsh, and her stride swinging. When I first met her, I bet myself twelve to one she was a lesbian, and I was completely taken back—right through the wall—when Giles coyly announced that they were getting married.

I couldn't conceive what he saw in her—or she in him.

Nor did I ever see any inordinate display of affection between them after they were married—any display at all, actually. Nor did I labor, particularly, to imagine what such a display would be like. He with his hulkish slouch, she with her solid lack of all the qualities I had taught myself to consider feminine.

Please!

And now, to commiserate with her on a death I had discovered was more than I could easily face.

But I had to. Aside from the requirements of common humanity, she was the one who would be most likely to tell me whether Giles had changed his habit and whether, just possibly, I was wrong to deduce murder from the condition of his clothes.

That is, I would check, but I had no fear, absolutely none, of being proved wrong. It is only the huge habits that people change without trouble. Communists can become Fascists with a day's notice and Conservatives can crawl into the Liberal bed (or vice versa) with scarcely an extra breath between; men can switch wives and mousy women can go liberationist—but show me a fellow who squeezes his toothpaste tube with his left hand, and I'll show you a fellow who will never do it with his right hand, except maybe to win a bet and even then he'll have trouble.

But I would ask. The wild Game of People is not won on generalities, however sound.

I chose the proper bank of elevators to reach the sixth floor, and found myself facing an arrow that said "Offices." I turned left and faced a glass door. I went through it and at once heard little Sarah's clear and precise accented English.

I followed it and it led me to Room 622. There were two rooms actually, the outer one containing a desk which presumably should have been occupied by someone who served as buffer between Sarah and the world. It was vacant at the moment and I walked into the inner room.

I did so slowly and softly, possibly because I did not want to attract Eunice's attention and have to confront her without the maximum possible preparation. (I never met a woman who looked less like her name—but that's a purely subjective reaction, for who knows what a Eunice would look like in someone else's imagination.) If it were my intention to avoid attracting her attention, however, it was effort wasted, for Eunice was not there.

It achieved another purpose, unintended, however, for Sarah Voskovek (I was getting to remember the name) did not hear me. Her back was to me, and she was looking at a series of large cardboard placards. Facing her, one side toward me, was a rather large, stout, white-haired, clearly uneasy man, who did give me a brief glance as I walked in, then lost interest in me at once.

I sat down quietly and listened. The only reason for interrupting would have been to ask the whereabouts of Eunice and I was in no hurry. This might be more interesting.

Sarah was saying, "But why four makeups on the same subject? Each one features the lobby." She held them up like large playing cards.

I could see that there were headlines on top, others (taillines, I wonder?) on bottom, and photographs in the middle. In between, there were wavy lines supposed to indicate print. The details would follow later, I suppose.

One of the headlines was "The Lobby-Lovely Hotel," which I thought was a phrase to set anyone mewling and puking in his nurse's arms. Another one was "From Lobby to Living, You'll Love It," which seemed only marginally better. I averted my eyes from the other two, so I'll never know what new depths were reached.

Sarah said, "I've spent the Memorial Day weekend here in the office, but I'm not letting this pass. Why the lobby? Who's interested in lobbies? The lobby is just an extension of the street, air-conditioned in summer and warmed in winter, but that's all. It's always crowded, always busy, always strange and cold. We're selling rooms, beds, closets, windows, dining rooms, ballrooms, conference rooms, every blessed thing but lobbies, and after all our discussions you come here with four lobbies."

The man managed to speak here in what I think he imagined to be an ingratiating tone. "I think they got the idea from you, Sarah. When we had that conference, they said you said you could tell a hotel by its lobby."

"I never said any such thing," said Sarah, staring the

man down. "I would like to know who said I did. Exactly who. Find out for me. Just ask and find out exactly who is willing to swear I said that. Even if I had done so, would that be worth four lobby makeups, with not even a single backup in case the lobby idea is sour?—which it is."

"But what are we going to do now?"

"You'll work all night, if you have to. If you had had this in last week as you were supposed to—"

"Come on, Sarah, you can't push these things too much."

"I'm trying to push them enough. Anyway, these are out. Remind everyone there's a recession on and we can't get by without something good—and these things are putrid."

She tossed the placards to the man facing her and sat there unhappily. I couldn't see her face, but if ever a beehive hairdo looked downcast from the back, hers was it.

The man got up, gathering the placards together and said, "Well, I'll call you tomorrow morning. And I think someone's waiting for you."

She turned around rapidly, and when she saw who it was, she reddened. I imagine she flushed easily; her skin was quite fair; almost startlingly so against her dark hair and eyes. Flawless, too—at least the parts I could see. It was a pity she couldn't be stretched out into something taller.

She said, "I'm sorry, Darius. I didn't know you were there."

The use of the first name caught me by surprise till I remembered we had placed ourselves on a first-name basis on our previous meeting. Actually, I liked the way she pronounced it.

I said, "It's all right. It was a pleasure watching you work."

She said, "I'm sorry again. I must have sounded petulant to you."

"They looked like lousy ads to me."

"Weren't they? It's not really my job to backstop design, but they do such stupid things when they're left to themselves. Imagine saying that I said you could judge a hotel from its lobby."

"You might be able to."

"Never. Ours is terrible. It's like Grand Central used to be. There's even a porno newsstand."

"Where?"

"Well, almost porno and never mind where. But I'm talking nonsense. I've been kept so busy that I've forgotten what a miserable time you had since I last saw you. I understand that you went up to the room and found your friend dead. I've been thinking you must have been suspecting such a tragedy or you would not have run off so—so—" (for the first time I heard her stumble over an English word) "—distrafft."

"Distraught," I said.

"Distraught. Did you expect to find him dead?"

"No. Never. Anything but that. Your remarks had just put it into my head that I had promised to run an errand for him and I had forgotten. By the time I got to his room—"

"He was dead," she said. "I hope there was no connection."

"I don't see how that could be," I said gruffly, but she had put her finger very efficiently on my particularly howling worry. "Did you tell anyone that I had run off like that?"

"Oh, no," she said. "I thought you might be in trouble and it was not my wish to make that trouble worse. Of course, if I had been asked directly, I couldn't very well have lied about it." She smiled, something I hadn't seen her do before, and she had nice, even teeth—front teeth, anyway. "I come from a land, you see, where you quickly learn not to volunteer information. Still, there are many around us who saw you run off."

"I know, but you're the only one who knew exactly what you said to me that made me run off. And talking about Giles, I understand his wife was here in this room and that she wants to see me."

"Yes, but how did you know that?"

"Ah," and I smiled, too, something it was a relief to be able to do, "but, you see, I don't volunteer information either."

"But I asked you. It is not a matter of volunteering."

"Does it matter that you do not know?"

"It always matters for a woman not to know."

"Sexist nonsense!" I said, and rejoiced (and by no means for the first time) at the weapon the liberation movement had handed over to the occasional male chauvinist. (I repeat, I'm a feminist—most of the time.)

"Very well, then," she said, coming dangerously close to a pout. "Yes, Mrs. Devore did say that she would like to see you. She is a very strange woman. Do you know her well?"

"No."

"Do you like her?"

"No."

"She seemed so in charge of herself, even though her husband was lying dead upstairs. Her voice did not tremble. Her hands were quite steady. I'm told she didn't even wince at the news."

I said, "She's a successful career woman who has schooled herself to take things as they come. She's forged her way through a male society before the liberation movement came to help, and that takes guts."

"I thought you said you didn't like her."

"I don't. But in some ways I admire her. Where is she?"

"She's upstairs. Waiting in the room for the Medical Examiner. In 1511."

I looked at my watch. It was edging past 3:40—not yet twenty-four hours since I had arrived at the convention.

"When the hell will he come?" I muttered.

"There are many—"

"I know; many bodies waiting. But you'd think they'd want to autopsy fresh meat."

She winced, and I said, "I'm sorry. That was a foul thing to say. It's just that I'm feeling tired and bitter."

"I understand."

I made a little quasi-salute gesture and left.

14 EUNICE DEVORE 3:45 P.M.

Back up to 1511. It was not my idea of anything I wanted to do.

I knocked at the door and after a while it opened a bit and the eye of Officer Olsen appeared there. I guess if you're a cop and are carrying a gun, you don't have to be as careful about asking who's there as ordinary people do.

I said, "Hi. Remember me?"

He did.

I said, "If Mrs. Devore's in there, can I get in to see her? Tell her it's Darius Just."

She must have heard me, for I heard Eunice's husky voice say, "Let him in. I want to see him."

Olsen opened the door for me and closed it after me. The room had been straightened out. Eunice was sitting in one chair and the policeman took the other. I considered the bed, discarded the idea, and sat down on the low bench-like affair next to the bureau, where a suitcase would ordinarily be put.

Eunice was looking particularly plain, rather more than the forty-two years I knew she was. She was a dozen years older than Giles, if you wanted another factor that made for the mésalliance.

She must have seen the quick glance I cast at the bathroom door just before I sat down and promptly read my mind, though that must have been one of the easier telepathic tasks.

She said, "He's still in there with a blanket over him. I suppose one of these days the M.E. will be over. It's silly taking an autopsy in a case like this, but necessary. You go through the routine to avoid trouble. If you leave out an autopsy, there may be legal complications of all sorts and better a thousand useless autopsies than one set of ensuing complications."

It was almost as though she were anesthetizing herself by talking like the lawyer she was.

I said, "Sorry for the delay, but I was told you were down in Room 622."

"I was," she said, "but I didn't stay." Her nose was shiny and her hair was bedragged. "If I had been penned in with that niminy-piminy any longer I'd have broken down the door to get out."

"What niminy-piminy?" I asked, even though I knew very well what niminy-piminy.

"That peewee with the voice. With her hair up and her mouth tight and her tits squeezed forward and upward and her ass hanging out behind and all the words coming out and being nearly bitten off. She's not human. It must take her two hours every morning to put herself together and three hours every evening to shake herself apart and pick up the loose pieces."

I guess she didn't like Sarah any more than Sarah liked her. Less, maybe.

Six hours before, I would have rejoiced at that little speech, and even now I had to admit it wasn't a bad word picture on the malevolent side. Still, Sarah had apologized to me manfully (womanfully?) and *she* was making it in a man's world, too. And for that matter, whatever Sarah's artificiality, I preferred it to Eunice's over-natural look. I wasn't close enough to Eunice to get a whiff of underarm odor but I bet myself even money it was there.

However, I didn't take up Sarah's part. I let it go. My task now was to keep Eunice in good enough temper to answer my questions.

I said carefully, "I'm terribly sorry, Eunice, about the —the tragedy. We were very close, Giles and I, for a while."

"Very close indeed, Just, if you had his key," she said dryly. "That's what I want to talk to you about. But not here. I've identified him, and that's enough for here."

I said to the policeman, "All right if I use the phone?"

"What for?"

"To get us another room to talk in with less company."

He shrugged.

Eunice said, "Who're you calling?"

I said, "The peewee with the voice."

It didn't take too long. I knew I could count on Sarah. In a while a key came up and we moved over into 1524, which was between occupants. We had till six, we were told. I sure as hell didn't want to spend any longer—if as long.

Still, there are amenities. I said, "You sure you want to stay here? Shall we go have a drink? Are you hungry?"

"No," she said sourly. "We'll stay here. I just want this over with. What I want from you is the story of what happened. How did he manage to die?"

I said, "Eunice, I don't know. When I came into the room, he was already dead."

"Yes, that's what you told the police, I gather."

"That's what really happened. And because it's the truth, I'm not telling you anything different."

"All right, then, tell me about the key. Giles hasn't gone homosexual, has he?"

"For all I know, he may have," I said icily, and managed not to point out I would consider it an improvement when compared to marriage with her, "but *I* haven't. He gave me the key last night so that I could run an errand for him, and I forgot. I did it today during the luncheon and he was dead when I got there."

"And is there a connection?

"Post hoc, ergo propter hoc?"

"You know Latin, I see," she said, without admiration.

"I know that much. Do you think that because he was killed after I had slipped up on my errand, that he was killed *because* I had slipped up."

She shrugged. "Why did you forget?"

"Irrelevant, immaterial, and incompetent."

"You've been watching Perry Mason," she said. "Well,

since you deny you're a homosexual, I suppose a girl was involved."

I kept quiet. She was a formidable harridan with an absolutely uncanny way of guessing what went on in your mind. I had experienced that before and I suppose it was a great help to her as a lawyer. How had Giles ever had the guts to marry her, even assuming he lacked the brains not to?

She said, "Well, then, that's it. He fell in the bathtub. They'll run the autopsy and give him to me. I'll see him buried, probate the will, if he's made one—I swear I don't know if he's made one—and that will be it. Do you know if he's got any family, parents, siblings?"

"Don't you know?" I asked.

"He never mentioned. I never questioned."

I shrugged. "He had a father some years ago who would send him money now and then, but I can't say where he's to be found, or even whether he's still alive. And I don't know anything about any other relatives."

She said, "I daresay they'll all show up, right down to the third cousin, each expecting to be remembered in the will and assuming Giles to be a lot wealthier than he was."

She put her hands on her knees, stood up with a grunt, and said, "That's all, Darius. You can run along now."

I found the grace of the remark somewhat less than lovable and would have longed to tell her so in my own inimitable fashion, but I was still playing for cooperation. I sat where I was and said, "But it's not quite all. Do you mind if I ask you some questions, Eunice? I promise it's for good reason."

She hesitated, looked at her watch, sat down again, and said, "Well, till the M.E. arrives, there's nothing to do, so go ahead." And then, as though her remark had been too ungrudging, she added, "Provided you don't take forever."

"How's Giles been lately?" I asked.

"Same steady son of a bitch he's been for quite a while."

Not perhaps the most loving remembrance of a freshly dead husband, but I wasn't going to dictate the nature of her feelings.

I said, "You don't know if he was on drugs, do you?"

"No, not as far as I know—and I think I would have known."

"Has he been seeing a psychiatrist?"

"No, not as far as I know—and I think I would have known."

"Has he changed any of his little habits?"

She let out a harsh squawk of laughter. "He? You should know some of his little habits. They never change."

I nodded and said, "That's the thing. When you came into his room, was it the way it was when I came in a little while ago?"

"Yes, essentially."

"Giles's clothes weren't in sight?"

"They were in the closet and they were being taken out and everything about them was being marked and itemized."

"There was nothing on the bed or chairs?"

"His clothes? No."

"You know how he takes care of his clothes."

She said, "None better. He blows in his socks and folds them and folds everything else and makes a neat little pile of them like Mommie always told him to do. You roomed with him once; you know."

"But he hasn't changed that habit?"

"You can bet anything you want he hasn't."

"All right then. How about this? When I came in and found him, his clothes were thrown over the chair and floor. You *know* that can't be him."

"It can't. So?"

"So someone else must have done that. Someone else was there. And why should the someone else have spread the clothes like that except to make it look as though Giles were taking a shower when he wasn't?"

Eunice said, "You mean we're faced with a murder made to look like an accident?"

For once her ability to read minds was useful. I didn't have to explain. "Well?" I said. "Doesn't it look that way to you?"

"Because the clothes are scattered? That's not enough. No jury would buy that."

"The hell with a jury; don't be a lawyer. I'm talking about you and me, so be a person. Would *you* buy the fact that it was murder on the basis of the scattered clothes?"

"It's an interesting thought," she said, unmoved. "It's possible. But there should be more evidence."

For a moment I thought of telling her about the heroin, but decided not to. There was absolutely nothing but its physical presence to connect it to Giles, and that physical presence no longer existed. In fact, I couldn't even absolutely swear to its being heroin in full certainty.

I said, "What about the shower bit? I never knew Giles to shower in the middle of the day."

"You don't know much," said Eunice. "He'd shower anytime if he had a woman with him."

I paused a moment. "Are you suggesting he had a woman with him, and he took a shower and fell and killed himself?"

"Why not? And the woman, not wanting to be involved, for which one can't blame her, quietly eases out and lets someone else find him."

"And his clothes," I said. "Would she scatter them around, after he had taken them off and folded them all neatly? Why improve on him?"

"Because the poor mutt might have thought that he folded everything neatly to make an impression on her and that if he had been taking a shower by himself, he would have thrown them about. So she threw them about to make it look as though no one had been there but Giles."

I was rattled. My God, it made sense. "Do you think that happened?"

"Not really. Any woman who knew Giles would know that was how the clothes were supposed to be, and any

woman who didn't know Giles would be far too panicky
to fool around with the clothes. She would just get the
hell out of the room."

"Then all this stuff about a woman with him doesn't
amount to anything. Why do you bring it up?" I was
irritated.

"Because any lawyer would, and by the time he was
through, your notion of deducing murder from messed-up
clothes would be shredded into nonexistence. I'm showing you. Besides—"

"Yes."

She seemed lost in thought for a moment, then she
said, "Besides, I don't think poor Giles had a girl with
him anyway. It is very hard for him to find anyone to
cooperate with him. Except me, of course."

The natural question would have been: Why not? I
hung back, though, and didn't ask it. For one thing it
would have been a clearly prurient intrusion on someone's private sex life, and for another, I wasn't sure I
cared to know.

But Eunice laughed and exercised her frightening ability
to see what I must be thinking. "Of course," she said,
"you want to know what I'm talking about, but you feel
it isn't gentlemanly to ask. Don't hesitate. I don't give a
damn whether you know or not. In these rotten per-
missive days, it doesn't matter if everyone knows.

"Look, when I met Giles, he was a virgin. He was
incapable of sex in the ordinary routine sense of the
word—I'm using 'routine' to cover a broad territory—
and he's still incapable of it. He had to be babied into
it, and I mean that literally. We stumbled onto that fact
more or less accidentally as a result of what teen-agers
might call 'fooling around' and it worked so well that
we got married.

"The thing is, he has to be undressed while he moves
his arms and legs aimlessly and makes little gurgling
sounds. Except that I guess I should use the past tense.
It wasn't easy, but he moved his body in such a way as
to help, though he pretended he wasn't. I had to make

soothing noises to him and take him to the bathroom and bathe him carefully, sometimes by shower, sometimes in the tub, depending on how much time we had. Afterward I had to dry him, powder him, right down to the Q-sticks for the folds in his outer ear. I had to pretend to suckle him and then, finally, he'd be ready for sex in the ordinary sense of the word. He could be pretty good at it if all the preliminaries went well."

I sat there frozen with horror. The man had occupied an adjacent bedroom to mine for over two months— and I had babied him, too, in my way. He had come in for help, like a little boy to his father, and, intellectually, I had fathered him as, more physically, Eunice had mothered him.

A big hulk like that, with a mustache like a black forest. God, height and weight and size and bulk could be as great a burden as lack of all of them. What was it like to look out over the heads of the world and to reject the role that sheer size had thrust upon you?

Eunice said, "For God's sake, Just, don't sit there looking censorious. If you want to know, I liked **it**. I liked every bit of it; it turned me on, too. Even if I hadn't, the end paid off. So what's to complain about? Since it's between consenting adults, who's hurt? Your sense of propriety? How do *you* get to the point? A drink, a giggle, a kiss on the shoulder, the slipping of fingers up a thigh?"

"I don't drink," I said. "Listen, is this the way Giles would want it with anyone?"

"It's the only way. Nothing else will interest him. Nothing else will bring him to the point." She grinned sourly. "If you know what I mean."

"Well, then, if you undress him, what do you do with the clothes?"

"I thought you'd ask. I fold them neatly in a cute little pile. Otherwise, he cries; I mean *cries*. I suppose it all traces back to his real mother, to the kind of compulsively neat object she was, and to whatever games they played." She sighed. "The hell with it."

"And he never went to a psychiatrist?"

"Why should he? It gave him pleasure and it didn't hurt him, or get in his way, either personally or professionally. Would you go to a psychiatrist to be cured of your vile impulse to eat when you're hungry?"

"And you liked it all?"

"Who knows what *you* like?"

She was right. I had to stop playing Puritan.

I said, "But what went wrong? If you like the game and he likes the game, why is he a son of a bitch now? Has he changed?"

"Of course he's changed. He found out he likes variety. You have to go through the same routine every time, but he likes to have different mothers, to experience different touches, different mouth odors, different nipples, who knows what? There was that bookstore owner downtown, the broad one. Now there's a motherly type for you."

Look who's getting into the judgment business now, I thought. And then it occurred to me that Eunice and Roseann were alike in many ways. If Giles liked one, why not the other?

I said, "You mean that they played the game, too?"

"I didn't take photographs, Just, but let's say they did. Bronstein, that's her name. Yes, they did. I'm satisfied with the evidence, even if a jury might not be."

"Do you think Roseann Bronstein might have been here in the room with him?"

"Is she at the convention? She's a bookseller; she ought to be."

"I met her in the hotel yesterday," I admitted.

"Then she might have been."

I said, "But she'd know enough not to mess up the clothes, whether he died by accident or she killed him."

Eunice said, with sour reluctance, "Yes, I suppose she would."

Then she said, "Well, never mind that. After Giles discovered the pleasure of variety, Bronstein didn't last long with him either. He left her and went after anything female, I think. And it was only after he was frustrated by enough refusals that he turned to me."

"Was he always refused?"

"Just about always. Eventually, though, he discovered he could buy cooperation and for the last six months he never turned to me once. The son of a—"

She let the phrase hang and sat there, shaking her head.

I said, "Does he always play the game the same way, all the way, with everybody?"

"What do you mean?"

"Well, look, suppose he found someone at the convention. There are bound to be some who wouldn't mind."

"Yes," she said, "some of us crazies. Yes."

"Very well. He got some girl at the last minute, but he hasn't cleared the situation very well with her; he might even have brought back a professional. Would he be desperate enough to accept some shortcuts? I mean, would it be all right to undress him but not to fold his clothes, as an example?"

"I've never witnessed the game with anyone else," said Eunice, "so I can't give strong evidence. I'm pretty sure that he wouldn't play. He would cry and he wouldn't go to the bathroom and you can't take him to the bathroom if he doesn't want to go."

"So it can't be a woman," I said. "Any woman who knew him would play the game properly; any woman who didn't know him would play it properly or it wouldn't get played. In either case, the clothes would be folded. If they were folded and Giles died in any fashion, why should anyone take the time to strew them around? Don't you see, it works down to this; that he had to die with his clothes on and that someone didn't know Giles's peculiarities, so he had to take the clothes off him while he was dead, toss them about, and take him into the bathroom. And why on earth do that but to convert murder into apparent accident."

"Except," said Eunice, "that it's been six months since

the last time I played the game and for all I know there
has been a change."

"Do you believe that?"

"No, I don't. Not for a moment. But a lawyer would
point that out."

"The *hell* with lawyers," I said desperately. "What do
you think? Murder or not."

"I don't think anything, Just. Let it be to hell with
lawyers but I'm one and what strikes me as important
is what the jury thinks. The jury would decide on accident
after listening to the evidence."

"Doesn't it bother you that juries can be wrong?
Doesn't it bother you that it might be murder whatever
they say?"

"Why? Suppose I say: It's murder. Does that bring
Giles back to life?"

"Do you want the murderer to get away with it?"

"What murderer? That's another thing. If you decide
Giles was murdered, you would have to think about the
matter of who murdered him. Who had a motive? And
who was strong enough to get his dead body into the
bathroom? He weighed two hundred and twenty pounds."

I stared at her thoughtfully and she stared back and
her lip curled. "You're wondering if it could have been
Eunice Devore. The first suspect in the death of a husband is the wife, right?"

I felt uneasy and shrugged. "I don't say that," I said.

"Say it, and let's go over the evidence. First, do I
have a motive? Sexual frustration, unhappy marriage, he's
been talking about a divorce. I'm sure he meant to con-
sult a lawyer right after his new book was published and
was clearly a best seller. If I kill him and make it look
like an accident, I spare myself humiliation, get a kind
of revenge, probably inherit the bulk of his estate, which
might not be a bad one at that, if this new book makes
a good movie sale, as it might. Going against that is the
fact that I am not a very sexually driven woman, that I
have no objection to a divorce, and that I make a good
living on my own.

"Second, the means. Could I have killed him? Why not? I'm as strong as a man and he's a flabby person. I could have made use of something that would serve as a bludgeon, break his neck and take the weapon away with me. Or I could have used a karate blow—"

"Karate?" I asked with sudden interest.

"Yes, I've taken lessons in karate. I work late at night in the city sometimes and a woman needs to know the art of self-defense, I'm told, though the fact is that I've never been attacked. The idea of karate came to me once when Giles told me that *you* were an expert in it. I'm not. I don't know if I could crack Giles's spine just under the skull with one quick sidewise strike of my hand. I imagine you could, however."

I said, "And how would I carry him into the bathroom?"

"You don't have to carry him, sonny. You drag him." She looked at my shoulders appraisingly. "I think you could do it."

I said, "Dragging would have left traces, I suspect. Or maybe not. I don't know. Anyway, what's my motive?"

She said, "Who cares? That's nonsense about motives. Anyone could have a motive and anything suits for a motive. He could have called you a little squirt or he could have said you were a lousy writer or he could have insulted your sainted mother. What's the difference? It was something that made you lose your temper.

"But let's go on to the third, opportunity. I was in the city all day; I have no alibi, I could have been here. So I've got motive, means, and opportunity—and the only catch is that I didn't do it. Did you?"

"No, I didn't," I said, dismissing the matter as though it were nonsense, which it was. "But tell me, how was it you were in town? How long have you been here?"

She raised her eyebrows. "Since about four P.M. yesterday. Do you want an explanation?"

"I can't make you give one. Do you want to offer one?"

"Nothing is easier than the truth. He called me. He had left a package at home—"

"A package?"

I have a feeling my eyes bugged at that one, for Eunice looked at me with amusement and said, "Yes, a package. Have I given myself away with that? Am I guilty?"

"No. Go on."

"He called me up, told me where the package was, asked me if I could bring it in. I said I would try. The point was, it would serve as a possible excuse to visit my brother, whom I hadn't seen in over a year for all we live only forty miles apart. I called him up and he was home, *not* out for the weekend, and he said, 'Come over.'

"I did. I brought the package with me. I called Giles's room, and he wasn't in. I didn't expect him to be—unless he were with a woman, in which case I don't think he'd answer. So I checked the package and left the ticket at the desk for him. They put it in an envelope, and put a message buzzer on the gizmo in his room; at least that's what they told me they would do. Off I went to my brother's—he lives about ten miles from here—and I spent the night there."

I shook my head. "I wish they had sent the package up to his room and had the maid take it in."

"Why? He got it, didn't he? I saw it lying on the bureau when I came in, just before they put it into a canvas bag with his other loose belongings. In a few hours I'll get it back. So much for bringing it in yesterday."

"That's the errand I had to run, Eunice," I said, in self-disgust. "He got the ticket last night and never had time to go to the checkroom. He gave me the ticket and the key and asked me to get it for him. I did, but not till lunch today and he was dead by then."

"Oh, well. Big deal."

I said, "When I first said I had forgotten to run an errand for him you asked if there was any connection with his death. Now you dismiss it as unimportant. Why? Do you happen to know what there was in the package?"

"Of course I know. He gets them all the time. *Pens.* His own special triangular blue pens with his name monogrammed on them. I'm the one who first got them for him. I couldn't stand his fiddling with the ordinary ball-points."

"I know," I said, "and dropping the springs."

"You were married to him, too, then," she said, with some sarcasm.

"In a way," I said.

"Well, they're his babies now, comfortable to his finger, comfortable to his ego, cheap, disposable. As far as I know, they have only two disadvantages. They don't last long, but run dry quickly. The other disadvantage is that he puts them back in his pocket when they're dry and its up to me to check the pens in his inner jacket pocket and throw them out if they're dry."

I nodded. I could guess now the nature of the fuss at the autographing table. Giles had tried to autograph books with a nearly dry pen (the one on the bureau in his room, no doubt, the one with which I had drawn the question mark, using the last dregs of ink that had settled down to the point after it had run dry on him). He didn't have the fresh supply of his pens since I had not brought them to him and he had had to use some non-monogrammed pen that didn't set well in his fingers.

That would have a lot to do with his annoyance with me; everything to do, in fact—and even recognizing his neurosis with respect to pens, I could scarcely blame him. But how would a dry pen contribute to his murder? It might make him murder *me* out of petulance, but it wasn't something to induce the murder of *him*.

It still meant, however, that I had contributed to his discomfort, frustration, and anger on the last morning of his life, and that would remain bitter in my memory.

I said to Eunice, "Apparently you didn't stay at your brother's. You left this morning."

"So I did, Just. I can't stand those kids of his and his wife is no bargain, either. I keep forgetting, but then when I visit I remember why I don't see him oftener than I do."

"How early this morning did you leave?"

"Right after breakfast."

"And came here?"

"No, I didn't come here. I wasn't here during the crucial hours when the death took place. Some stores were open and I went shopping."

"Did you buy anything?"

"No, but I wasn't seriously intending to. Nobody I knew saw me. I told you; I have no alibi."

"But why did you come here?"

And for the first time, Eunice grew uneasy. Her eyes, which had been staring into mine with almost insolent carelessness, dropped. Her voice lowered.

"I thought I might see Giles. It had been a rotten night last night. I knew he was signing books this morning, and I thought that might put him into a good humor. I thought he might be willing to— If I stayed overnight here, I—"

I sat there, appalled. This solid block of woman was coming apart with no warning whatever, and I didn't want to have to try to put her together again.

She said, "But instinctively he knew I was coming and rather than have anything to do with me, he bashed his head or arranged to have it bashed for him and said goodbye to me once and for all. The son of a—" And two large tears overflowed and furrowed down her cheeks.

I stared at her helplessly.

She said, "You're going to sit there and watch me cry? Well, screw you, sonny, I'm not crying." She took a deep breath, passed the back of her hand over her eyes, and said, "I'm going back to his room. Maybe the Medical Examiner is there. I've got to arrange for the funeral."

She went to the door, opened it, and walked through, turning to the left toward 1511. She didn't bid me farewell, and that didn't bother me. I looked at my watch. It was past five.

15   ROSEANN BRONSTEIN   5:15 P.M.

I didn't have much of a desire to leave the room. Not

at once. I had till six before I would be forced to go and what bothered me was that I had nowhere to go, nothing to do.

Wherever it was I went, whatever it was I did, it would have to be aimed at solving this damned puzzle. In two or three days, probably, Giles would be buried and I would have to attend some sort of memorial service, I knew. And I *must*, for my own piece of mind, know something by then. (Or was I just setting myself deadlines, as I was accustomed to do in connection with this chapter or that in my novels, in order to force myself to get them done?)

Well, why was he murdered? So far, I had a trivial complication to his life and a serious one. The trivial one was the dry pen owing to my failure to deliver the package. I didn't see how the pens could have anything to do with it. (Or was I just trying to rid myself of responsibility?)

There was also the serious complication involved in the sexual frustration of two women, Eunice and Roseann. (Who would ever have thought of Giles Devore as an *homme fatal* driving two women to distraction!)

Of the two, I was sure Eunice hadn't killed him. She guessed, two quickly, that I was hinting at murder. Surely, if she had been a murderer she would have been very careful not to see my hint at all. She would stubbornly have veered away from the word and concept. (Or am I just being a romantic?)

What about Roseann?

Where could I find her? I might try wandering about the hotel, looking for her, but the fact was that I could wander forever and never bump into her by accident, even if she were in the hotel—which was as large as a small town. And she might not be in the hotel in the first place. Nor could I think of anyone whom I might ask and who might know where she was.

I thought awhile, staring out the window at an unappetizing section of walls and windows as seen blurrily through an off-white curtain.

Roseann must have found out about Giles's death. Henrietta would have had it announced, and it might even have made the radio and television news by now. And if she had heard, and she had been in the process of desperately trying to win him back to that horrible game he played with obliging women, surely her reaction would be one of despair. Would she go to a bar and get drunk? Would she jump off the roof, shrieking imprecations at fate? Would she go home and sob herself to sleep?

I couldn't check every bar in town, and if she had jumped off the roof, I had a feeling I'd hear about it soon enough. As for home, that was easy enough to check. It required only a phone call and there was a phone in the room. Of course, it didn't belong to me and the tab would be placed firmly on the wallet of the guy who was arriving to take the room this evening. I refused to worry about it, though, and told myself I would straighten out the matter with Sarah.

The phone was of the type where dialing 9 would give me an outside line automatically. That was good, for it meant I didn't have to go through the operator, who might, after all, object to completing a call from an un-occupied room (or would she know it was unoccupied?).

I dialed 9 and then the number of the bookstore, which the telephone directory had been kind enough to give me. The bookstore wouldn't be open on Memorial Day, I supposed, but she lived in several rooms above it. She probably had an extension upstairs.

I let it ring fifteen times on the theory that she might not have an extension upstairs and might have to hurry downstairs to pick up the phone. I bet myself, fifteen to four, no one would answer. I lost my bet by a nose when the receiver was lifted on the fifteenth ring.

The voice was a low croak, absolutely unrecognizable, and I suspected a wrong number. "Roseann?" I said tentatively.

"What the hell do you want?" came the voice, some-what stronger. I recognized it now.

"It's Darius Just."

"I know it is. What the hell do you want?" She didn't call me little fella. She was really in a bad way.

"I'm sorry, Roseann, but have you heard about Giles?"

"Yes, I heard about him. You'd think that rotten bastard could keep on his feet in the bathtub."

That made two women who called him names for daring to be dead.

I said, "Roseann, did you see Giles since you and I talked yesterday?"

"No, I didn't, and what business is that of yours anyway? Did *you* see him?"

I could have told her I had, but to what end? No point in repeating what he had said. Not now. I said, "Roseann, I'm puzzled about something."

"What are you talking about?"

"Look, when I came into his room—"

"You found him. Yes, I know. Maybe you pushed him."

She was being completely unreasonable. I said, "Listen, Roseann, when I came into his room, he was already dead. He was in the bathtub as though he had been taking a shower, and his clothes were thrown all over the room. It was as though he had taken them off and just tossed them every which way as he was getting ready for his shower."

There was silence at the other end for so long that I was about to jiggle the contacts, then she said, in a more normal voice than any I had heard her use. "But that's impossible. He *always* folded—"

She stopped, but I had two things. I was certain now that Roseann had played the game with Giles, and the second was that she clearly agreed that the clothes could not have been strewn by Giles.

She said, "You mean someone else tossed those clothes around? Some woman— No, he wouldn't let that happen." Then she, too, made the leap which, it seemed to me, declared her innocent. "You mean someone killed him and then spread the clothes around to make it look as if he had an accident while he was taking a shower?"

"Do you think that's possible?"

"I don't know, I— Yes, of course it was possible," she exploded suddenly. "It was *Eunice*."

"Eunice?"

"Of course. If she couldn't have him, then no one could."

"That can't be, Roseann," I said, deliberately lying to see if she had reason to say it or was the simple prey of spite. "Eunice has a rigid and solid alibi."

Roseann made a croaking sound that might have been intended for laughter. She said, "Do you suppose she would do it herself. She hired somebody. You don't have to invest much these days to get someone killed."

"Do you have evidence for that, Roseann?"

"I don't need evidence."

"You do, legally, if you're going to say things like that. Besides, it may occur to someone that your motive is the same as Eunice's and as strong."

"*Mine?*"

"If you can't have him, then no one can."

And she screamed, "Oh, don't be a goddamn jackass," and crashed the phone into its cradle.

Much more slowly and gently, I hung up.

Well, what had I accomplished? Both got my hint at murder without trouble, which made me tend to eliminate them from suspicion. To be sure, Eunice had not been able to accept the possibility, even for the sake of accusing Roseann, which she had clearly wanted to be able to do. Roseann, on the other hand, could and did accuse Eunice at once. That, however, might merely reflect the fact that Eunice was a lawyer and Roseann was not.

And meanwhile Roseann had brought up the point of a hired killer. Why not? It didn't sound likely, but why not? That would mean that alibis meant nothing. And perhaps the trace of heroin I had found was the sort of thing that a hired killer might have left behind. (Why? I couldn't say why.)

It was no use. In the last five hours I had thought harder and longer and steadier and more monotonically than I had ever done for an equal period at any time in my life. Not even when I was plotting my novels had I thought harder and longer—and yet it had all brought me exactly nothing. I was no wiser now than at the start—less wise, for others had suggested complications I would not have thought of myself.

But it was almost six and a customer would be arriving at any moment. I placed the key on the bureau, walked out the door of 1524, and locked it behind me. I was still thinking.

16 GWYNETH JONES 5:55 P.M.

The elevator took its time, but as it happened I was in no great hurry.

Since I couldn't believe (and didn't want to believe) that the murder depended on the triviality of the pens and my failure, and since it didn't seem to me to involve either Eunice or Roseann, the motive had to rest elsewhere—another unsuspected woman, the heroin, a homicidal maniac (no, would a homicidal maniac bother to arrange an accident?).

In search of that motive, it might serve to track down everything Giles had done from the time he left me nearly twenty-four hours earlier to the time of his death.

The elevator still wasn't coming. It was approaching dinnertime and people would be going up and down at an above-normal rate. Life went on. People were hungry.

I wasn't.

When I last saw Giles, he was leaving with Henrietta Corvass. If I began with her—

The elevator came to the floor, going down. It was full and there was a halfhearted squeezing backward to make room for me. I stepped in. I don't take up much room: I'll say that for me.

I gave the group in the elevator one sharp glance to see if I recognized anyone. I was in no mood to talk.

Luckily, there was no need to. With thousands at the convention, in any random group of a dozen or so I would know no one.

I turned to face the front. The others were all conventioneers. They all wore badges. I sighed and tried to be unobtrusive about taking mine off.

I got off at the fifth floor and found the interview room still open. It surprised me; I had assumed it would have closed at five and I had gone there only to make sure of that.

There was only one person inside, a young woman with straggly hair, unobtrusive breasts, and sneakers. Her legs were spraddled apart as she slouched back in her chair and looked thoughtfully at what I assumed were releases. She had a sheet of paper in the typewriter and would undoubtedly begin typing in a moment. I looked at her legs, but that was unrewarding, so I looked at her nameplate and that said, "Gwyneth Jones."

"Gwyneth!" I said to myself in disbelief.

I said it to myself just a touch too loudly, for the young woman assumed I was trying to attract her attention (which I meant to do in a moment), looked up, and said, "Yes?"

I said, "You wouldn't know where Henrietta was, would you?"

The girl looked at me thoughtfully and said, "Henrietta Corvass?"

I said, out of curiosity, "Is there another Henrietta around?"

"No. She's the only Henrietta here."

"Then why did you ask me?"

"We've got to be accurate."

"I'll start over. You wouldn't know where Henrietta Corvass was, would you?"

"As long as we're starting over, who are you?"

I fumbled for my badge and showed her and got a blank stare.

"I'm a writer," I explained. "Now what about Henrietta? Do you know where she is?"

And after all that, Gwyneth said, indifferently, "No."

I said, "Look, sweetheart, pretend it's an emergency. Suppose your bra strap broke and Henrietta had the only spare in the place. Where would you look for her? Guess, if you have to. Give me a start."

She said. "I don't wear bras. I think I heard her say something about the Sewall, Broom party tonight. Maybe she'll be there."

"Thank you, sweetheart. And where will the party be held?"

"I don't know, but I think there's a flyer somewhere around." She looked about the top of her desk half-heartedly and said, "I'm behind in my work, you know."

"I know," I said. "I could tell. But spend five more minutes looking for it, will you?"

I bet myself eight to five she wouldn't find it and I lost. She got to it in less than a minute. She was a short girl and uninteresting but I kissed her on the cheek and said thanks. She didn't look overwhelmed with gratitude.

I went off to find a men's room, where I took care of my biologic needs, washed my hands and face, looked earnestly at myself to see if I looked as crummy as I felt and decided I did, but what the hell. I'm not strikingly handsome, but I'm not grotesque either. I fall into that broad in-between that's called "attractive" in various tones of voice and that's about the best I can do in describing myself.*

I leaned against the towel dispenser and studied the flyer. The party was not in the hotel but at a restaurant nearby, and it was slated to start at 6:30.

I had some twenty minutes, so I found myself a seat in an odd, sequestered corner of the lobby and let my

---

* It's the best *Asimov* can do, or cares to do. Any reasonable consensus would have me "strikingly handsome."

          —DARIUS JUST

I would suggest, Gentle Reader, that you settle this matter for yourself. Just get a copy of any one of Darius' books and look at the jacket photo.

          —ISAAC ASIMOV

eyes close. I remember wondering if that might be the place where the semi-porno bookstand Sarah had referred to could be found. I lacked the energy to look for it, so I thought of Sarah herself for a dispassionate moment and somehow fifteen minutes vanished between two ticks of a wall clock I could hear above my head.

I started rather violently and checked my pockets to see if a sympathetic pickpocket had lightened the load of a clearly weary man. I was still in one piece and, feeling better for the few moments of unconsciousness, I left the hotel.

17 THOMAS VALIER 6:40 P.M.

I suspect that there is scarcely an hour of the day on any day of the week that somewhere a party isn't being given, complete with bartender, free drinks, and lavish buffet.

And with enough guests imperfectly known to those in charge, it becomes possible for anyone to enter provided only that he maintain an air of cheerful self-possession and wave, now and then, to people at the other end of the room.

I am sure there are some people who manage to provide themselves with much of their food supply for the year by attending such parties—but, of course, at a price. There is the noise and the stale tobacco smoke and the crowds and the gradual accumulation of drunkenness and the indifferent food and having to watch, *ad nauseam*, people striving to maintain an image, make a contact or an impression, broach business, or stab an enemy.

Generally, the price is too high for me, but I notice that when I do attend such a party, I become as bad as the rest. For all I know, every single person at any such party is convinced that he (or she) alone is a real, decent human being and that everyone else is to be condemned as a phony or worse.

I didn't have an invitation, but I had my ABA badge and, if questioned, I could prove my status as a writer, if not as a bookseller. However, I wasn't questioned and I don't think the fact that I wasn't actually wearing my badge bothered anyone. Presumably, the publishing firm of Sewall, Broom and Company was investing its money in the hope of obtaining goodwill among the booksellers and any touch of nastiness in keeping out anybody, even if justified, would introduce an unpleasantness that would turn them all off. Better some wastage on party crashers than a negation of the entire purpose of the evening.

The drinks were, of course, of no interest to me, and I passed them by except for a quick study to see if Henrietta was in view. She wasn't. I had a horrible notion that if I did see her I wouldn't recognize her, for I couldn't seem to bring her face before my mind's eye. If I could hear her speak, though, I would have no trouble. My memory for hearing is much better than for seeing.

I moved over to the buffet, which consisted largely of a mountain of fried chicken and was overcome by a feeling of *déjà vu*, of having done all that before. Except that it wasn't the illusion one usually describes by that French expression, but the real thing. I had done all that before. The night before, I had stepped through a room with a bar, stopping only to look for someone, and then passing on to the buffet. Last night it had been Giles I had been looking for; this night it was Henrietta. And as I hadn't seen him last night, I didn't see her this night.

I concentrated moodily on the fried chicken. It looked and smelled good and my appetite was with me in a bound. (I may get too upset to eat from time to time, but that state never lasts for long and I consider this to signify that I am a healthy human being.) I helped myself to a leg and a breast because I hate to have to pick and choose between white meat and dark meat, ladled on two or three sausages and some French fries. That, plus a salad and, later on, a cup of coffee and a sliver of cake, would represent all my inner man would need. After that, I could devote myself to finding Henrietta if she was there to be found.

In moving about in search of an empty table, I passed

the gantlet of a set of senior editors of Sewall, Broom, one of whom was a woman who headed a subsidiary house and whom I had known when that subsidiary house was an independent. I greeted them all with my head full of smiles and my hands full of food, managed to lean forward to kiss my friend without spilling anything, and got into the other room. The kiss meant my credentials for attending the party were full-blown and evident—not that I had worried about it.

Sewall, Broom isn't a bad firm. I wouldn't mind working with them, if I could be sure they would let me have my own way. Prism Press, at least, doesn't interfere with me and that's an advantage that balances out quite a bit of money.

I suspect that thought passed through my mind because somewhere out of the corner of my eye, I became aware of Tom Valier, my esteemed publisher and the Prince of Prism Press. He saw me, too, more clearly than I saw him, for I had not as much as gotten one somber bite out of the chicken leg (and remembered that I had had one for lunch, too) when he joined me.

"Hello, Darius. Terrible thing," and he shook his head solemnly.

I knew what he meant, of course. "Yes, terrible thing," I said, and went on eating.

He said, "You found the body, I heard."

"I was the lucky man," I said.

"He fell in the bathtub and killed himself?"

"That's what it looked like," I said.

"Terrible thing," he said.

"Terrible."

He shook his head. "It happens all the time. Slipping in the bathtub, I mean. There must be thousands of people every year injured that way. The tub is a deadly weapon. Poor Giles."

"Terrible thing," I said.

"Terrible," he said.

Not for one minute did I think he had come just to tell me what a terrible thing Giles's death was, and his indoctrination of me into the dangers of the bathtub interested me.

I said, "Spying out the competition?"

"I've got good friends at Sewall, Broom," he said feebly, still brooding, apparently, over what a terrible thing it was.

I finished my chicken leg and had a few French fries before tackling the salad.

He said, "You know, Darius—"

It was coming. I said, "Yes?"

"What we talked about yesterday?"

"About Giles leaving Prism Press?"

"Not leaving. He was talking about leaving. He hadn't left yet." He smiled in a deprecating way. "Under the circumstances, I don't think we ought to mention that unnecessarily. The man's dead, you know."

"Yes, I know. Terrible thing."

Tom looked suspicious, but I suppose the point he was making was too important to take off on side issues. "I mean, let the dead lie in peace. Why bother with useless scandal?"

"There's no scandal in changing publishers," I said. (Maybe publishers thought there was, of course—if they were on the losing end.)

"Yes, but nothing came of it, you see, so why talk of it?"

"Sure," I said. "I have no reason to talk about it, Tom. I'll consider it confidential."

"Thanks, Darius."

And as though I had relieved him enough to make it possible for him to think of food, he said, "I think I'll get something for myself."

He came back a few minutes later with chicken on his own plate and by then I had had a chance to think a little.

"We've got to look at the bright side, Tom," I said. "His book will do better than ever. It's not every author who dies in the middle of a promotion campaign."

"Oh, no," he said uneasily, "we don't want to capitalize on a thing like this."

"Why not? What about the signed books you were going to hand out as door prizes? Are they all gone?"

He frowned and looked shocked, as though deploring my bad taste. "Oh, no. I've got them. We can't hand them out now. It wouldn't be a fit thing to do."

"You're right," I said. "If you hang on to them till *Evergone* is a clear best seller, you can auction them off. I wouldn't be surprised, considering these are the last autographs anyone will get, if they don't bring a couple of hundred apiece."

"No," he said, "I don't even want to think of anything like that." (But he was thinking of it, I knew, and I bet myself five to two he would do it eventually.)

"Come on," I said, "take advantage of the headlines. It's happened at the ABA Convention. It would mean a lot to the booksellers and they'll push the book. You know, 'Death at the ABA.'"

For a moment, I recalled Asimov's *cri de coeur* of the night before; of his obligation to write a book called *Murder at the ABA*. I swear to you I was so desperate to make sense out of the whole thing that I had a passing flash of Asimov having arranged the whole thing in order to have his plot—or publicize his book.*

Tom said reluctantly, "I suppose sales *will* improve, but I don't care about that."

The corners of my mouth quirked a bit at that thoroughly ridiculous statement that no publisher (certainly not Tom) could possibly have said without instantly

---

* Absolutely sick. I told Darius it would be ridiculous to include that bit, but he wants it in because he says it's so. If he wants to be made to look like a ninny, on his head be it.

—ISAAC ASIMOV

I don't know why Asimov should think he's above suspicion. The interested reader might be wondering if he were writing this book from a jail cell.

—DARIUS JUST

Well, even if it spoils the suspense, I am *not* writing this book from a jail cell. I'm right here in my office.

—ISAAC ASIMOV

making himself a liar. I held steady though and said, "For that matter, you can jack up the price for movie rights to *Evergone*, and you can bring out Giles's first novel again at a higher price and probably sell as many copies as you sold the first time, if not more. The cloud has a silver lining, literally."

"Oh, well," said Tom. "It's not an appropriate subject for discussion. The loss of those books he might have written can't be made up for." And he filled his mouth with chicken.

We both ate quietly and I went for my coffee and cake, being thoughtful enough to bring some for him, too.

Those books that Giles "might have written" wouldn't have been Prism Press books. It was no loss to Tom. He only gained.

Could he have done it? There was the anger over Giles's leaving the house and frustration over the financial loss that might represent; and add to that the gains his death would bring. Was it guilt that made him urge me to say nothing of his troubles with Giles, to hide the motive? Was it guilt that made him steadfastly refuse to accept the bait of greed I dangled before him, to hide the motive? Was that why he talked so prattlingly of accidental deaths in the bathtub? Was he anxious to make sure that there was no hint of murder in the air?

But it was all conjecture. He might really think it was accident; he might really be embarrassed at seeming to profit out of tragedy. If Eunice were there, and if she read my thoughts, as seemed to be her habit, she could probably tear my conjectures concerning Tom's guilt to shreds and ribbons.

Oh, well. I changed the subject. "Have you seen Henrietta, I wonder?"

Tom registered polite inquiry. "Henrietta?"

"The interview secretary of the ABA. Plump girl. Longish face."

Tom shook his head. "I'm afraid I don't know her. Teresa might. She arranged the autograph session along with the Hercules Books people. The Devore autograph session," he explained, and his voice dropped as he said it as though he had just placed a phantom hat over his heart. "I suppose Teresa would have had to have some contact with the interview secretary."

"Sounds reasonable. Where's Teresa?"

"She went home. She developed a sick headache after hearing about Giles."

Well, if Tom was a Macbeth, Teresa was no Lady Macbeth. That is, provided she really did go home with a sick headache (God, I was beginning to suspect everything).

"I won't be coming in tomorrow myself," Tom said. "I'll let the girls run the booth. This thing with Giles has spoiled the convention for me."

"Terrible thing," I agreed, and eventually he got up and left.

Eventually I got up, too, to find Henrietta, if she was there.

18   HENRIETTA CORVASS   7:45 P.M.

The party was crowded, filling two large rooms, with a corridor in between. It was not as though the people were stationary and I could simply go from group to group, studying the faces. They were moving around, brushing past me, shifting and changing.

Nor was it as though I were invisible and could carry on my errand undisturbed. I knew perhaps one out of ten people there and each one, it seemed to me, hailed me.

I was a celebrity, getting more mileage out of the fact that I had found the body than out of all four (and a fifth in press) of my books put together.

There wasn't, as far as I could see, any diminution of gaiety at the party from what might have been expected if all were well; there was no trace of solemnity over and above that which might have resulted from a momentary difficulty in getting to the bar, or from a conversation that might have come to rest, for a while, on the matter of the loss of a job, of a book, of a buck. Life goes on.

Here was the case of a man who, some nine hours before, had been one of the stars of the convention. And, some six or seven hours before, he had met with death, violent and unexpected. It was a pity, it was a shame, it was a shock, it was terrible, and then life went on. Giles was swallowed up by the inexorable advance of time and it was as though he had never been. Here's to the next man who dies.

And if it had been someone else who found the body; if I had been in no way involved; if I had not been late with the package of pens; would I have been any different? I didn't have to make any bets with myself. It was a dead certainty that I would have been no different.

Life goes on.

If every human being on earth were to die in one gory moment, whatever else of life on the planet was left would go on, unconcerned, and nothing else in the entire universe would give a damn. Nor should they? The universe goes on.

I was getting more and more morbid as I went from group to group, being engaged at times and disengaging myself at times, and coming to the decision that the needle I was hunting for wasn't there, and thinking I would see her tomorrow anyway—

And then, about a quarter to eight, I heard her voice. I didn't see her at first. I turned in the direction of her voice and, with that as guide, I recognized her at once.

I joined the group quietly and listened, trying to work myself in, temporarily, as a member. I wanted to abstract her from the group and I didn't want to do it very ostentatiously. Being unobtrusive is easier for me than for most. I don't take up much room, and I'm not one of those noticeable characters, either for reasons of sheer bulk as Giles had been or out of a visible glow of self-satisfaction as Asimov is.

When I had been standing there long enough to be taken for granted I managed to lock eyes with Henrietta. Recognition on her part was instantaneous, but after a second or two, she looked away quite deliberately.

I nudged my way next to her and tapped her very lightly on the elbow. When she turned, I said, "I want to talk to you." I mouthed it so that I practically made no sound.

She said, "Why?" talking normally.

I said, still quite low, "It's important."

"About—"

She didn't finish the phrase, not because I interrupted her, or because anyone or anything did. She just didn't want to finish it and that gap in sound was as clear an ending to the phrase as a word would have been.

"Yes."

"Can't it wait?" She was looking angry.

"Please," I said.

She looked rapidly from face to face as though hoping for some sort of rescue, but her momentary withdrawal from the general conversation meant, merely, that it flowed past and over her and it was as though she were not there at all.

So she said crossly, "Well?"

"Not here. Please. Come with me."

I've felt reluctant arms in my time. I've led girls in directions they were not sure they wanted to go. Generally, I expected to be able to change their minds and make them glad they had come along. This time it was different. Henrietta's arm felt stiff and unyielding and I didn't have the self-assurance of delights to come to lend me plausibility.

I said, "Let's go outside. We can't talk here. Just outside. Five steps outside," I said urgently. "No more."

She came with me.

It was the darker half of twilight outside, with the sky slate gray, and the air motionless and mild. The traffic was gaudy in its headlights and taillights. The street was wide, not too full of people, and there was a hip-high wall of concrete about the building in which the restaurant was. Through a break in the wall there was a wide, shallow stairway that led down to a sunken patio.

It had been my notion to go down to the patio, but it carried an overflow of people from the party at the small tables there, so I motioned her, instead, to sit down on the wall. I placed my hands on it and lifted myself up to sit on it with my feet dangling.

She said, "That was a terrible thing. Talk about the wrong kind of publicity! It will be in all the papers."

"I don't know about that, Henrietta. The hotel will do its best to keep it quiet, and what is there to a guy falling in the tub? He's not exactly a household word. He might become one after this, but he isn't yet."

I was trying to soothe her, loosen her up. I swung my feet and grew chattier. "You know," I said, "when the movie actor James Dean died in a road accident about twenty years ago, he got exactly two inches in the newspapers. I noticed it at the time because I had seen him on a TV show and had admired him. Then his final movies came out, and he became a soaring teen-age idol. If, two years after his death, he could have come back to life and died again, there'd have been no type large enough for any newspaper in the United States to announce the fact. It might be that way with Giles two years from now, but right now it's two inches—maybe one inch."

"I'm the one who had to make the announcement."

"It's your job."

"It doesn't mean I have to like it."

"All right, don't like *it*. What you're doing is disliking *me*, just because I brought the news to you. I don't like *it*, either. How'd you have liked to have been there and—"

"Shut up!" Rather to my surprise, she seemed on the point of tears.

I did shut up, and waited till I saw whether she was going to tip toward tears or dry eyes.

It was the latter and she said, "What are we doing out here?"

I said, "Look, he was a friend of mine. You were there last night and he didn't want to go with you, remember?

I made him go, and because I did, he couldn't pick up
a package he wanted to pick up and he asked me to do
so and—uh—I didn't get a chance to do it. It's important
to me, now, to make sure that my failure with that package didn't lead to his death. This could mean a lot to me.
Just remember that I'm stuck with my misery now because I did you a favor last night. I'm trying to find out
as much about this whole thing as I can, now, and you
can return the favor and help me."

She wasn't buying it, though I was using my most
sincere and insinuating tone of voice. She said, "How
could the package mean anything one way or the other?"

I shrugged. "They were pens. He always used monogrammed pens and he had left his supply home. I didn't
get them to him, so he autographed books with the one
pen he had and it ran out of ink and that upset him. If
he hadn't been upset he might have gone to the book-
and-author lunch afterward. Since he *was* upset, he went
up to his room in a huff and decided to take a shower
and cool off and, I suppose, fell. So that makes it all my
fault in a way."

"If that's the way it was, what can I do about it?"

"You can help me show myself that I'm wrong; that
there may have been some other reason he went up to
his room, some other reason he was upset, some other
reason he slipped. I don't want to have to think I helped
kill my friend, if I can avoid it. And you can help me."

"But how?"

"I just want to know everything that happened after
the last time I saw him alive last night, and you walked
off with him."

When she hesitated, I said, "I'm not a policeman,
Henrietta. I can't make you tell me. I'm just asking you
to tell me out of common humanity."

"But there's nothing to tell. We went to a TV station
and we taped a show."

"How did you go? Where? Who did the taping?"

"We went by taxi. We picked one up just outside the
hotel and it took us to the studio. It was a morning talk

show with what's-her-name." She waved one hand in the air. "Sandra someone." (I knew whom she meant.) "We taped it and that's all."

"Did you have to wait long before you started?"

"Five or ten minutes. You know how it is. They *always* make you wait just so that you know who's boss."

"How did Giles take that?"

"He just sat there, looking straight ahead, puffing out his mustache. I was a *little* nervous because I had insisted he come, and once or twice he looked at his watch and then at me, but he didn't say a word."

"And how did he behave during the taping?"

"Like a doll, actually. He was very good. They're going to run it in about three weeks to fit in with publication day. If they have any brains, they'll push it ahead now. I wouldn't be surprised," she added bitterly, "if they run it tomorrow morning while the convention is still on."

"Not a chance," I said soothingly. "They have commitments, too. What did they talk about?"

"About what you'd expect. She wanted to know about his book and what it was about and whether there would be a movie sale. Then she got onto his writing habits. Since he had said the book dealt partly with the Watergate crisis, she asked whether he didn't think there were fantasy aspects to that. He said 'surrealism' was the word he would use and explained what he meant. He was very good. It was a good show."

"I'll have to watch," I said. "Did she ask about his publishers? Anything at all?"

"No, she didn't." Henrietta sounded surprised. "Should she have?"

"I don't know," I said ingenuously. "I'm just asking because Prism Press are my publishers, too, and I was wondering if they got any of the publicity."

"Oh, sure. When they mentioned the name of the book at the beginning and end of the program, they mentioned the publisher, too."

"At no other time? Nothing else?"

"Nothing that I can remember."

"And what happened after the taping was over?"

"Nothing. We went back."

It was quite dark by then and I couldn't see her face clearly in the streetlights. Her voice, however, had gone dead.

I said, "After you took him to his room, I mean."

Her voice gained a sudden edge. "Why do you say I took him to his room?"

"You were going to, weren't you? The last thing you said when you left with him was that you would see him safely back to his room."

"Oh, I see what you mean," she said, with a sudden air of indifference as though it all meant very little. "I went up the elevator with him to his floor."

It would have been utterly unconvincing in any case, but now that I had talked to Eunice, I knew exactly where we stood and she didn't have a chance with me. "Of course," I said, "he asked you into his room."

"No-o-o," she said feebly.

"Henrietta," I said, "be reasonable. He asks *every* woman into his room." (I didn't know that for a fact, but I felt absolutely safe.) "And you must have gone in, or you wouldn't be in this state."

She didn't answer and she turned her head away. I'm sure she had started to cry.

I said, "I promise you, I won't repeat anything you say. You don't have to go into any details. Just let me know, roughly, what went on."

She looked about to see if there was anyone near us. There wasn't. There's a kind of freemasonry of humanity that keeps anyone not completely outside the pale from coming too near any man and woman engaged in what seems an intimate conversation. She said, "There's nothing *I* have to be ashamed of, but it's all so unpleasant."

I said, "Henrietta, I know Giles better than you think. I have an idea of what he is capable of. He didn't—hurt you? (Even though I was doing my best to use words that would keep her calm, it hurt me to use that Victorian pause followed by that Victorian euphemism.)

"Oh, he didn't," she said, grateful for the euphemism, I'm sure. "He just asked me to come in and tuck him in, because I said—joking, you know—after the taping was over that now I would take him right back to the hotel as I had promised and tuck him in.

"I laughed, because I thought he was joking, too, and said that I hoped he would have a good night's sleep. But he took my wrist in his hand and said, 'Oh, come on in for a while.' Well, I didn't like to make a scene and I couldn't believe he had anything really—you know—" She paused in confusion.

I said, "You didn't expect him to try to use force on you, you mean?"

"Well, I thought he might try to persuade me to come to bed with him"—she was suddenly more businesslike, as though she felt it to be beneath her dignity to be caught being too coy—"but I had no doubt he wouldn't succeed. He didn't appeal to me at all and I have a lover who's quite satisfactory. So I let myself be pulled in and the door closed behind me and then I said as coldly as I could, 'Really, I have work to do, Mr. Devore,' and his *voice* changed."

"His voice changed?"

"It became high-pitched and squeaky— Do I have to go on?"

"I wish you would. Please. Just roughly. You don't have to give me every word."

"He wanted me to undress him. He called me Mommy."

"What did you do? Undress him?"

"I didn't know what to do. I didn't want to start screaming; I didn't want to create a stupid scandal. I thought I'd humor him a little and perhaps calm him down. I mean, I'm not a virgin and I'm not afraid of men. I took off his jacket, his tie, his shirt, and I helped him off with his shoes and socks. But that was as far as I could go, really. And he said—he said, he wanted me to bathe him. I mean, he said, 'Bathe me, Mommy,' and that was just too much. I just dashed for the door and out."

"He didn't try to stop you?"

"*No.* He just cried. After I closed the door, I could hear him crying inside, like a little boy. So I went down to the bar and I had a couple of drinks and, thank God, I didn't meet anyone I knew. Then I went to my room and took a sleeping pill."

I waited a while to let her recover, then I said, "When you took off his clothes—those items of clothing you did take off, that is—what did you do with them?"

"Oh, that! That was another weird thing. He directed me. He made me put the shoes in the closet with the points inward. He made me hang up his jacket with the buttons facing left, and I had to fold his shirt in some very careful way."

"How did he make you?"

"Well, he told me, in his baby voice, in a whiny sort of way. So I did it—I told you I was trying to keep him under control. He wanted me to blow in his socks before folding them. That I wouldn't do and he got petulant and said he wanted to be bathed and I ran."

That was it, then. I had what I wanted. As late as last night, he still insisted on having his clothes folded.

Henrietta said, breaking in on my thoughts, "So you have what you wanted."

"What?" I looked up quickly. Was another one reading my mind?

"It was over me that he was upset, not over the missing pens."

"Are you guessing that or did he tell you that this morning?"

She got down from her seat on the wall. "Oh no, I didn't see him this morning. After I left him last night, I never saw him again. I had no intention of seeing him. When I got up this morning, I had breakfast in my room, and I called down at five after nine and told them I wouldn't be in till after ten. He would be autographing then and there would be no chance of running into him."

"Then you weren't at the autographing session?"

"Certainly not!"

"Didn't someone go for him in the morning?"

"I wouldn't know, but it wasn't I. I was through squiring *him* around."

Yet I had the distinct impression there had been a woman with him in the morning before ten. Someone had told me so. There was even a name given me. . . . No use, I drew a blank.

I said, "Look, Henrietta, don't start thinking it was over you that all this happened. It could have been something else altogether. Did Giles say anything at all to you last night that indicated he was disturbed about anything?"

"Not a thing."

"Well, think about it for a while. Did *anything* happen out of the ordinary? Were you stopped by anyone at any time? Did someone speak to Giles? Did Giles say something puzzling? Did he look funny at any time I mean, not with respect to his sex games. Is there anything, as you think back on last night, that puzzled you at the time?"

She said, "Not a thing! Nothing!"

Well, I had to accept it. I couldn't beat her into remembering. And at that point, even if there was something to remember, I suspected that she wouldn't—just to be done with it all. In fact, I didn't think I could keep Henrietta there much longer. She showed distinct signs of getting ready to leave. I said hastily, "When did you leave him last night?"

"I didn't look at my watch. It felt something like elevenish, but I don't know. Look, I don't want to talk about it any more and—you know—it's confidential."

"Absolutely. And thank you."

She turned and hurried down the steps, and I turned in another direction and walked down the street toward the hotel.

19 SHIRLEY JENNIFER 9:10 P.M.

What was I to do next? I knew what Giles had done

up to possibly 11 P.M. the night before. At 10 A.M. he was autographing. Nobody had said he was late and it would have been remarked on if he were. What had happened in those eleven hours of night and morning that might account for what happened toward noon?

There was a woman with him toward the end of the period. Of that I was certain even if I couldn't remember what it was that made me certain. The question was: Who was she and had she been with him all night?

I tried to put myself in Giles's place. As long as he was with Henrietta and he was engaged in his game, it would surely never have occurred to him to look at the bureau and note that the package and key were not there. Once she left, did he find another woman with whom to continue the game and was it not till morning that he noticed the lack? Or did he go to sleep in frustration after Henrietta left, too much the little boy of his sexual fantasies to notice? Or was it that he *did* notice but thought the cloakroom was closed after eleven and was he too frustrated and too little-boy to do anything about it?

As usual, when I asked myself a series of questions such as these, I had no answer.

I was entering the lobby of the hotel when I heard the cry that I suppose I had been dreading, subconsciously, ever since lunch.

"Dari-i-ius, I've been looking for you all da-a-a-ay."

I don't think she had, but it was the nice thing to say.

"Hello, Shirley," I said dully. "I'm sorry. I've had a terrible day."

"I kno-o-ow. Everyone is talking about it. How awful! And you had to be the one to find it. I suppose that was the reason you never came to my booth when I was signing." She picked that moment to light a cigarette. She knows I hate it and I decided that despite her claim to understanding she was getting back at me for standing her up.

I said defensively, "I was spending the time with the cops, and it was no fun."

"Poor baby," she purred.

It was odd how remote and immune I felt. I said, "I feel pretty sick about it and I guess I'll go home and give myself a chance to recover." I backed away a little.

She looked surprised and a little annoyed. "Home?"

One minute before, I had had no intention of leaving just yet, but now it seemed the thing to do. I could think of no other way of avoiding another night with Shirley, and I *had* to avoid it. Perhaps after a while I could go back to her, but not that night, not while I was so aware that if it hadn't been for the night before, I wouldn't have been the one to discover Giles's body. If I think about it now, I don't see much sense in my attitude, but at the time it was different. It made more sense to me than anything else that had happened the entire day.

"I better do that, Shirley. I'm worn out with the afternoon I've had." I managed a yawn, and suddenly found it wasn't difficult. "Will you be here tomorrow?"

She looked indifferent. "I don't know."

"I'll be here. Maybe I'll see you." And I about-faced and walked out of the hotel. Ten hours earlier, I would have been willing to bet a hundred to eight—more—that I would spend another night with Shirley, but even very short odds win on occasion.

Now I made a bet at the same odds—a hundred to eight—that she'd never speak to me again. I won't lie to you. I was sorry about that; damned sorry.

I walked home. It was a healthy walk to the park and then along its long side, but I wasn't in a hurry to try to make it to bed. I kept thinking, with my mind going around in the same circles and ending nowhere.

When I found myself in my apartment with the door locks clicked shut behind me (all three of them) and with my typewriter gazing reproachfully at me through the door to the bedroom (as it always seems to do when it is neatly covered and has been unused for longer than two days), I couldn't remember the walk from the hotel at all. It was a more-than-a-mile walk and I couldn't remember a step of it. My passage from hotel to apartment might have been by instantaneous mass transference, like something out of Asimov's silly science fiction stories.*

It was only about 10:30, too early to go to bed, really, and yet I did not want to stay awake. I went through the preparations for bed, washing my teeth and all the rest of it, half in the hope that it would wake me, but it didn't.

Of course, it was possible that, going to bed early, I might wake up at 3 A.M. with all my sleep done. I thought of Henrietta taking a sleeping pill, and while I disapprove of that, I would have taken one if there had been such a thing in the house.

I put out the light, got into bed, and left the window open so I could hear the hypnotic sounds of traffic and city life seeping upward from twelve floors below. (It's hypnotic to those bred in the city, that is.)

Just before I went to sleep, there was one last thought I had. Isaac Asimov had been the second author at the autographing session. He might have seen Giles come in with somebody. What's more, Asimov was slated to be on some panel the next morning—11 A.M., I thought— I'd look it up in the morning—it was something I had thought—might be in—teresting—anyway—

And I slept.

---

* As I recall, I merely thought of science fiction stories generally at this point. You can depend on Asimov to put himself in here as though he were the only writer of science fiction stories the world has ever seen.

—DARIUS JUST

One of my better stories, "It's Such a Beautiful Day," which you'll find in my book *Nightfall and Other Stories*, has a plot involving mass transference. Since Darius, after some tedious cross-examination, admitted he had read that story, I maintain that my interpretation here is as close to the truth as need be.

—ISAAC ASIMOV

Part Three

TUESDAY

27 MAY 1975

1 DARIUS JUST 6:00 A.M.

But I didn't sleep really well. I had bad dreams of which I don't remember the details. Though I didn't wake up at three, I did flip my eyes open at six and found I had a rotten taste in my mouth and that my head was resting on a pillow damp with perspiration.

I stared at the ceiling for a while, sorting out the nightmares my imagination had constructed from the nightmare of yesterday's realities, and decided I wasn't going to be able to sleep any more that morning. So I pushed out of bed, took care of my day's assurance that I would require no laxatives, showered, shaved, and then had to make the decision about breakfast.

The contrast with the breakfast of the morning before was too extreme, and I decided not to fool with the eggs or the English muffins or the coffee. I didn't even want to be alone. It was a bright morning, the temperature was 59 and that would mean comfortable walking in a jacket, so I walked to the hotel.

Actually, I jogged partway since I was feeling guilty over having stayed out of the gym for the length of the convention.

The coffee shop at the hotel was respectably full even though I was there by 7:30 A.M., and after I had ordered my pancakes and ham (no use getting something I could make for myself at home—and I never made pancakes) I listened to the conversation about me.

Muhammad Ali, it seems, was the big hit of the convention. He had been big and brash, and I suspect there is something exciting to the audience in seeing a man who could flatten you into a grease spot with one blow if he wanted to exert himself—something like being in the same room with a tame lion and with no bars in between.

I also heard comments on Joe Namath's mother. She had made a hit, too, pushing the biography she had written of her son.

A bookseller (I caught just enough of his badge to see he was from Dallas) complained that no editor or publisher ever came to his store, so how could they know the problems of the bookseller? And the salesmen, he said, just wanted to unload books and didn't care if the store went broke.

I took a circuitous route on my way out after I had finished, deliberately attempting to overhear conversations. There were complaints about the discounts on textbooks (not high enough), on the nature of the packages the books came in (not easy enough to open), on the quality of the books that came in (not undamaged enough), and loud bitching about the Postal Service (not *anything* enough).

At one table, there was a discussion of the relative merits of religious books and occult books and how both were selling well, and I had a momentary impulse to lean over and say, "Religious books *are* occult books," just to stir something up, but didn't. It wasn't my business, after all.

I heard only one comment from the other end of the spectrum, which isn't surprising, since most of the attendees at the ABA were booksellers, after all. There must, however, have been two editors talking in the corner, for one was complaining that booksellers by and large didn't read books and how could they sell what they were not interested in?

I wasn't just being a nosybody, you understand. I was curious as to the extent to which Giles's death had taken over the convention. The answer was simple. Zero, that was the extent. I caught exactly one comment that was Giles-oriented.

A fellow from Poughkeepsie said, "Someone fell and killed himself in the shower yesterday. Hear about that?" He couldn't even use his name.

The answer was, "What I say is, don't take showers. A cousin of mine—" and he was off on a dull story I didn't want to hear.

Life goes on.

2 SARAH VOSKOVEK 8:45 A.M.

It was about a quarter to nine when I went to the elevator and punched the "up" button. I doubted that the hotel chief of security would be at his desk yet, and in any case I didn't know where his desk was. I did know where Sarah was, so I went up to the sixth floor. Undoubtedly she wasn't in yet, but I would wait a reasonable length of time.

I was wrong; she *was* in. The girl at the outer desk still wasn't there, but I could see Sarah in the inner room. I knocked on the doorjamb and said, "Hello."

She turned, saw me, and said, "Come in."

She didn't smile; somehow I felt smiling didn't come easy to her, but she didn't frown, either. She was wearing a dark-green outfit in which the collar stood up behind (I don't know the technical terms and I refuse to try to learn them). It was cut narrow and low in front, just low enough to show a pleasant cleavage between breasts of light cream. It was a pleasant sight for the morning.

She said, "How are you, Darius? You look a little worn."

"Bad day followed by bad night. It's all right."

She changed her cool expression into one of quiet sympathy. "It's Mr. Devore's death, of course."

"Yes."

"If I had not come to see you at the luncheon—"

"What's the difference? I was about due to remember, and something else would have kicked it off if you hadn't."

She said, "You know, the Medical Examiner came at about seven-thirty last night and took the body away."

"I assumed he did it at some time in the evening. What happened to Eunice? I mean, Mrs. Devore?"

"That I do not know. I presume she went home. Would you like me to get you coffee?"

"No, I've just had some. What I'd really like to do is to get, say, six hours of rest in which my brain was turned on to nothing *but* rest—preferably in your arms."

Why I said it, I don't know, because she didn't appeal to me, but when you reach middle age and have as checkered a career with women as I have had, these things come out without real planning—like slicing bread.

Even as I heard myself say it, I expected her to turn icy, but she didn't. Rather shockingly, she smiled and sat back in her chair. "Well," she said, "don't do anything that will get me fired."

She caught me by surprise and the moment passed. Her muscles tightened and she was sitting up in her chair once more, her posture excellent.

"But is there anything in the business way with which I can help you?" she said.

"When does the chief of security come in? His name is even harder than yours or I'd call him by that."

She looked at her watch. "It is Masogliani." (She pronounced it "Mahr-soh-LYAH-nee," which is how I tried to say it afterward.) "He's usually quite early, but I don't know if he's arrived. And if he has arrived, he may not be at his desk. Is it that you want to see him?" she asked, lapsing into non-English word order, which just made her sound cuter.

"Quite a lot," I said.

She shrugged. "I'll call him for you, but you know, he was a little annoyed with you yesterday."

"Did he tell you why?"

"He said you were a busybody. No details."

"I *am* a busybody," I said. "At least right now I am. For instance, before you call him, would you tell me something?"

"Depends."

"Is there a drug problem at the hotel?"

"Drug problem?"

"I mean, is the hotel involved in some way in the sale or distribution of drugs—dope—heroin?"

"Certainly not!"

"All right. Not the hotel. But is it taking place here *without* the hotel's connivance? That's what I mean."

She stared at me thoughtfully. "Why are you asking this?"

"I said I'm a busybody."

"You are, indeed. It's not your business to ask a question like that, nor is it mine to answer. If you must ask, you will have to ask Mr. Marsogliani, but I don't see why he should answer you, either."

"Would you call him?"

She did. He answered. At least I suppose he answered, since she talked as though he were on the phone. She explained that I wanted to see him and said, in a cajoling tone of voice, "He only wishes to see you for a moment." She had to guess that, for it was not derived from anything I had said.

I got the impression he wouldn't have agreed to see me if I hadn't been working through Sarah. Chalk up one good decision for me in seeing her first, and one good turn from the little woman.

"Thanks, Sarah," I said. "I wouldn't want to do anything to make you lose your job, but it requires restraint on my part."

She smiled a little.

Just as I was walking out, the receptionist walked in. She moved behind the desk in the outer office, put down her purse, and looked at me and then at Sarah with a kind of wise tolerance in her eyes. She was a good-looking black woman, about thirty, I should say.

I lifted both hands as though surrendering. "Business," I said. "Strictly business."

She laughed genially. I didn't think she'd mind if it weren't.

3 ANTHONY MARSOGLIANI 9:20 A.M.

Marsogliani wasn't smiling when I reached his office, which was also on the sixth floor. He made me wait while he went over some papers leisurely, making it perfectly clear he wasn't rushing. I sat there, my mind detached, prepared to show no signs of impatience but letting my eyes follow him in all his movements. He wasn't smoking a cigar but he smelled of stale cigar smoke just the same. I guess he always did. And he looked about the way he smelled, sour and uninviting.

It was well after nine when he finally wore himself out at the game of doing nothing under my unswerving gaze and said, "What can I do for you?"

I said, "Would you be able to find out for me whether anything in Mr. Devore's autopsy shows him to have been a user of drugs?"

"No," he said. "Call the police or ask his wife. Anything else I can do for you?"

"The police wouldn't tell me and it would be rather rough bothering his wife on such a subject at such a time. Why can't you tell me?"

"The police won't tell me, either. It's none of my business."

"Isn't it? There was heroin in the hotel room."

"I didn't see any."

"It was there. Someone brushed it away."

He reddened very slightly. "Who is the someone? Me?"

"I'm not accusing anyone, but it was there, and after a while it wasn't there. It seems to me important to know if it had anything to do with Devore. If he was not a drug user, then it may have been left over from the previous occupant of the room." (I didn't plan to say where I had gotten that notion; I felt Marsogliani wouldn't welcome having his underling suggest such a thing to me and I didn't want to do anything to endanger Strong's job, any more than Sarah's.)

"Even if it was, so what?"

"So would it be an isolated incident? Or is there a drug problem at the hotel?"

"I don't know what you mean by a drug problem."

"I don't know, either. Something that would make it undesirable to have anyone locate heroin in a hotel room."

"That would be undesirable at any time for any reason."

"If you found it, would you report it to the police?"

"Of course."

"Or is it something you would try to take care of quietly yourself, so that you would perhaps manage to avoid informing the police?"

Marsogliani looked at me for a long time from either side of his thick and majestic nose. Then he said, "These days there is the problem of drugs everywhere. It would be impossible not to have incidents in any hotel. Whether there is anything that could be called a *problem* is quite another thing. If there were, I would certainly tell the police, and I would certainly not tell you."

"You wouldn't, for instance, just quietly brush the heroin into an envelope and take it away?"

"No, I wouldn't, and I guess you're lucky you're such a little pipsqueak or, for suggesting it, I would pick you up, break you in two, and throw the pieces out of the office one at a time."

"I'm glad I'm small, then," I said very politely, and stood up.

"One minute," he said. "What's your name again?"

"Darius Just," I said.

"Mr. Just, I suppose all this is because you still think that the man in 1511 was murdered. Have you given your theory to the police?"

"No. After the reaction I received from you, I felt I had better dig up stronger grounds."

"I see. Well, then, Mr. Just, let me put it this way. Either the man in 1511 was not murdered or he was. If he was not murdered, your investigations will come to nothing, but they are likely to be a pain in the neck to the hotel and I may eventually find myself unable to resist unscrewing your head. If he *was* murdered, then your unauthorized and clumsy investigations may encourage whoever murdered him to try to do the same to you just to get rid of an annoyance. Think it over."

"Either way, I'm not long for this world then?"

"Think it over—but do it outside." He reached for a cigar and put it into his mouth and that was hint enough for me. I dislike cigarette smoke, but I detest cigars with a passion.

So I walked out, having accomplished nothing. Before speaking to Marsogliani, I was reasonably sure that he had brushed away the heroin, and if so, it was to protect the hotel. Having spoken to him, I had nothing with which to change my mind or to increase my certainty. Status quo.

4 SARAH VOSKOVEK 9:35 A.M.

I leaned against the wall outside Marsogliani's office, thinking it out for a while and getting nowhere. I looked at my watch, found it a bit past nine-thirty, leaving me an hour and a half before the panel I wanted to attend. What to do? I didn't have a room in the hotel, so I couldn't go there and stare out the window. The exhibit booths would be opening at ten, but there was nothing I wanted there.

I walked down the sixth floor toward the elevators, feeling very much the complete failure. There was the glass door that led to Room 622 on my right, but I had no excuse to go in there, or anything useful to do once I was in.

The matter was taken out of my hands. Sarah was standing there, her spike heels bringing her eyes nearly to a level with mine. She said, "Mr. Marsogliani just called me. He said he does not wish to see you again for any purpose. I imagined you'd be coming down the hall therefore, and I *hoped* in reasonable health. He sounded furious."

"He *was* slightly furious. He didn't hit me because I'm so little."

"There are advantages to it, then."

It was about what I had said to Marsogliani, but what I say and what other people are allowed to say are two different things. I said, "Thanks," rather angrily.

She looked at me speculatively; the kind of look, I think, that I give to some girls. She said, "If there were even one person in the world who despised you for your height as much as you yourself do, you would then have reason for complaint."

"Two nights ago," I said, "you—"

"Ah," she said, clasping her hands, "but I have apologized. That is not kind."

"You're right," I said quite sincerely. "My turn. I apologize." I felt so gentlemanly that, if I had had a hat, I would have tipped it. As it was, I raised two fingers of my right hand and made an outward gesture at eye level. I turned away.

"But wait," she said. "I want to talk to you."

I turned again, expectantly.

She added, "If you have the time."

I looked at my watch automatically, though I knew the time. "I have some time," I said.

She said, "There is a room I can use sometimes. Would you come to it with me? Here we will be interrupted. I'm expecting the art director."

"Won't he leave if you're not here?"

Her lips set dangerously. "He will not. He will wait for me." She leaned back, past the doorway, and said to her receptionist, "Ginger, if anyone comes for me, they are to wait. Don't let them leave. I'll be back soon. ... Will you come to the room, Darius?"

It seemed only natural, almost inevitable, to grin, look knowing, and hope that the room had a bed in it. But I didn't say a thing. The trouble was that I never saw a woman look so—no, not innocent, I was quite sure there was nothing innocent about her in the old-fashioned sense and hadn't been for some years—well, so divorced from seduction.

"Gladly," I said, and there was no seductiveness in that, either.

We went up the elevator to the tenth floor. Others got in the elevator and she moved away and let them separate us. She did not look at me—or look away from me, either. She met my eye, occasionally, and without any particular interest whenever chance would have it so. She was a woman loaded with common sense. I felt myself liking her more per inch than I ever had almost any woman, but that didn't make the total liking very high, unfortunately.

She stepped off at the tenth floor, certain that I would follow, and I did. A third person stepped off, a youngish man, but he turned in the other direction. He wasn't wearing a convention badge.

She opened the door to a room quickly, and I followed her in just as quickly. She placed the "Do Not Disturb" sign outside and closed the door.

I said, "What will they think when they see that sign?" nodding in its direction.

She said, "Let them think what they will think."

She sat down. "This is a staff room. There are several of them. They are useful when a member of the staff must stay overnight, or does not feel well and wishes to lie down. In great emergencies they are rented, but ordinarily not—not even with a convention like this in the hotel."

"Very convenient and pleasant."

She said, "Now tell me—You were asking me about drug problems. Is that what you asked Mr. Marsogliani, too?"

"You said I should."

"I said he was the person to ask. I did not think you would, or should."

"Well, I did."

"But why? Why do you ask about the drugs?"

"Why should you want to know, Sarah?"

"So that I might give you information in exchange."

"That is the payment; that is not the reason. Why should you wish to know?"

She said, "Because I'm afraid you think Mr. Devore was murdered."

I paused and considered, but there was nothing to consider. I hadn't the faintest idea whether it would serve my investigation (or, perhaps, from its general failure to accomplish anything, I ought to give it the

disgrace of quotation marks and call it an "investigation")
to admit it or hide it. All things being equal, I decided,
tell the truth.

"Yes," I said. "I'm sure he was."

"Oh, for goodness' sake," she said, looking far more
troubled than that miserably mild expletive would justify.

"I know," I said wearily. "It would be bad for the
hotel."

"Yes, it could. I'm thinking of Dr. Asimov and his
book about murder at the ABA."

I had forgotten about that completely. "Oh, boy,"
I said.

"Have you told *him?*"

"No, I haven't, but if it's murder, it will come out and
then Asimov could use it if he wanted to. But don't
worry. I know him well enough to know that by the time
he's through prettying it up and translating it into his
own milk-and-water style and changing all the characters
to suit his own pseudo-romantic notions, no one would
recognize the truth behind it. And I tell you what, I will
personally guarantee that he will not name the hotel
or in any way give hints that would identify it."

"But that's prior restraint, isn't it?" She seemed in two
minds as to whether to smile or not, and ended not
smiling.

"I've changed my mind. Now, what are you going to
tell me?"

"That the whole thing may be more complicated than
you think. I scarcely like to say this." Her voice had
lowered, nervously.

"If you think the room is bugged," I said, "I'll turn
on the radio loud, and you can whisper in my ear. Or
let's go out somewhere."

"Oh, it's not bugged. I just don't like to say. . . . It's
so disgraceful and I'm not supposed to know. . . .
Darius."

"Yes?"

"Darius, there *is* a drug problem. I've heard talk
about it."

"Are you guessing? Or is this hard information?"

"Not rock-hard, but I would bet on it."

"As much as eleven to five?" I said. (I never gamble, actually, though I keep score in my own head of the bets I make with myself. I'm about three hundred fifty dollars ahead, as of now.)

She said, "Better. Three to one at least." She seemed to have no problem falling in with my betting game.

"Okay. What's the problem?"

"This may be a clearinghouse for drug distribution."

"*Here?*"

"Why not? Thousands of people pass in and out. Anything can happen here anonymously. If Mr. Devore was killed, who could find the murderer in the crowd? Who could identify anyone who went to his room? Who would see such a thing? Who would be interested? There is scarcely anywhere as anonymous and safe from oversight as a huge hotel."

"So they could use it as a clearinghouse? Someone gets the drug and someone distributes it here?"

"I suppose. I know very little about it."

"Well, then, why doesn't the hotel report this to the police? Or has it already done so?"

"I don't think it has. The evidence, perhaps, is not clear, and Mr. Marsogliani—"

"—wants to save the reputation of the hotel?"

Sarah shook her head. "That is not quite it. If he can gain more evidence and present the whole to the police, then not only is police involvement less long-drawn-out, but the hotel's work can be praised. What was bad publicity could be made into less-bad publicity, even into almost-good publicity."

"And I'm threatening to upset the whole scheme, just over a little thing like murder."

"You don't really know that it's murder, do you? And suppose it were, how can you be sure it had a connection with the drug traffic?"

I said, "There was heroin in the room."

She looked shocked. "Are you sure?"

"No, I'm not sure in the ordinary sense of the word. There was no time to analyze it, for it disappeared—and the disappearance is analysis enough for me."

"Was Mr. Devore a drug addict?"

"I'm sure he wasn't. I tried to get Marsogliani to check that for me, but not a chance."

"Even if he were not a drug addict, is it your theory that he might be part of the chain of distribution? Would that explain his murder? Is it that he was not behaving in such a way as to please the—please the—"

"Syndicate?"

"Yes, so they—they—"

"Rub him out?"

"Yes. Is that what you believe?"

"No," I said—but that wasn't quite true. Again someone was handing me something I hadn't thought of and something that seemed disturbingly plausible.

She said, "But if Mr. Devore were himself a drug pusher, wouldn't it be more important to expose the whole ring than to find one little small-time killer and allow the head men of the ring to escape? Shouldn't you leave the investigation to professional people?"

"I don't think professional people will accept the death as murder."

"But don't you see that if he were killed and if drugs were involved, surely desperate people are involved, and *you* will be in danger if you get too near the truth?"

That sounded very much like Marsogliani's warning, and the hell of it was that it made sense. And I'm no hero.

I said, in a troubled way (for since I felt troubled, how else could I say it?), "I'm not out to get killed. I'll be careful."

She smiled suddenly and said, "Good. Let Mr. Marsogliani handle it. He'll know when to go to the police."

It seemed to me that she had reacted too quickly and too sunnily. Marsogliani had warned me and he had then called Sarah and set this up as a further pressure. It was all a game, with Sarah maneuvering me into cooperation by playing on my cowardice. What the devil made her so sure it was there to play on?

I said coldly, "I must go. I'm catching a panel." I left quickly.

She must have been astonished at my sudden change in manner and my abrupt leave-taking, but it had occurred to me, further, that she chose that route to persuasion because she assumed that a small man was bound to feel fear of violence.

Damn her! And damn myself for feeling that fear!

5 MICHAEL STRONG 10:40 A.M.

I went down to the third floor and, in a mood of disconsolate anger, took my seat in an otherwise empty ballroom. It was nearly a quarter to eleven before the audience began to gather for the panel, which was called "Explaining the Unexplained." There was some time to go, but I have a moderate experience with audiences and I could tell already that it would be a light one. It would not come near to filling the room and it was quite clear that the interview room, which was in charge of these panels, would be mightily disappointed.

It didn't matter to me. I was emotionally uninvolved.

In the panel, that is, but not in Sarah Voskovek. I went over the previous conversation in my mind. There were the trappings of intrigue—the special room, not to be interrupted, the secret to be given away. It was a matter of atmosphere, wasn't it, designed to play on my fears and shut me up. The more I went over it in my mind, the longer the odds grew in my private book that the attempt had been made to play me into the net of shut-up.

And it bothered me because I had been starting to think that Sarah was a nice person. I was beginning to count on her, to rely on her for little things, like getting me an empty room or getting me in to see Marsogliani. And I was just being set up—

I could feel myself flushing.

"Mr. Just."

I looked up and blinked my eyes into focus. Michael Strong, the security guard, was standing in front of me.

"Hello," I said. "Off duty again?"

"Early lunch hour," he said. "I want to hear the panel." He added conversationally, "This is the most interesting convention we've had during all my stay here at the hotel. May I sit with you, Mr. Just?"

"Why not?" I said. "You're not going to throw yourself out for not wearing a badge, are you?"

He laughed feebly, and sat down in the seat next to me. Considering the fact that there were several hundred unoccupied seats in the room, this anxiety of my company betokened either a strong personal affection for me or an order from his boss to keep an eye on me. I had told Sarah I was leaving to attend a panel and there had to be only so many—perhaps only this one—at this time. He had no difficulty finding me.

Strong produced a yellow pad from his jacket pocket, then carefully chose a pen from the inner pocket in clear preparation for taking notes. He was going to play his cover well.

I said, "How's your boss?"

Strong turned a pair of wide eyes upon me. "In a foul mood, Mr. Just."

"About me, do you suppose?"

"I don't know. Why do you think it's about you?"

"I advanced a theory about that heroin."

"What heroin? What are you talking about?" He dropped his voice to a low whisper though there was no one within twenty-five feet of us.

I didn't want to induce apoplexy in the poor fellow, so I lowered my voice, too. "I told Marsogliani," I said, lying somewhat to see what would happen, "that I was pretty certain that the hotel was a center for drug distribution, and that hotel personnel themselves were involved and that was why he wasn't reporting it."

I got what I wanted, for a look of what anyone would interpret as the purest astonishment crossed Strong's face.

That was it as far as Sarah was concerned in my book.

Strong might be unbrilliant and he was certainly not a man in whom Marsogliani (who, for all his temper, struck me as a fine-edged sharpie) would confide. And I could see they hadn't bothered telling him what the setup was with respect to me.

But if there was no setup, if there really was a drug problem it was much more likely that Strong had heard the rumors than that Sarah had. So since Sarah reported it and Strong was clearly astonished out of his pants at what I had said, it *was* a setup.

For once I was proud of my capacity for weaving a logical net.

I said, "How long have you been working here as a guard, Mike?"

"Uh—two and a half years." He stuttered the phrase badly.

"And in all that time you've been aware of no such thing—drugs and matters of that sort?"

"N-no," he said earnestly, staring at me in horror. "You must have been crazy to say something like that to Mr. Marsogliani."

"Not if it's true."

"But it *isn't* true. I'm surprised he didn't kick your butt."

"I'm too small a target."

Strong stared at me in continuing horror. "You haven't been talking like that to anyone else, have you?"

"Just Marsogliani this morning about nine A.M. and now you." True enough. I hadn't told it to Sarah. I had *asked* her and *she* had then told *me*.

He said, "I wouldn't talk about that if I were you."

"Bad for the hotel?"

"Sure. Especially when it's not true."

"Okay!" I said indifferently, and slumped back in my seat.

Strong said, abruptly and nervously, "You didn't tell Mr. Marsogliani that I said the powder might belong to a previous occupant like as if"—he faltered—"like as if it might be a common thing to have that stuff in the place."

I felt for him. It was quite clear to me (odds a hundred to one at least) that Marsogliani would kick Strong out of the hotel and into the middle of the street on his left ear if he knew of that little remark. I had no intention of losing the poor fellow his job; finding another would be hard work in the Ford recession.

So I said, truthfully and as earnestly as I could, "I did suggest that the powder might have been there all along, but I didn't say you had suggested that. I didn't say a word about you. Not a word."

He looked unconvinced, disturbed, and he stared at me as though he were trying to weigh my integrity. I let him. There was no way in which I could help him convince himself I was an honest man. I would have to throw myself on the mercy of his, perhaps defective, judgment in such matters.

6 ISAAC ASIMOV 10:50 A.M.

A new voice broke in and I looked up. It was Asimov, walking in some ten minutes early.

He said, "Darius! You've come to hear me say my piece. I'm touched."

I think he really was. Why else did he refrain from calling me Darius Dust and then choking himself red in the face on the wit of it? However, fair's fair. Since he gave up Darius Dust for that one time, I didn't let on that it was strictly an ulterior motive that had drawn me into the room.

I said, "I can count on you to be interesting, Isaac."

Apparently that merely heightened his philanthropic mood (which the clear absence of much of an audience did not seem to dampen) and he said, "Would you like to meet the other panelists?"

"Why not?" I said.

I turned to Strong and said, "You'll pardon me, I hope?"

He mumbled what I thought was an affirmative (what else can anyone give under the circumstances?) and off I went. Later, when I looked back, I didn't see him. Clearly, he had left to report to Marsogliani on me. I was vaguely sorry I had had to upset him in my desire to double-check on the duplicity of Sarah Voskovek.

Actually, the panelists were a rather impressive group. With an air of eager and cheerful proprietorship, Asimov introduced me to Carl Sagan, an astronomer at Cornell, tall and slim with dark hair and dark eyes and a quick way of speaking. Asimov introduced me as a "real writer," a remark, I presume, designed to elicit assurance that he, too, was a real writer.*

Sagan nodded amiably but I have a sure instinct for people who have heard of me. Sagan hadn't.

Walter Sullivan of *The New York Times* was the moderator. He was even taller than Sagan, and thinner; white-haired, ruddy of complexion, and so eager to please that when I was introduced as a writer, he said, "Oh, yes," as though he read himself to sleep with me every night. I was nearly fooled.

Asimov didn't know the other two personally, but they required no real introductions. One was Charles Berlitz, who had just written a book on the "Bermuda Triangle," tall, round-faced, and gray-haired, and the other was Uri Geller, the Israeli semi-mystic who is supposed to bend keys by telekinesis, to read minds, and so on. Geller was young and very attractive both in appearance and in conversation.

It was clearly Asimov and Sagan versus Berlitz and Geller, with Sullivan trying to remain impartial, but unable to resist toppling over onto the side of rationality. The panel discussion, however, lacked excitement. I don't know whether the poor attendance dampened the spirits

---

* Needless to say, it was *not* so intended.
                                                   —ISAAC ASIMOV

Modesty then? Please!
                                                   —DARIUS JUST

of the panelists, or whether some precognition of the lack
of clash had kept the audience down. Either way, it was
a quiet hour.

Or most of it was. Toward the end, there was a chal-
lenge from the floor when someone dared Geller to
subject himself to an audience of magicians, doing so
in somewhat provocative language. Geller, who was used
to this sort of thing, was careful not to betray himself into
losing his temper. He simply stated that he would never
do any demonstrations before magicians because it was
useless to do so; they would never believe anything he
did was anything but trickery, no matter what the circumstances.

That seemed to stir Asimov. He leaned over to whisper
something to Sullivan and was duly recognized.

"I do not think," he said, "that the problem of the
refusal-to-believe on the part of magicians is a serious
one. It is paralleled by a far greater, *far* greater, and far
more intense refusal-to-disbelieve on the part of almost
everybody else.

"I do not wish to speak specifically of Mr. Geller,
though this applies to him, for it is true of anyone who
invades the area lying outside the narrow and constricted
boundaries of what scientists will, without serious argument, accept.

"The parascientific fringes are intrinsically glamorous,
they are exciting and delightful, and they court belief.
Millions will grant the belief and will not be deterred by
anything scientists will say, especially since scientists
cannot counter with anything equally evocative but can
only grumble a spoilsport 'It isn't so!'

"In fact, so eager are people to believe the essentially
incredible that they will resent, even with violence, any
effort to advance evidence in favor of disbelief. If some
mystic, with a wide and ardent following, were to disown
all his previous statements, if he were to declare his
miracles frauds, and his beliefs charlatanry, he would
lose scarcely a disciple, since one and all would say he
had made his statements under compulsion or under a

sudden stroke of lunacy. The world will believe *anything* a mystic will say, however foolish, *except* an admission of fakery. They actively refuse to disbelieve.

"Is there, therefore, anything to be accomplished by arguing against mystics, or by trying to analyze their beliefs rationally? As a healthful exercise to improve and strengthen one's own rationality, certainly. As a hope to reform fools, never.

"But it doesn't matter. My own attitude is to bid the world, believe! All of you—believe! Believe whatever you want, for in doing so, whatever misery you bring upon yourself and others, you will nevertheless never affect reality. Though all earth's four billion swear from top to bottom and left to right that the earth is flat and though they kill anyone who dares suspect it might be an oblate spheroid with a few minor irregularities, the earth will nevertheless remain an oblate spheroid with a few minor irregularities."

There was a polite patter of applause and the hour came to an end. I didn't applaud—even though I once again marveled at how easily, and I suspect unconsciously, Asimov could shift from the essential triviality of his social personality to the intense intelligence of his professional one, and back again—since Asimov's little speech took all my painfully gathered grounds for certainty and shook them badly.

I believe in the murder of Giles Devore and so far had refused to accept any reasons advanced to support the contrary. Were there any conceivable reasons I would accept, or was I a true believer, dedicated to my belief though the heavens fall? If Giles himself were to rise from the dead and swear that he had not been killed but had slipped in the bathtub, would I not reject that, too? Would I not say that whatever had happened, whatever the attack, it had been so sudden and came from a source so trusted that Giles himself was mistaken and took murder for accident?

And if I were a true believer, would my belief, however firm and inalienable, in the least change reality?

7 ISAAC ASIMOV   12:15 P.M.

I looked up and again Asimov was standing before me. I said, "That was a very eloquent little speech you made at the end. I was impressed." (I must have remained in a brown study for longer than I had thought, for the audience had dispersed and only a handful remained at the door, talking to Charles Berlitz.)

Asimov grinned broadly, as he always does to any compliment, from anyone about anything, and grew mellow enough to say, "Well, then, come have lunch with me, if you have nothing better to do."

Since lunch with him had been my hoped-for aim in attending the talk, I said, "Sure thing!" Politeness forced me to say, "What about your panelist friends?"

"They're off," he said. "They just came in for the panel."

"In that case, in default of anything better for you, I will join you for lunch."

"Come on," he said. "Don't be falsely humble." (That remark was hard to take, coming from him, but I managed.)

Apparently he had not yet come to the end of his good humor, for he added, "And lunch is on me."

I might have argued the point, but, frankly, the offer was so uncharacteristic of him that it took my breath away—so in default of objection on my part, lunch was on him.*

---

* This sentence went in only after prolonged argument. I defy any-one who knows me to say honestly that I ever allow anyone to pick up a check except under overwhelming pressure. The remarks made a little later concerning my eating habits are grossly exaggerated, too.

—ISAAC ASIMOV

All right, I admit that my remark about Asimov's parsimony is hyperbolic. However, as to his eating habits— In an earlier footnote, Asimov suggested you look at my photo on a book jacket to settle a point. On the same note, I suggest you have lunch with Asimov. If you can get anything more than a monosyllable out of him while he

It was Asimov's idea that we leave the hotel and find a Chinese restaurant. I was delighted. I had had my surfeit of fried chicken and I was precisely in the mood for pressed duck and sweet-and-sour pork. Off we went.

During the five-block walk, Asimov said, "Say, do you remember that little girl with the breasts that tackled you Sunday night?"

"I remember," I said grimly.

"She didn't know who you were when she handed it to you, you know. She came to see me just as the autographing session was about to start yesterday and apologized very humbly—which was nice of her. Then she asked who you were and you should have seen her turn sick when I told her you were Darius Just."

"Not Dry as Dust?"

Asimov laughed, as he recognized, once again, the wit of this play on words. "Don't be so damned sensitive," he said. "Anyway, look her up, and give the poor thing a chance to make it up to you."

"She already has," I said, "so we can forget it."

Asimov seemed taken aback at my tone of voice, but nothing takes him aback for longer than a second and a half, and in no time he was talking again. During the remainder of the walk, he prattled on about articles he had written denouncing astrology and various other lunatic-fringe beliefs and the letters these had educed. I answered in a desultory fashion, preferring to concentrate on my own thoughts, and finally we reached the restaurant, which, as so many Chinese places seem to be, was a kind of haven of dimness and quiet—something I welcomed.

Once we had taken our seats, Asimov fell to studying the menu, and insisted on ordering for both of us, which suited me fine since he got the pressed duck and sweet-and-sour pork I had casually mentioned as we sat down,

---

has food in front of him, I'll pay the tip. If you can finish before he does, without choking to death in your haste, I will pay for the whole meal.

—DARIUS JUST

plus some soup and hors d'oeuvres. The waiter took it, after favoring us with a look of contempt when his invitation that we submerge ourselves swinishly in a variety of alcoholic beverages was haughtily rejected.

I said, "You seem in high spirits, Isaac."

He said, "Well, I did my autographing stint yesterday and my panel today and now, after lunch, I can go home, take care of my mail, and get to work on an article that's about due."

"And what about *Murder at the ABA?* Do you have all the local color you need?"

"Enough," he said airily. "I won't need much of it, I suppose."

"Do you have it all plotted?"

"No. I never do. But I have enough to get started, and I have my gimmick, and I'll make it up as I go along."

"What happens if you get tangled up in the middle and can't get out of the tangle?"

"Never happens," he said cheerfully. "It always works out."

I sighed inaudibly. I wondered if some of us couldn't arrange to picket him.

About this time, the waiter filled the table with a dish of appetizers, and I knew that would be followed by the soup, and that by the main courses (very efficient, the waiters at these restaurants) with tea in between, so that there would be no use in continuing the conversation. Once food is on the table, Asimov is a spent force as far as social chitchat is concerned. His universe then consists of himself and food only. I ate quietly and made no attempt to keep up with him.

I said, as he speared and devoured the last bit of the pressed duck, "And who will you kill off at your version of the ABA convention. Giles?"

It was as though I had pulled the chain and turned out his light. Even the afterglow of a good lunch seemed to fade.

He said, "You know, I feel bad about Giles. I feel

bad about him because I *don't* feel bad about him. Do you know what I mean?"

"I don't," I said.

"Well, I do an awful lot of kidding with an awful lot of people. You, for instance. I can't make myself say what people really mean to me; I just drown it in horseplay. Then when people die, you wish they were back so you could say what you really felt. If you, for instance—"

"I know," I said, "you'd want me back to tell me that after all you never really noticed how short I was and that all your short jokes were not meant for me, but for someone else—for your friend Ellison, if that's his name."

He turned red. "Maybe something like that, Darius. But in Giles's case, that's not so. There's nothing I want to say to him now that he's dead. Darius, I didn't really like him more than just a little bit." He owned up to it as though he were confessing a crime.

I said, "No law against it. I didn't like him, either."

"But I don't like not to like people."

"You can't always have everything you like. . . . Does that mean you won't use Giles in the book?"

"Not by name, of course. Not by anything identifiable. Who wants trouble with Eunice? Still, after making all necessary changes, it's possible that I'll let Giles inspire something. Of course, it would have to be murder, not accident."

I thought: Well, let's try once again. Aloud, I said, "I think it *was* murder, not accident."

You would think that what the "it" in that sentence referred to was obvious but people fight off unpleasantness and Asimov held it off one conversational exchange by saying, "*What* was murder, not accident?"

"Giles's death," I said.

He stared at me for a long moment, then he said, in a voice half an octave higher than normal. "The police say he was killed?"

"Not the police," I said. "They think it's an accident, as far as I know. So does everyone else. I think it's murder. As far as I know, only I think it's murder. And I'm trying to find evidence to support it, and I want to talk to you about it."

"To *me?*"

"Why not? You owe me a little help. Damn it, your final speech at the panel shook me up and made me uncertain of my own certainty of his murder. You made me think that perhaps he wasn't killed."

Asimov looked relieved. "Good. I'm sure he wasn't. Drop it, Darius."

"I can't. I failed him night before last and I've got to find out that that didn't contribute to his death. And even if I knew it didn't, I've got to make up for that failure."

"It won't bring him back to life."

"Oddly enough, Isaac, I realize that. Getting this settled, though, will help me continue to live with myself. Just a little, anyway."

"Well, then, what do *I* do? Play the role of Watson?"

"Not unless and until I can be Holmes and, judging by what's happened these last twenty-four hours, that will be never. No, I just want you to help me fill in the time between my last sight of Giles alive and my first sight of him dead."

"How can I help you there? I saw him two nights ago briefly and then never again—except for the autographing session. And besides"—he grew thoughtful—"I'm not dying of eagerness to get involved. Once you start being a witness, heaven only knows how many hours you have to waste with the police and the courts—and I've got deadlines to meet."

It was the mention of deadlines and the knowledge that he had at most three months to write his mystery novel that impelled me to attempt a peculiar bribe. I said, "Look at it this way. If this turns out to be a murder, as I think it will, you may find yourself with a plot ready-made for your damned mystery."

"But then you'll want to write it."

"I? Never. I have better things to do than write stupid puzzlers.* *You* write it."

I could see Asimov thinking quickly in the direction in which quick thought was his specialty—that of constructing a book. He said, "I could write it with you as first person and introduce myself in the third."

I said, "Provided you don't libel me."

"I'd have to describe you as five feet two inches tall. That would be the most interesting thing about you."

"Five feet five, damn it."

"With elevator shoes."

"Look. You do what you want within the bounds of good taste and let me see the manuscript first and argue it out with you and maybe add a footnote for clarification now and then. And we'll put it in writing, both of us."

"All right. But first let me call up my Doubleday editor. I don't want to get involved in this if Larry Ashmead vetoes the idea."

"Go ahead!"

He was gone for about three minutes—which I spent wondering whether I ought to get into this, and rather hoping that Ashmead would say no. I doubted that Asimov knew anything worth the bribe, and he probably would have been as helpful as he could be, without it (with a little coaxing), so why the devil had I offered it?

And then I thought—well, damn it, if it *is* murder and I can *show* it is, and work out the details, then why shouldn't I get some of the credit for it? Asimov himself had wondered if I wanted him to be my Watson, and why shouldn't he be?

Once I had convinced myself I was doing it all out of a respectable drive for self-aggrandizement, I was

---

* It's the usual ploy of writers who aren't clever enough to write good mysteries to pretend such productions are beneath them.

—ISAAC ASIMOV

I won't even bother answering that ridiculous statement.

—DARIUS JUST

satisfied and began to hope that Ashmead would say yes.

He did. I could tell that from Asimov's grin when he was still at the other end of the room. He said, "Larry's out to lunch, but Cathleen says I can do it any way I want to and she's sure Larry will feel the same. So now give me all the details and we'll—"

"*No!*" I said sharply: "Nothing now. We have to see how it works out first.* For now, I just want to discuss the autographing session."

"It's got to be written by August, Darius."

"That's *your* problem. If nothing comes of this, you'll have to work on the plot you've already made up. You'll be no worse off than you were ten minutes ago."

"Well, go ahead. What do you want to know about the autographing session?"

"When did Giles arrive at the session?"

"He came about five to eleven. I was there, seated and waiting. I believe in being early, damn it. I figure, what the hell, if people are kind enough to—"

"I know," I said. "But he wasn't late, was he?"

"About five minutes before, as I said."

"Who was it who brought him in?"

"Brought him in?" Asimov looked blank.

"Some woman dragged him in and made sure he was on time. I was told that." (I still didn't remember who told me that, but I was sure of the fact.)

He shook his head. "I didn't notice anyone."

I said impatiently, "Well, then, what kind of mood was he in? How annoyed was he? Was he shouting?"

Asimov looked blank again. "I didn't hear anything. Listen, there were a hundred people crowding round me and I was thoroughly occupied. There was the little dame showing up at the last minute and apologizing."

---

* Actually, the whole thing worked out better than I expected and, for the most part, Asimov did well enough with the book.

—DARIUS JUST

Aha!

—ISAAC ASIMOV

"I remember," I said in annoyance. "Go on."

"So Giles wasn't of great interest to me. I became aware of him sitting down at the other end of the stage about ten feet to my left. I shouted, 'Hi, Giles,' and he looked at me with one of his basset-hound expressions. He struck me as being angry but there was no time to weigh and analyze his expression and my impression. They were waiting for me to sign and I had two hundred and fifty or so copies of *Before the Golden Age*, Volume Two, to hand out."

"But he did make a fuss eventually, didn't he?"

"Oh yes, I couldn't miss that. For one thing, he stopped signing and that meant there was a pile-up. After all, everyone who got my signature passed on to get Giles's. When Giles stopped signing, the line stopped moving."

"Did you know what was wrong?"

"Not right away. I said, 'What's the matter?' and someone in the line said that Mr. Devore's pen had run out of ink and I said I had a spare—you know, anything to get the line moving—but someone else gave him a pen, and then *that* ran out of ink—"

"Again?"

"Oh yes, twice in five minutes. Then Nellie Griswold of Hercules Books ran over with a pen and there was a little mix-up there of some sort and then everything settled down and that was it."

"And what about Giles? I presume he was swearing at me?"

"No. I didn't hear him swearing at you. Why should he swear at you?"

"Damn it, Isaac. He gave me a ticket to get a package for him out of the cloakroom, with a supply of pens in it, and I never got it for him. That's the errand I failed to run. That's where I messed him up. And he didn't say a word about that?"

"Not that I heard. But I see now why you're feeling bad about this. Why the hell didn't he hand over the ticket to someone who was reliable?"

"You walked out on us, for one thing, if you're talking

about yourself. . . . The hell with it. What you're saying,
Isaac, is that the whole fuss, all of it, was over pens
running out of ink. Nothing else was involved at all?
At all?"

"Not as far as I know."

"I want something else to be wrong. Something else
that I'm not responsible for."

"I can't help you. I told you all I know." Asimov had
signed the check, signed the credit-card slip, put away
his credit card. He was clearly getting ready to leave.
He said, "I wish I could do the dramatic thing. I wish
that at the last minute I could remember something for
you, some little apparently unimportant event that would
break the whole case, but I can't do it. But why should
that bother you? I was ten feet away and completely
busy with my own signings. I'm not your best witness.
Why not ask what's-her-name?"

"Nellie Griswold?"

"No. I mean, you can ask her if you want to, but that's
not the one." He snapped his fingers. "I *hate* to forget
anything. I'm always afraid that it might be the first
sign of approaching senility."

I tried to be helpful. "Eunice? What would she know?"

"Not Eunice! Damn it, the woman who's your editor,
too. The gal from Prism Press, what's-her-name."

"Teresa?"

"Teresa Valier. That's it."

I was surprised. "What's she got to do with it?"

Asimov stood up. "She was sitting next to him, opening the books to the title page and handing them over
for him to sign." He looked aggrieved. "No one did that
for me. I had to fumble the pages of two hundred and
fifty books and sign them, too."

I said the natural thing. "Why the hell didn't you tell
me this in the first place?"

He gave me the natural answer. "I assumed you knew."

How could he assume I knew that if I hadn't been there?
There was no point fighting over that, however. I looked
at my watch and it was well past two.

Asimov said, "Will you be seeing her? Do you want me to come along?"

"I may see her. But if I do, then—no, I don't want you along."

He shrugged. I guess he didn't really want to be involved and his momentary urge toward active Watsondom abated.

So we separated and I didn't see him again during what remained of the convention.

8 TERESA VALIER 2:20 P.M.

It was twenty after two, which was borderline. Teresa might be back from lunch or she might not—or she might not have come to work today—or she might be at the convention, though I doubted that strongly, not if she had gone home with a sick headache after she had heard of Giles's death.

But I was only two blocks from the Prism Press offices and it was home away from home for me, anyhow. Why not walk over?

I did and found myself playing in luck. The elevator door was closing as I walked into the building, but the elevator operator knew me well, and having caught a glimpse of me through the closing door, opened it again. When I walked in, I found Teresa there.

Her loud, glad greeting was a little less loud and a lot less glad than usual and when I said, "I've got to have ten minutes, Terry—it's about Giles," it got dramatically less glad still. In fact, when we got off at the eighteenth floor, she was crying as she rushed past a startled receptionist.

I followed quickly. "Come on, Terry, they'll think I made a pass at you."

"I don't cry over passes," she said, "and I don't want to talk about Giles, Darius."

"Please, just a little," I said. We were in her office but we hadn't dashed in so quickly that I had lacked the time to note that Tom was not in *his* office—which was good. I didn't want him to interfere.

I closed the office door. "Come on, Teresa. I've got to know what happened."

"What's to know? He fell and was killed and I just *hate* people I know dying—especially when I've been hating them before they died. It makes me feel so—damned responsible."

The tears were still rolling and she was snatching paper tissues out of a box on her desk.

I felt distressed for her sake. "I mean what happened at the autographing session? That's what I've got to know." Then desperately, "Don't cry, Teresa, don't cry. If you just talk to me, I promise that you'll see it was my fault, not yours."

"*Your* fault? You had nothing to do with it."

"You heard Giles say it was my fault, didn't you?"

She was looking at me suspiciously now, eyes still shining, but not actually overflowing. She said, "He didn't say anything at all about you. What are you talking about? Unless it was while I was gone."

I sighed. "Please, Terry, tell me about it and then I'll explain why it wasn't your fault, and I'll go away."

She looked at her watch. "I'm expecting someone—"

"They'll wait, whoever it is," I said urgently. "I've waited for you often enough. Come on. Begin at the beginning."

Teresa said. "The beginning was months ago, when I made the arrangement for having Giles autograph his new book at the convention and promised him I'd open the books for him. That pleased him and helped persuade him to agree to do the signing. You know the kind of man he is—was. It made him feel important to have the publisher open books for him.

"Of course, then the business started about his leaving us and for a while I thought he could go to hell, but Tom wanted to go through with it. You know, smile through the tears, make everything look normal to the last possible minute."

She made a feeble gung-ho gesture with her right arm

and went on. "So I was there fifteen minutes early and so was the other guy who was autographing, raising the roof and hugging the girls and making me all the more nervous about Giles—you know, why couldn't *he* be early? And then he was there—"

I interrupted. "It's my understanding that he was more or less dragged in by some woman. Wasn't he?"

She stared at me. "Was he? I didn't see anyone with him."

"Well, was he angry?"

"I don't know. *I* was angry, because I'd had a fight with Tom over the whole business. I was sure Giles wouldn't change his mind, and I said the hell with it. Tom said maybe if I humored him and it was a good autographing session, I might get a chance to make one more try. And I said, 'What do you mean, humor him? How far do I go?' and he— Well, it was rotten. So I didn't look at him particularly, just enough to know he was there, and then I was ready to open books for him. But I didn't have any pens."

"Were you supposed to?"

"It's routine. Some authors arrive without pens—too ethereal to think of any such mundane things—or they bring their special pen that doesn't work. Giles is different, however. He always insists on using his own pens—his special monogrammed ones, you know—and won't use any others. Well, ordinarily, I would bring pens anyway, just to backstop, but this time I thought—well, screw him. I had to show my hostility somehow, so I didn't bring any pens."

By then, I had gone through all the flagstones that had laid out the fine path to my failure, and here was one that was later than any that had been laid for me.

I said, "Does that make you responsible for his death?"

"In a way, I suppose it does," she said, but she wasn't crying now. "If I had had pens, the whole damned fuss might not have taken place and he wouldn't have been so upset that he would—would—"

"Storm upstairs for a shower and be so blind with

fury that he slipped, fell, and killed himself?"

"It could be that."

"I suppose so, but the fact is that I was supposed to bring him a supply of pens the night before and I had forgotten to do it. So you see, the primary fault is mine and not yours. Now please tell me what happened. Give me the details of the fuss."

"I don't know what I can tell. For nearly half an hour, nothing happened. He signed every book I put before him the same way: best wishes, his name, the date. He didn't say a word, he didn't smile, he didn't look up. I could hear the other fellow—what's-his-name —the one who writes all the books—"

"Isaac Asimov."

"Yes, I could hear him babbling constantly, talking to each one, flirting with the girls."

"I know," I said. "I know his corn-ball routine."

"All right. People enjoy it. They leave him and come to Giles, expecting more of the same, and all they got was dead silence."

"He was upset over my failure to get him his pens," I said. "Little failures in accustomed routines upset him."

"If what you did upset him, why take it out on the general public?"

" 'Why' is a crooked letter, my old man used to say."

That stopped her for a moment. "What does that mean?" she asked.

"I'm not sure, but it sounds good. Please go on."

"Eventually his pen gave out and he just sat back. I said, 'What's the matter?' and he said, 'Out of ink,' in a high-pitched voice, with his lower lip pushed out. He just sat there. Naturally the line stopped and Asimov stood up and wanted to know what was wrong. I was just sitting there, too thunderstruck to do anything. Asimov offered a pen and so did whoever was waiting for the autograph. He pushed his pen toward Giles and took the pen Giles was holding—for a souvenir, I suppose.

"Giles had to stir himself up to the point of using the new pen and then for five minutes everything seemed smooth and then the *new* pen ran out of ink. It was like a nightmare. It was as though God were punishing me for not having brought spare pens."

She was gasping for breath and her voice faded out as though she were reliving the experience too closely. I said, "What did you do?"

"I just got up and left to get new pens. I forgot Asimov had offered one and pushed past him. I couldn't think of anything better to do than go down the escalator to the hotel desk. I was just completely derailed, that's all. By the time I got back, I found that a girl from Hercules Books had given him a pen. Apparently there was a fuss about that, too, but I had missed it, thank God, and I don't want to know about it. The signing went on to the end without any other hitches. I tell you, it was the longest hour I've ever spent outside a maternity ward.

"After it was over, I left. I didn't speak to Giles or look at him. In fact, I never saw him again, and when I heard he was dead, it just knocked me over. I knew that all that fuss over the pens had just sent him off his rocker. I went home with a migraine."

I said, "But you're better now?"

"A little," she said woefully. "Thank God, Tom is bearing up."

"Oh yes, he's bearing up," I said. "And you say that while the fuss was on, he didn't say anything about me?"

"Nothing—unless it was while I was gone."

"How long were you gone?"

"I don't know. Five minutes, maybe."

"Funny."

"What difference does it make whether he said anything about you or not?"

"Well," I said a little abstractedly, "if he didn't say anything about me all that time, maybe it was something else that was bothering him. Look, Teresa, was there anything Giles did, anything at all that you can think of, anything that would indicate that something was bothering him besides the matter of the pens?"

Teresa shook her head emphatically. "As far as I know, it was the pens, pens, pens."

"Did he say anything, or did anyone else say anything, or *do* anything for that matter, that struck you at the time as odd; or that strikes you as odd now that you look back on it?"

"No," she said.

I threw up my arms. "I was told he complained about me."

Teresa said, "Maybe that girl from Hercules Books heard him. She was with him when I wasn't there."

"Maybe you're right. In that case, can I use the phone in the conference room for a while?"

"Go ahead, provided no one else is using it. Close the door, if you want privacy."

"Thanks," I said, and left.

9 HENRIETTA CORVASS 3:15 P.M.

I did want privacy. It wasn't that anything I intended to do at the moment was private, but that I wanted to think. I visited the men's room, thought there for a moment, then went to the conference room and thought there for a longer time.

Periodically, I wanted to think—as though something would happen if I did, as though something would break and, at the center of that something, I would find the answer. But not so. No matter how closely I examined the events hovering about Giles in that less-than-a-day after I had seen him alive, I could find nothing that could serve as a reasonable prelude to murder.

Well, one step I might take would be to fill the remaining lacuna at the autographing session, so I put in a call to Hercules Books. It would take too much time to walk there and back, and too much money to taxi there and back, if Nellie Griswold wasn't there. If she *was* there, it might serve the purpose to talk by tele—

"Hercules," the telephone told me.

I asked for Nellie Griswold and the telephone operator

was agreeable but the voice that answered the proper extension disclaimed the identity. She told me in a semi-childish semi-treble that Miss Griswold was at the ABA convention.

"Are you sure?" I said, which was a silly question. How could anyone be sure?

The owner of the voice wasn't so semi-childish as not to see that point. She said cautiously, "She's *supposed* to be."

"All right. I'll walk over. Thank you," and I hung up.

I looked at my watch. It was well after three. If she was there, she would remain there for perhaps two hours.

I went back to the hotel, still thinking, braced by the fact that it was a sunny, mild, and entirely pleasant afternoon.

There were two things—no, three—that puzzled me.

First, was there any connection with drugs? God knows, I have no gift for looking deeply into a man's soul, but I had lived with Giles and I knew him to an extent. He despised coffee because of the caffeine; he worried about food additives; he was forever on the verge of toppling over into natural foods.

Of course, a man can compartmentalize his life. I knew lots of natural-food freaks who inveighed against the damage chemicals did while peering through the smoke of chains of cigarettes out of eyes whose lids were covered with oily colored gunk.

There was his writing. I had known it well in its early stages and there were numerous sections that I would consider as representing views incompatible with drug addiction. And yet might that be taken in reverse? Every stick pointed in two directions, one opposed to the other.

The second was the question of his complaint against me. He had gone through torture during the autographing session and Sarah had heard him mutter my name in anger. I would like to get corroboration of that and perhaps greater detail, and Nellie Griswold might supply it.

Finally, there was the question of the woman who

had brought him in that morning. Had no one seen her? The more I thought of it, the more it seemed to me she might have been with him all morning, and all night before, too, for that matter, and might represent the entire key to the matter.

And with my foot virtually on the escalator to the exhibition floor, the thought of that unknown woman overcame me and I decided to postpone Nellie—for just a little while.

I took the elevator to the fifth floor.

The interview room seemed as hectic as ever. Leo Durocher had just been interviewed concerning his autobiography and I just caught a glimpse of him leaving. For a minute, I stopped to stare at his back, remembering the time twenty years back and more when I had been an ardent baseball fan and he had been one of my villains.

The flash passed; it may have lasted five seconds, not more; and I was grateful to him, then, for supplying me with five seconds in which I totally forgot the convention and its miseries.

But it was only five seconds. It was gone and I turned to look for Henrietta Corvass. She saw me, I suppose, before I saw her, for when I detected her presence, her back was to me and she was just out the door.

I moved quickly and overtook her in the hall about three doorways down and seized her elbow. She shook me off.

"Wait," I said.

She turned, her eyes narrowed and bitter. "What the hell do you want?"

Clearly, she regretted having talked to me the evening before; she resented the hold I had over her in knowing too much about her. I spread out my hands and said in a low voice, "Nothing about last night. Nothing."

"Well, then?"

"The morning."

"What about the morning?"

"You said you hadn't picked up Giles yesterday morning. Please, think again, and don't twist things. If you *did* pick him up—"

She turned to face me full and placed her clenched fists on her hips in an old-fashioned gesture of exasperation I hadn't seen in years. "You must be crazy," she said. "Right out of your mind. Do you think, after what happened, I'd go *near* him?"

"You wouldn't want him to be late for the autographing session, would you?"

"I didn't give a f— for the autographing session." She said it as loudly as she could, and I didn't wince because the emotion with which she charged it made it the *mot juste*.

"But somebody brought him. I know that. Who was it?"

"I didn't send anyone. I told you, I wasn't even there. If anyone went of their own accord, that's their business."

"Who would it be?"

"I don't know. I don't care."

"Would you find out for me?"

"No, I won't. Find out for yourself."

And she walked away, her heels making a muffled sound on the carpet of the corridor.

I stared after her nonplussed, and then went back to the interview room.

10 GORDON HAMMER 3:40 P.M.

It was hard to tell which of the individuals were functionaries of the interview department, but I picked a young man with pinched-in cheeks, pale blond hair, and a thin, nervous look about him.

"Listen," I said, "you're working in the interview room, aren't you?"

"What about it?" he asked suspiciously.

"I'm Darius Just; I'm a writer."

He relaxed visibly. He even smiled. "Oh, sure, I've heard of you. My name's Gordon Hammer."

"Thank you, Gordon," I said. "Could you tell me something?"

"I can try."

"How many women are working here for the convention besides Henrietta?"

"It's hard to tell. Some are just volunteers who run errands."

"Ah, I'm after the errand runners. Which of them went to get Giles Devore yesterday morning to see that he got to the autographing session?"

He looked confused. "I don't think anyone did that. It's not our job."

"Someone did," I said, firmly positive. "Could you find out for me?"

He said weakly, "I don't see how—" But then he walked over to one of the girls and talked to her in a low voice. Then to another. I kept my eye on him and waited.

When he returned, he was scratching his head. "I don't think anyone did."

"Is everyone eliminated entirely? Think, please."

He said, "It might be Stephanie."

"Stephanie who?"

"I don't know her last name."

"Where is she?"

"She isn't in today. She just worked Sunday and Monday. She's back in school now."

"Do you know her home address?"

"No, but Henrietta might know it."

"Okay."

But as I turned to go, he touched me very gently on the shoulder. "Mr. Just?"

"Yes?"

"Has Stephanie done anything wrong? I mean, she's only fourteen."

"No, no," I said hastily. "I'm just checking on something. Giles Devore was a friend of mine and I'm trying to find out as much as possible of his last day for a—for a—eulogy I'm writing."

It seemed to carry conviction, for a look of great relief came over his face. "I see. Okay."

Of course, it wasn't okay. I didn't relish the thought of having to ask a fourteen-year-old what had transpired that morning, considering what *might* have transpired. It was not so much the thought of the futility of expecting useful answers that troubled me, as the possibility of inducing a fit of hysteria that would bring parents down upon my ears.

Yet some fourteen-year-olds these days—or perhaps any days. After all, Juliet was fourteen—

No, that was silly, and I had no time to follow up at the moment. It was almost four and it was time to find Nellie of Hercules.

11 NELLIE GRISWOLD 3:55 P.M.

Although I didn't know her, I had no trouble detecting her at the Hercules booth. She had been described as "nice" with that particular roll of the masculine eye which gives that bland word an unmistakable flavor, and what I saw fit that exactly.

She was five feet ten or eleven inches tall, with her brown hair at shoulder length, with a narrow waist that rather emphasized the caboose effect of her rear end. Her breasts were perfectly shaped and were encased in a brassiere of the type chosen by women who strongly suspect their breasts to be perfectly shaped. Her nose was a little long and her eyes a little small, which meant she was no raving beauty, but they did combine to give her face an open look of good nature that substituted surprisingly well.

I said, "Miss Griswold."

I had put on my badge to get into the exhibit area and she looked at it, then said excitedly, "Mr. Just! I admire your books very much."

There's no such thing as a better opener than that, and she went on immediately to improve on it.

She said, "You know that Hercules is interested in doing a paperback of your new book."

"I *don't* know." I said.

"The Valiers have shown us some of what you've done and it's made a good impression on our editor in chief. I read it, too, and I *love* it."

And I love *you*, lady. She looked so damned good to me at that point that I would have given my second-best typewriter to be able to forget Giles and invite Nellie to dinner, and maybe end up by not doing right by our Nell, if she were willing.

But Giles came first just at that moment and Project Nellie had to be postponed. I said, "That's great, but if you don't mind, I won't count my chickens. We'll see how you and Hercules like it when it's done."

"Will that be soon?"

"If I can be left alone at my typewriter, maybe two months. In actual fact, probably four. But look, would you answer some questions?"

"What kind?" She seemed just interested, not in any way suspicious.

"Well, you were at the autographing session yesterday with Devore and Asimov—"

"Yes. Asimov is one of our outstanding authors, you know."*

"I know," I said. "But it's Devore I'm interested in. You brought him a pen, I understand."

"Oh, yes, and what a bummer that was. Were you there?"

"No, I wasn't."

"Well, let me tell you what happened." She was the first person I had questioned on the subject who seemed *eager* to talk.

I said, "Please."

She said, "I was there mostly for Asimov, making sure

---

*She did *not* use the adjective. Typical of Isaac to throw it in.

　　　　　　　　　　　　　　　　　　　—DARIUS JUST

She used it to *me* often enough. Being overliteral is not the surest way to the truth.

　　　　　　　　　　　　　　　　　　　—ISAAC ASIMOV

he had enough books and that things were going smoothly."

"He was a little annoyed you weren't opening books for him," I said, getting in the needle just a bit on Isaac's behalf.

She dismissed it with a wave of the hand. "I was more useful keeping the line in order. Besides, whatever Isaac said, he loved it. You know him, he just eats it up; he can sit there signing books for twelve hours, grinning and scribbling. So my attention wandered to Giles Devore and, boy, he was different. He looked as though he were suffering."

"He was," I muttered.

She paid no attention to the comment. "His pen ran out of ink and for some reason Teresa Valier, who was next to him, didn't have any spares, which I thought was pretty irresponsible of her, but then he changed pens with the man in front of him. It looked as though the trouble was all over and then came crisis number two the second pen went dry.

"Devore seemed to fall apart. He just sat there with his face working and Teresa simply ran off the stage. Well, the line stopped and I could see Asimov getting out of his seat and beginning to look nervous, and I was in charge of *him*. So I dashed over to Devore with another pen. I had plenty.

"He took it automatically, as though he weren't really there. He didn't even look down as he started to write with it. After a second or two, though, he stopped and said in a thin whisper, 'It's red.' I had given him a red-ink ball-point, you see. It was crisis number three. I said, 'It's all right. Fans like it red.' So he started writing again.

"By then, Teresa was back and she had a pen, but it wasn't needed. Devore was continuing to sign in red and there was no more trouble. Of course, when the session was over, he threw my red-ink pen against the wall and walked away without talking to anybody, so he was clearly annoyed. I guess I was lucky he didn't throw it at me.

"And then, two hours later, he was dead and I— Oh my, you were the one who found him, weren't you?"

I nodded. "Yes, but never mind that. What were you going to say?"

"Just that I wondered if he was so upset that he couldn't keep his footing in the tub, and that maybe it was my red pen that was the last straw."

I said, "Everyone wants the credit. The fact is that I had his set of pens and I didn't get it to him. If I hadn't muffed it, there would have been no trouble, so if there's credit, it's all mine."

She looked sympathetic (she was clearly a very warm girl, and I made another silent check mark in her favor) and she said, "That's too bad."

"Never mind. Listen, Nellie, tell me, was there anything in what he did, or said, or looked like, or *anything*, that gave you the impression that it was anything at all, other than the pens going dry or being red, that was upsetting him?"

She thought a while, then shook her head wistfully. "If it was anything else, there's no way of telling that I can think of."

"Okay, one more question. Did you see who it was who brought him into the room?"

"You mean at the beginning of the autographing session?"

"Yes."

She shook her head again. "I didn't even see him come in."

I stood there for a moment, frowning. No one had seen him come in with a woman and yet the distinct and overpowering impression that he had done so remained. Who had told me that?

I remembered! It was quite sudden. I saw the face; I heard the voice. It was the checkroom woman. When Giles had come to question her about the package to which he had no check, he had been urged on by the woman accompanying him. She even called her by some name.

It was like having the roof cave in and every bit of plaster fall on my head. I said, "Look, Nellie, when you were near Giles, did you, at any time, hear him mention *me*, express anger in any way about *me?*"

"No. As far as I recall, he never said a word that I heard except 'It's red.' "

"Thanks," I said. "Thanks. I think I'm in love with you, so keep me in mind." And I ran from the exhibit area, as well as I could for having to dodge people.

12 GORDON HAMMER 4:15 P.M.

It was getting riskily late, but I had to take time to clear up the loose ends. Unless I were certain, I wouldn't have the clout to drive it home.

It took me a while to get out of the area, and another while for the elevator to come. It seemed like a much longer while than it took but eventually I was back up on the fifth floor.

I found him—Gordon Hammer, the young man with the pinched-in cheeks—and grabbed his shoulder and shook. He looked startled. I said, "That fourteen-year-old you told me about—What did you say her name was?"

"Stephanie?"

"Yes, yes. She's a little girl, right? You said only fourteen." I was holding my arm out at shoulder level—*my* shoulder level, which would make her quite small, but maybe not for a fourteen-year-old.

But Hammer's lips swelled and he sputtered for a moment or two.

Finally he said, "No. She's taller than you are—if you don't mind my being personal."

I suppose I looked grim enough to show that I did mind so that his moment of laughing faded into anxiety again. Then he said, "And she's fat, really fat. No one would call her little."

13 DOROTHY 4:25 P.M.

That removed the last possible source of confusion—
the last one I could think of unless some entirely unknown
factor had entered into it. It was back down to the
second floor and my watch showed the time to be nearly
half past four. I had a notion it was too late to find the
next person I needed—the one who had seen the woman.
When the elevator didn't come after fifteen seconds, I
damned it quite loudly and dashed down the stairs.

I probably didn't beat the elevator but there was no
way in which I could stand still, even to save time. I
ran across the lobby to the cloakroom, dodging through
the crowds, and then pushed past the two or three people
standing there

"Listen," I gasped. "Where's the attendant?"

"I'm the attendant," said an elderly woman, still pretty,
with white hair, metal-rimmed glasses, and a refined way
of speaking which she probably cultivated very carefully.
Her nameplate said: Dorothy.

"Not you. The other one. Dyed yellow hair, fat arms,
tinted glasses, nose twitches. I don't remember her name.
. . . Excuse me, excuse me. This is important. I'll be out
of your way in a minute." That last was to the other
people waiting there, who looked increasingly exasperated.

The elderly attendant—Dorothy—smiled as though she
recognized the picture without trouble. "That's Hilda.
She gets off at four."

"Do you know where she lives?"

"No," she said briefly and disapprovingly. (Come on,
I thought impatiently, you *can't* think for a minute I
have anything improper in mind.) She turned to the
other people, clearly dismissing me.

I said, "Well, wait, let me ask **you** one question. Is
there a woman around here that you and Hilda call Little
Pepper."

She smiled again. "Oh, sure, that's the—" Then she
stopped and said primly. "I don't know what you're

talking about, and I'm busy."

But I was off and running again. It was someone familiar, someone both she and Hilda knew, someone who was little, and peppery, and well known to them. Now to get to the sixth floor at last, and it was still well before five.

14 GINGER 4:35 P.M.

The inner room looked empty. I didn't have to go in to check its corners; it had the unmistakable look of emptiness, and my heart sank. I was bubbling over with resentment and I wanted things straightened out right now.

The good-looking black receptionist, or secretary, or whatever, was at her desk. I remembered her name. Sarah had called her Ginger. She was eyeing me with a controlled amusement and I was quite certain she remembered me.

"Can I help you?" she said.

"I don't know. Can you tell me where Miss Vosto— Voskovek might be?" In my impatience, I found myself still stumbling over the name.

I felt there was no use asking. She was gone.

But Ginger said, "I don't know where she *is*, but I know she'll be back. Won't you wait?"

Her voice was friendly, and she continued to be amused. I wasn't sure what it was she was amused about, but it made me feel uncomfortable.

I sat down abruptly and fidgeted. I had nothing to read, and although I consulted my watch often enough, its capacity to console and distract me was sharply limited. Ginger's equanimity, her apparent warm and confident acceptance of the fact that Sarah would be back, was all that kept me in my seat after a while.

15 SARAH VOSKOVEK 5:00 P.M.

It was just about five o'clock when I heard her footsteps outside. I had no doubt it was she—short footsteps, fussy but firm, with the high heels making sharp clicking noises. I stood up.

She walked in, looked at me, stopped in clear consternation, and said, "Is something wrong, Darius?"

I said, "I want to speak to you."

She said, "Can you wait a bit till I clear up some things?"

"Will you have to rush away to go home then?"

"No," she said doubtfully. "Not if it's something important."

"It's important."

"Then please wait." She didn't seem unduly disturbed.

I sat down again and returned to my fidgeting. After a while, Ginger stacked some papers neatly at one side of her desk, made some scrabbling noises under the desk which I interpreted as getting her shoes on, and took her purse out of a desk drawer.

She said in a brisk voice, "I'm leaving, Sarah." I took it she was giving fair warning that we would be alone together. She smiled at me as she left—wishing me luck, I think, which was nice of her but inappropriate to the occasion.

Sarah's voice came back, clear and serene. "Very good, Ginger. Have a nice evening."

Two more minutes passed. Sarah came into the outer room, looked casually out into the hall, then closed the door softly, pulled down a shade, and motioned me into the inner room.

"If you want to talk further about our last topic of conversation," she said, "we couldn't do it with anyone else here, you understand."

I sat down on the couch in her office. She remained standing.

I said, "Did you know the hired hands around here call you Little Pepper?"

"I've heard the phrase," she said indifferently. "Where did you hear it?"

I ignored her question. I said, "You heard Giles Devore

speak my name in hatred. Through clenched teeth, I imagine."

"Clenched teeth or not, he did."

"I'm sure of it. Not, however, at the autographing session. There were three people near him part or all of the time. There were Isaac Asimov, Teresa Valier, and Nellie Griswold, and not one heard him say a thing about me."

She said, "I didn't say it was at the autographing session. I believe I said 'later.' "

"I don't remember your exact words," I said. "I got the impression, however, that it was at the autographing session. I was wrong, I suppose. And I'm not surprised, since I'm a very poor detective. I'll accept your statement now that it was later—but might it not have been earlier?"

"Why earlier?"

"You were here at the beginning, weren't you, when you apologized to Asimov and asked after me."

"I told you about that."

"Yes, and about the time when Asimov was talking to you, he became aware that Giles was present, so I suspect you two came in together."

"I leave you to your suspicion."

"It's more than a suspicion. None of the press people will admit to having escorted Giles to the autographing room, but *someone* did, because the cloakroom girl saw him that morning. He tried to get a package for which he didn't have the ticket and the cloakroom girl said, Little Pepper urged him onward lest he be late. How about that, Little Pepper?"

Sarah took the seat behind her desk, placing three feet of steel between us. She said, "I haven't lied to you. He *did* make it clear that he was furious with you and there *was* unpleasantness at the session, and I *had* apologized to Asimov and *had* also found out who you were. I came to warn you of Mr. Devore's fury and that was it."

"I have no quarrel with that, but you didn't tell me the whole truth, did you? You didn't say you had been with him before the autographing session." I paused a moment, then decided to say it. "Or, possibly, the whole previous night as well."

I was prepared for a storm, but she only reddened a bit, and clasped her hands tightly together so that the knuckles whitened as they interlaced on her desk.

"If I had," she said, "then it would be no business of yours, but, as it happens, I hadn't. I was at home that night, in my own bed and alone. If you don't believe that, there's no need for you to sit here asking me any more questions."

"But if there was nothing to hide, why not tell me you had been with Devore before the autographing session?"

"Why on earth should I tell you? I told you all I felt it was appropriate for you to know. I didn't know the man was dead at the time and that you suspected murder later on. And if I had known, there was still no reason to tell you, since you aren't the police. You still aren't, right now, and I don't have to tell you anything."

I said, "No, I'm not the police. Still, if you're worried over my getting into trouble over this matter of drugs, then don't mislead me and let me run the chance of getting into trouble through ignorance or misapprehension."

"The death of Devore can't have anything to do with drugs."

"I don't accept that, but if there's anything you can tell me that will show that you're right, I will change my mind. So please tell me. Tell me everything that happened from the moment you saw him yesterday morning."

She stirred uneasily in her chair. She said, "All right. This is how it went. About nine A.M. yesterday, not long after I got to work—"

"By the way," I said, "how is it you were working Memorial Day?"

"I've told you, haven't I? We've got a major advertising campaign coming up and the art department has flubbed it, so I've been here all weekend and so have they."

"And the security chief, what's-his-name—Marsogliani. He was here, too. Is he involved in the advertising campaign also?"

"No, he's not," she said, with just a touch of acid, "but he's always here when there's a major convention at the hotel. Why? Do you think we all got here on an off day to work out a conspiracy against your friend?"

I felt a little foolish under the lash of her contempt and said, "No, I'm just trying to ask all the questions I can think of." I added, humbly, "I'm not very good at it."

She was mollified. "All right. But don't worry about us. We make up any off days we lose."

"Well, then, what happened at nine A.M. not long after you got to work?"

"I got word from the desk that there were peculiar phone calls arriving from Room 1511."

"Why did they report that to you? Why not to Marsogliani?"

"Marsogliani hadn't arrived yet, and in any case minor troubles come to me occasionally. I have a perhaps exaggerated reputation in the hotel as a fix-it of miscellaneous mix-ups."

"Well, what did you do?"

"I checked on the occupant of the room and it was Giles Devore. That concerned me because he was a VIP at this convention and if something was wrong with him, it might mean unpleasant publicity. I decided to go up to the fifteenth floor."

"What were the phone calls about?" I asked, without the slightest doubt as to what they were about.

"The desk clerk who had received the calls wasn't sure. He said they were garbled and incomprehensible and, at one point, it sounded as though he were weeping. The clerk suggested that I call a doctor."

"Maybe you should have."

"Not at all. If a resident at the hotel wants a doctor, that's one thing. You can't force a doctor on him, however, without his consent, unless you have reason to think he is in no position to give consent. I went up to check.

"He answered the door, fully dressed, but with his hair grotesquely uncombed and with an oddly feverish look in his eye. The room was in complete disarray. He said, 'Are you the cloakroom woman?' I told him who I was and he said, 'Please come in and help me.'

"I went in. I was upset at his obvious misery. I've read his book, you know, and I admired it; and here was the author—"

"Yes, yes," I said. "What happened after you went in?"

She said, "He sat down on the bed with his face all twisted as though he were on the point of crying. He said, 'I've looked all over. It isn't here.' I said, 'What isn't here?' He said, 'The package. It's not here. It was supposed to be here last night but I forgot. I was busy.'"

I seized upon that. "He was busy. Did he say with what?"

Sarah shook her head. "I can't repeat what he said exactly. It was all very confused and repetitious and it's not as though I had a tape recorder there."

"Tell me what you can."

"I'll give you the impression I gathered. He had come to his room fairly late the night before from some television taping session and he hadn't been entirely well. There was a woman with him and he had needed help badly, but she was a bad woman—"

"A bad woman?"

"That's what he said, over and over."

"He didn't name her?"

"No, he didn't. And I didn't ask."

"No, of course not. Please go on."

She said, "He had needed help, and she wouldn't help, or not enough, even though he had begged and pleaded, and when I asked, in what I hope was a cool and business-like voice, if he wanted a doctor, he said no, very emphatically. He then went on to explain, quite repetitiously, that he had needed help and she wouldn't help him. He was very sorry for himself, almost disgustingly so. He was destroying my respect for him and I was embarrassed to be there."

I said, "Was it your impression that he was under the influence of drugs?"

"The thought didn't occur to me, but if it had, how could I have possibly been able to tell?" She hesitated for quite a while, and since it seemed to me she was trying to say something, I kept quiet and let her struggle.

Finally she said, "I shouldn't tell you this, It's confidential. The autopsy has been performed and Security received a copy a couple of hours ago. I saw it—and there are no signs that he had been taking drugs."

I was glad to hear that. "Then that's one thing we can eliminate."

"As I told you, drugs had nothing to do with Mr. Devore's death."

"Yes, but you didn't tell me why. At that, though, he didn't have to be an addict. Drugs could have been involved in his death if he were a pusher."

She grimaced. "Do you think he was a pusher, that poor, flabby little boy?"

"Little boy! He was a hulk!"

"What's that got to do with it? Little boys come in all sizes. I could see him as an addict, but not as a pusher."

"I can't either, to be honest with you, but it's got to be something, doesn't it, to account for the murder?"

"Not at all. His death could be an accident. Everyone but yourself is sure it was."

I shrugged. "Well, go on."

She said, "He went on to say that he had felt so ill after this unsympathetic woman—he kept calling her 'bad' —left that he just went right to sleep without ever thinking about the package."

"Do you think he was telling the truth?"

She said, "Why should he have lied?"

"I don't know. Do you think he was telling the truth?"

"How can I possibly know?"

"What was your impression?"

"I assumed he was telling the truth. As I look back on it, I'm reasonably sure he was. He was too upset and too out-of-control to lie. Unless you're pathogenic about it, it takes considerable effort to make up a lie. Was he a pathogenic liar?"

I thought about it. "No. I can't say I recall him lying to me, not even under provocation."

"You knew him well, then?"

"I lived with him for a considerable time," I said dryly, "in the nonsexual sense of the term."

"Then I would say he was telling the truth."

"Let's assume he was. Then, after the woman left, he went to sleep, and can we further assume that he had awakened not long before your arrival?"

"Some time before. There was a cup of coffee on the telephone table that was half full and had probably been made with the electric coffee maker."

"You mean that he hadn't called room service for breakfast?"

"No, I don't think he did. It's easy enough to check that out with room service, however."

"Well, if we have to, we will. But if he slept all night, then that would mean he hadn't left the room, and possibly the hotel, in search of a woman who *would* be sympathetic. And if he hadn't done that, then we lose a large possible source of motivations for the murder."

"You're still convinced it was murder?"

"Yes. And if the night is closed off, that leaves us with the missing package as the only unusual thing that could explain the whole tragedy. I dislike that."

"Because it isn't motive enough?"

"I don't see how it can be, but mainly I dislike it because I was supposed to bring it to his room night before last and I didn't. That was the errand I told you I had forgotten yesterday afternoon. . . . Unless, of course, there's something we still don't know about. In all the time you were with him, Sarah, did he say anything, do anything, give you any impression at all, that something was bothering him other than the package?"

"The woman of the night before, whoever she was, was bothering him," she said firmly, "but except for that, it was the package all the way."

"All right, go on, then."

She said, "Once he woke up, he said, he remembered the package and started looking for it. He was in a state of fury, I suppose, that made him pretty irrational, for he tore the bed apart, had all the towels on the floor, the blankets out of the closet, and so on. He might have had some dim thought that you had hidden the package in order to annoy him."

I shook my head. "It would never have occurred to me."

"Then he called the desk. I gather he was trying to ask if the cloakroom attendant still had the package or, if not, to whom she had given it."

I said, "Listen, when he came back the night before, he could have gotten the package, couldn't he? How late are the cloakrooms open?"

"Till midnight."

"And if he didn't have a ticket?"

"That could have been complicated. Still, if he had been able to identify the package, it could have been opened in the presence of the assistant manager."

"Did he tell you what was in the package?"

"No. Do you know?"

"Yes, I do. Pens. Monogrammed pens. Total worth, maybe ten dollars. And if he had had it opened, his name on those pens would have proved his ownership. That idiot! Dead or not, I've got to call him an idiot. If he had just held on to his damned ticket, he could have gotten his package when he came back."

"There are many people like that," said Sarah. "They take precautions. They worry about taking chances. I suppose he thought that if he didn't ask you to get the package for him, he would worry all evening long that the cloakroom might be closed when he returned—"

"And that would have affected his television taping. Yes, I suppose so. Please go on."

"It was about nine-thirty by then and he said he had

an autographing session at ten. So I said, 'Well, let's clean up your room and go. I'll see to it that you get your package if it's still in the cloakroom.' I was trying to calm him down, you understand, because it seemed to me he was dangerously close to going out of control. ... Are you sure, Darius, that the package contained only pens?"

"Not sure," I said cautiously, "in the sense that I ever saw the contents, but Mrs. Devore said they were pens in there, and I'm sure it's so. You have to understand that Giles is compulsive. When things don't follow the scenario he has prepared, he goes wild. Besides, he was trying to change publishers and, between being afraid of losing a big chance and being afraid he was being unethical, he was probably very much uptight and on edge. And besides—"

I wanted to go on and say that since he had failed to work off his little-boy syndrome with Henrietta the night before, he was still a little boy—Sarah had described him exactly that way, as a matter of fact. Certainly, he acted like a little boy over the pens going dry. But I kept it to myself. I wasn't going to give her anything that would guide her in what she had left to tell.

I said, "So you cleaned up the room?"

"Yes. I didn't vacuum it, you understand, but I put back the blankets and towels, and made the beds. He didn't help much."

"His clothes were neatly hung up or put away?"

"Oh yes. They were that way to begin with."

"You didn't leave any clothes hanging around on the chairs or bed?"

"No," she said firmly. "By the time I was done, it was about ten minutes to ten and I felt it was my responsibility to get him down to the autographing. It wasn't too hard to lead him, though I kept thinking that I had a robot by the elbow, one who would go wherever pressure impelled him but would stop if he were released and just stand in one spot indefinitely.

"Once we were in the elevator, however, he did insist

on going to the cloakroom. I was in no position to make a scene since the elevator, I assure you, was not empty. So we stopped off at the second floor. I knew it would be difficult to negotiate anything quickly with Hilda— she's a rather hard-bitten attendant and we only had a few minutes. When she balked at handing over something without a ticket, I urged Devore on, telling him I would get the package for him in a few minutes, as soon as he was safely delivered to the autographing session."

"But you didn't get the package, did you?"

"No," she said, with a shake of her head. "I was just keeping him quiet. Besides I didn't think there was any point in getting it till he was through with the autographing. It never occurred to me that he needed it *for* the autographing; and he never told me what it was. Even if I had known it was pens, though, it would have seemed to me that the world is full of pens and you could borrow one from anyone about you."

"Not a monogrammed Devore pen out of which to manufacture a monogrammed Devore book."

"Well, I didn't know that, you see."

"All right, go on."

"We got into the autographing room and he pulled away from me at once as though he were coming to life again. I let him go, figuring he could find his way to the stage himself, and he did. I saw him in his seat after a while."

"And no one saw you come in with him?"

"People saw him and people saw me, but I don't know if anyone saw us both together. The place was crowded as we walked in because another autographing session was just finishing up, and Devore pulled away from me at the threshold."

"You must have stayed there, though. You knew about the fuss Giles had made. Or did someone tell you?"

"No. I remained. I noticed Asimov standing there and I felt impelled to go to him and apologize for my attitude the night before. I had come on a little strong but, you know, I was having trouble with the art people and the pressures on me were a little intense. He was nice about it, and I asked him who you were and he told me and that rather flabbergasted me."

"But you didn't run to me at once and apologize," I said, with what must have been an annoying touch of irony.

She refused the bait (and I was relieved at that, for it hadn't come out the way I had intended). She said, "No, I wouldn't have known where to find you, though it did occur to me I might get to you at the luncheon—as I did, you know. Meanwhile, I stayed there because Asimov amused me. Have you ever seen him sign autographs?"

"Yes," I said unenthusiastically.

She smiled. "He's such a feckless lecher. Pants indiscriminately after every girl who shows up. An absolute democrat, who pays no attention to race, creed, color, age—"

"Or previous condition of servitude," I said. "I know. I guess it is fun the first time you watch it."

"Yes, it is. He turns every statement, however innocent, into a heavy-handed double-entendre and manages it in so inoffensively self-delighted a way that somehow no one minds. He's like a big puppy dog bouncing around and—"

I got her off the subject. "And you stayed there all the time till there was the fuss in connection with Giles?"

"Yes. And then I stayed on to the end because I was still feeling responsible for him and because I was afraid that something unpleasant might happen that would result in the kind of publicity that the hotel would not want."

"You didn't hear him say anything about me during that time?"

"No. Not then."

"When did you hear it?"

"When the autographing session was over, he threw the pen he had been using against the wall. It hit and fell to the ground—"

"The red-ink pen?"

"I don't know what kind it was, but he was clearly furious and perhaps out of control. He stood up and walked to the door. Some people tried to stop him and talk to him, but he paid no attention. It seemed to me he was swaying and I was afraid he would collapse. My feeling of responsibility overcame me again so that I followed after him quietly, took his arm, and led him to the elevators."

"And what happened then?"

"As we were walking to the elevators, I asked him if he wanted to stop at the cloakroom for his package and he said, 'Too late.' And then, in a kind of whisper, 'That Darius. That Darius Just.' He said it with such *hatred* that it just chilled me. There was a homicidal edge to his voice, and even though he struck me as being a child, he's such a physically large man and you're so—"

"Small?" I suggested when her hesitation had grown perceptible.

She hurried on. "I felt you ought to be warned."

"But you didn't run and warn me right then, did you?"

"As I told you, there was no way I could have found you then. Besides that, I had to take him up to his room."

"And what happened when you did that? Did you leave him there? Did you walk in with him? What?"

Now she was in trouble. She took to shuffling some of the papers on her desk. Then she looked up and said, in a small voice, "I've told you everything that's important."

I said, "Why not just lie to me and tell me you took him to his room and walked away without entering?"

"How do you know that would be a lie?"

"Because I've discovered things about Giles. We can be reasonably sure that he was left frustrated by the events of the night before, and there had been no relief since then. The failure to get the package, the fiasco at the autographing session, must all have accentuated the needs he felt. I am quite certain that even if you wanted to leave him in his room, you wouldn't have been able to. He took you by the arm, didn't he, and drew you in. And what could you do: he's so large and you're so—small."

She said miserably, "Yes, he drew me in."

"And once he had you in, he began to cry and then he asked you to undress him and give him a bath."

She looked me straight in the eye and said bitterly, "You know, then. You've lived with him. Does he do it all the time? And he's never tried to get help?"

I shrugged. "My living with him has nothing to do with it. I just found out about this yesterday. And why should he get help? If he finds a girl who doesn't mind cooperating, who's hurt?"

She didn't say anything and, after a few moments, I asked, in a flat, quiet voice, "Did you cooperate?"

She rose from her chair so she could lean toward me and for the first time I saw her actively angry. "No, I did *not*. When he told me what he wanted, I left."

"You couldn't have left, if he tried to stop you."

"He didn't try to stop me. I left quickly, in a hurry. I was near the door—and out. He couldn't have moved fast enough to stop me."

"I see."

Sarah said thoughtfully, "I suppose that woman the night before had also refused."

"Yes, she had."

"And that's it."

"Is it?" I said. "You got him up to his room after the autographing session. Shall we say eleven-ten?"

"About that."

"And you came to the luncheon and warned me of Giles's anger with me at about one o'clock, nearly two hours later."

"I couldn't have found you immediately. Did you expect me to wander about the hotel aimlessly, trying to meet you by chance?"

"What did you do during those two hours?"

"I was in my office. I had plenty to do."

"Who saw you there?"

"No one. My receptionist was out. It was Memorial Day, remember?"

"You have no alibi."

"Why would I need one?" Her eyes were fixed on mine and I could see the anger surge upward again.

"Your story is unsupported," I said. "Giles said he slept all that night and was not with a woman, and if he said so, as you reported he did, I would believe him. But I have only your report to that effect. I have only your report as to what happened before and what happened after the autographing session. You could be lying."

"Lying? What do you imagine *did* happen?"

"You're a small woman," I said easily, lounging back on the couch, "but a dominating one. You run a department here with authority and you're used to putting down large men. You may even like it. Now, here was a large man who wanted to be dominated. You might have stayed with him all night. Or, if not"—I waved aside the beginning of an angry statement from Sarah—"and I admit it sounds unlikely, then you might well have helped him out Monday morning, especially afterward."

Sarah was back in control. "Go on," she said out of tight lips.

"You said you had been feeling responsible for him all morning. You led him by the arm back to his room, felt sorry for him, and might even have enjoyed undressing him and bathing him. There's no harm in it. Two consenting adults and all that."

"I see. And if so, what are you getting at?"

"Why, if so, you might well have been there when he died." I sat up suddenly, and said sharply, *"What happened?"*

And it was as though all the anger died in her at once and washed out. She laughed in complete good humor and said, "That's funny." Then she laughed again.

I began to feel foolish. "What's funny?"

"The way you did that. Sitting up suddenly like a schoolteacher who was going to trap me into saying something I didn't want to say."

"But you're not answering."

She said, in total good nature, "Because there's nothing to say. You don't really believe I'm lying. You're just testing me and, I assure you, I pass. I brought him up about eleven-ten A.M. and it couldn't have been much past eleven-fifteen when I left, eleven-twenty at the outside. I left him there crying, poor fellow, but I assure you I had nothing more to do with him than I have told you. Of course—"

"Yes?"

"I do have a little sadness over not having, perhaps, been a little kinder. When he tried to take his shower by himself, in his condition—"

"Everyone tries to be responsible," I said querulously. "Now, look, are you certain now that when you left there were no clothes scattered about the room?"

"I tell you"—and her usual precision of language became even more pronounced—"that when I left he had his clothes on his body. Not one item had been removed."

"All right. Now, then, when you left, was anyone in the corridor?"

"No."

"Are you sure?"

"Quite sure. Look, Darius, I've made love, you understand, and with a certain reasonable variety of technique, too, but this was something quite new and repellent to me and it was advanced by someone whom I found completely uninteresting, sexually, and I felt shocked at the whole thing, even though I wouldn't have thought anything sexual could shock me. . . . Why are you looking like that at me, Darius? Did you think I was a virgin? I'm thirty-two years old and have a seven-year-old son."

I spread out my hands. "Sorry. I hadn't really thought of it at all. Except that your name fits your accent, so I thought you were unmarried. Of course, you could have married a fellow countryman, and your husband's name—"

"Or I could be divorced and be working under my maiden name. Isn't that possible, too?"

"Oh, is that it?"

"Does it matter? Are you interested?"

I didn't really know what to say, so I settled for the truth. "No, it doesn't matter, but I guess I'm a little curious."

"I'm divorced," she said. "And your marital status?"

"I'm single," I said quickly.

"Always."

"Never been married, though I guess it won't shock you if I tell you I'm not a virgin either."

"I wouldn't have believed you if you had said you were," she said ironically. "But let me explain how I know the corridor was empty. When I left Devore's room, I felt somehow dirtied and I had an intense desire for no one to see me leave the room. I felt that too much, perhaps everything, could have been guessed from my appearance."

"Your clothes were mussed?"

"Don't be foolish. It was a purely neurotic feeling. In any case, I didn't want anyone to see me and I took special note of the fact that no one did. There was no one in the corridor."

"No one at all?"

She hesitated. "Well, I did have the impression that there was a flash of movement in the direction of his room when I turned into the elevator-bank recess. It might have been a bit of fearful apprehension."

"Anything more specific than just a flash of movement?"

"No. Since I didn't want to be seen, or worse yet, be caught by Devore if he was following me, I slipped down the staircase to the floor below and took the elevator there."

"Too bad," I said. "Was there no impression of any kind other than the flash of movement? Could you tell whether whatever you saw was large or small, man or woman?"

"No. Nothing."

"Too bad. If you did leave by eleven-twenty and if I found him dead two hours later, at which time he had been dead for some time, isn't it possible that the flash of movement you saw was of the murderer coming up to see Giles?"

"Goodness!"

I sat there for a while, unable to think of any further questions to ask her. It was well after six.

I said, "Do you have to go home?"

"I usually do, eventually."

"I mean, I suppose you have to get back to your son."

"No, he's with his grandmother, my ex-mother-in-law. They have rights in him, too, and the divorce was not an excessively unfriendly one. It wouldn't be, since I asked for no alimony."

"Oh. Well, then." I grew suddenly animated. "Would you care to have dinner with me?"

"Will we be talking about Mr. Devore?"

I decided to be honest. "We might, a little, because that's all I've been able to think of for about thirty hours now. But I promise I'll make an honest effort to talk of other things."

"In that case, all right. I accept your invitation, Darius."

16   SARAH VOSKOVEK   6:20 P.M.

We both took time out to wash up, both literally and euphemistically, and then there was some discussion as to where we might eat. We decided on a small Armenian place I knew, one with booths and one that was not likely to be crowded on a Tuesday evening. And it was close enough to walk to, and somehow I felt like walking.

It was one of those pleasant evenings when you're not aware of the atmosphere, it is so perfectly suited to human requirements. The air was neither too warm nor too cold, nor too damp nor too dry. It wasn't so still that the layer next to the skin grew warm and moist, nor was it moving briskly enough to be annoying. There was even a fresh smell from the park that one could detect in the interstices left by the automobile exhaust.

The sun was on our backs as we walked, pleasantly warm, and lending the streets a brilliance. We didn't even mind the traffic.

Sarah seemed in a good humor, almost lighthearted. If she had been wearing sensible shoes, she might have skipped. I think she was relieved to have told the details of that difficult morning and to have gotten rid of its fester.

As for me, I had a little less to be thankful for. I had now traced Giles from the moment I had left him on Sunday night to a time two hours before I had found him. . . . And I had nothing.

There was nothing that would account for what must have happened in that two-hour hiatus. I couldn't say who had murdered him or why. Worse yet, I had no idea at all as to what to do next.

Yes, I did—I was going to have dinner with Sarah Voskovek, something that I would have considered utterly unlikely as recently as lunchtime.

Our shadows stretched before us as we crossed the avenue, the lights permitting, in a leisurely stroll. For a moment they seemed strange, distorted, and unnatural to me—and then I realized why. My shadow was longer than hers. For that matter, her arm resting in my elbow exerted the faintest pressure downward instead of upward. It was an odd feeling, and rather exciting.

"You know," she said, when we were finally seated opposite each other over the wooden table in one of the alcoves to the rear of the restaurant, "I'm grateful to you for inviting me here and taking my mind off the ad campaign. I want you to know that. I'm so *tired* of it. To-morrow we make the final decisions, no matter what, and then I take off for a week, and that will be a pleasure."

"Where will you go?"

"I'm not sure. But then I might just stay at home and

sleep all day every day, or watch television. Why do I have to go somewhere?"

"I suppose you don't have to—but everyone does."

"I know. It's the mark of the mobile society," she said. "We all go somewhere—in automobiles, or planes—or ships, maybe—with oil burning and with churning—churning. *We* go *there* and *they* come *here*."

"Hotels couldn't survive otherwise."

"I know—and it bothers me sometimes. So many of us live at the expense of high-energy bustling. What happens when the energy for the bustle runs out?"

So we talked doomsday for a while. Then, over the stuffed grape leaves and salad, we talked natural foods. I've lost track of what we talked about except that the ball kept bouncing back and forth briskly, never went out of bounds, never hit the net, never got lost in the underbrush.

I found out about her early life. Her father was a government official in her homeland and he had fallen out of favor under conditions where such a fall meant prison or worse. Fortunately, he got out with her and they made it to the United States. That was ten years ago and he had died since. She had married soon after arriving here—too soon, and it hadn't worked, except for producing a son.

"I knew English when I came," she said. "It was to be my profession, and I was going to be an English teacher. I love the language; it just seems to fit me. I used to think I spoke it perfectly, but here everyone can tell at once I am European."

"You speak it *too* perfectly," I said. "Can you still speak your native language?"

She laughed and spoke rapidly in something that sounded Slavic. I tried to repeat a few words and we went back and forth over the moussaka. She said, "You're not a linguist."

"I know that," I said. "It's all I can do to handle English. My copyreaders weep over my manuscripts. What was it that I was trying to say in that gibberish you were making me repeat?"

"You ask too many questions."

"Oh, come on. It's only natural for me to want to know."

"No, no, that's what we were saying. The words you repeated meant, 'You ask too many questions.' "

She asked questions, too, just the same, and I spoke an incredible deal of nonsense over the baklava and coffee about how I had gotten started as a writer.

And then, unaccountably, her fires seemed to sink, and a frown, like a cloud, came over her face.

I said, "What's the matter, dear?"

The "dear" slipped out unintentionally. I was feeling friendly.

She shivered a little. "I don't know. I'm beginning to see things."

"What things?"

"I think it's because I was telling you I had seen that flash of movement when I left Mr. Devore's room. It seems to have put me into a melodramatic mood."

It was the first time that Giles had been mentioned since we had entered the restaurant and I felt his unseen presence come gritting down over the smooth evening sunshine that had seemed to fill the meal. "Well, what? Put a name to it."

"When we were walking here, it seemed to me that someone was following us."

"Following us? I didn't see anything."

"You weren't watching. Well, neither was I, but I saw a man."

"There were thousands of men all about us."

"I saw him several times, always somehow near us, but not too near. And then just now, he came into the restaurant."

I turned, of course, for my back was toward the door, and she said, "He's gone. He only came in for a moment, as though to make sure we were still here."

"Did you recognize him?"

"He was a complete stranger."

"Was he the same man you saw in the street?"

"I can't be sure. I just had a glimpse. But why should anyone just come in and leave? The man just looked around and left."

I looked up at the clock on the wall over our heads. I pointed and said, "He drifted in to check the time and he wasn't the same man who was in the street, and the man in the street wasn't following us. And besides, you need fear nothing when you're with me. Don't let my size fool you. I tell you what, let's take a walk. It's not late at all."

She smiled. "Where shall we walk? Let me guess. To your apartment?"

I felt myself flush, for, of course, my apartment was within walking distance. I said, "Innocent, your honor. If you were to beg to come to my place, I wouldn't refuse you, but, my word of honor, I have nothing evil in mind."

"It depends on how Darius Just defines evil," she muttered.

"I have a walk in mind," I said, "an honest-to-God walk along the side of the park in the fading twilight. I am suggesting a walk through beauty. It's just two days after full moon and in the clarity of tonight's evening air, we will see it rise nice and fat and orange over the park. And when we're through, if you live anywhere within ten miles, I will take you home by taxi; or, if you'd rather, I'll put you into a taxi and pay off the driver in advance."

"Goodness," she said, "you block off all reasonable paths to a kind refusal. What if I tell you I think I'm coming down with a headache?"

"Then I'll tell you that the smell of the fresh spring foliage from the park will prove a sovereign cure."

"Then that's it. By all means, let's take a walk, Darius."

The waiter had brought back my credit card and I carefully computed the tip, and we were out.

17 SARAH VOSKOVEK 8:30 P.M.

It was about half past eight when we reached the park, and the twilight was well faded. In fact, if I hadn't talked about fading twilight so that I had a vested interest in it, I would have considered it night. The three stars that one can see in the city sky were out and the automobile headlights twinkled merrily on every side.

I put my arm about Sarah's waist and said, "Are you cold?"

She said, "Not a bit," but I left my arm there, just in case she became cold later, and she put hers around mine, perhaps for the same reason.

We were walking toward my apartment, but I said nothing about that and I swear I had no intention of maneuvering her there. It was the purest coincidence that we were walking in that direction.*

The moon was exactly as I had predicted it would be and she told me that back in her apartment she had a field glass which she sometimes used from her apartment-house roof to look at the moon's craters, Venus' phases, and the four major satellites of Jupiter. I had never seen the satellites and I said so, and she said that someday she would show them to me; a promise which, at that moment, I treasured and meant to cash in.

She had apparently gotten over her grisly moment in the restaurant, but I wasn't particularly aware of that, since, to tell the truth, I had utterly forgotten about it.

In fact, between the odd, and therefore erotic, feel of the waist of a mature woman in a position I had

---

* Asimov is deliberately having me overprotest here to make me look ridiculous.

—DARIUS JUST

All I can say is that I wish I had thought to use a tape recorder. You should have heard Darius swear, cross his heart, and kiss his pinkie finger to heaven as a sign that his motives were pure. Not that I believed him for a minute.

—ISAAC ASIMOV

never felt before, and the utter placidity of the moment
after the hectic almost interminable, stretch of the convention, I felt an odd storybook romanticism of a kind
to which ordinarily I am a stranger.

I said, in melting tones that I would not have recognized as my own if I could have listened to them from
outside, "What a pity the park is off-bounds."

"A pity indeed," said Sarah. "It could be so beautiful
on an evening like this; so peaceful to escape from the
hectic city into the serene greenery."

It was exactly what I had felt and a sense of wild
grievance overcame me, a feeling of cruel deprivation.
"This," I said, "is the result of a self-fulfilling belief.
Once the rumor spread that the park was dangerous at
night, the public began staying away, and a deserted
park becomes, by that simple fact, dangerous. And since
the wolves flocked for what prey remained, since their
isolation made them easy picking, it grew still more
dangerous."

"I know. It's a terrible pity."

"But I tell you what. We need not penetrate its depths.
Why not a bench near the edge with a light conveniently
nearby? We can at least sit down and be shielded, just a
little, from the traffic." (I'll be honest, I was thinking
we might kiss a bit.)

She said, "Oh no. After all, if something happened—"

"Nothing will happen. And if it does, I'd take care
of it."

"Oh no," she said softly. "Don't indulge in bragga-
docio." It seemed to me in the uncertain light of a not
too close streetlamp that she smiled condescendingly for
a flickering moment.

I suppose I had just been talking. Kisses or no kisses,
I don't think I had really had any intention of walking
into the park—but what could I do after that?

I said, "Don't go by the fact that I'm 158 centimeters
tall and 55 kilograms in weight." (Damn it, if she was
European she could understand that.) "I can take care
of myself—and of you, too."

We were passing one of the entrances and I said, "Come on," and steered her toward it.

She tried to hang back. "Now, Darius, it's not funny."

"Come on. Don't be afraid. We won't be harmed. No one will bother us."

I insisted. I used my not inconsiderable strength and she had to give in. I wasn't actually feeling too good about it, and I was relieved when we found an empty bench perhaps twenty feet inside. It was just far enough from the street outside and the automobile road inside to give the illusion of isolation, and just near enough the edge of the park to give the illusion of safety, too.

"There," I said. "Perfect!"

18 ANONYMOUS 9:00 P.M.

There was enough light from a lamp half hidden by the fresh new tree leaves to show me her face, and enough darkness to make it look very desirable. It seemed to me perfectly natural to kiss her. Why else had I come into the park? Why else was she here?

Yet somehow I lacked the self-assurance I generally had on such occasions. There are body signals one recognizes. With experience and a certain amount of common sense at the game, one knows what is welcome and what is not and how far to go without suffering the humiliation of rejections or the greater humiliation of the use of force, however slight.

In Sarah's case, I was confused. She had been friendly in a completely non-flirtatious way. Did she or did she not want to be kissed? To my chagrin, I found myself back in my teens. I found myself slowly reducing the distance between my face and hers, watching for the first sign for a clear go-ahead—or a pull-back.

For a while, I though I'd make it, but then she pulled back—sharply, and without any sign of coyness or disapproval. It was a matter of sheer fright.

"*Darius!*" she cried out in a strangled scream.

I suppose I was more wrapped up in the game than

she had been. She noticed; and I never would have. It is somewhat more soothing to my ego to put it this way, though: she was facing in the right direction and I wasn't.

I turned quickly and was on my feet.

"What the hell do you want?" I demanded.

He was some fifteen feet away as best I could judge in the dimness, but I could tell nothing about him but that he was a man, a white man, moderately tall and stocky. He had on a dark jacket, dark shirt, dark pants, and if it weren't for the pale light on his hands and face, he would have been quite invisible except as a shadow.

"It's the man from the restaurant," said Sarah in agitation.

"You can't tell," I whispered, never taking my eyes from him.

"The same shape. The same—something. I'm *sure.*"

"What do you want?" I shouted again. They might hear me in the street, but I had no great hopes of any hero dashing in to protect us. Everyone would hurry past, pretending not to hear.

"Don't move," I said.

But the shape was moving, with small steps, and now there was light glinting, more efficiently, in a new place.

Sarah whispered, "He has a knife."

I didn't need to be told that. I said, "Do you want money?"

There was no answer, and I could wait no longer.

I pushed Sarah roughly to one side. "Stand clear," I said in a low voice. "If we start fighting, *run.*"

I stepped back onto the grass, putting the bench between us for just a moment while I kept my eyes on him and weighed the situation. At least he didn't have a gun (or wasn't using it if he had one) with which to shoot me down from a safe distance. But then a quiet killing would give him a longer time to get away.

I was sure it was a killing that was intended. A funny thing. You meet and know so many men in your life, so many women, so many names. And then you may meet one person whose interaction with you is the most intimate of all—killer and killed—and you don't know him at all. All the names of your life trickle by one by one and the whole thing ends at last with Anonymous.

Gingerly, Anonymous was circling the bench, to get at me. He wasn't going to throw the knife, I was sure. Throwing a knife is something that requires more skill than you might think and very few have it—and if your knife misses, you are left unarmed.

I backed as gingerly away, but let him get round the bench. I knew what I would try to do and I wanted the empty space between us.

I said, in as near to an ordinary speaking voice as I could manage, "Just move behind him, Sarah."

I knew she wouldn't move. How could she? She was probably frozen in terror; helpless—or running away, perhaps, though I had heard no rustling of grass, no cries. I was sure Anonymous would know she wouldn't move, but people are human. However completely the man with the knife knew there would be no one moving toward his rear, his eyes would have to flick in the direction of Sarah and it was for that moment of inattention that I waited.

With a loud cry, I lunged forward, my right foot shooting out straight for his testicles. I was well out of range (he had the knife, after all) and I couldn't have trusted the accuracy of my thrust anyway, so I had neither the hope nor even the intention of scoring a bull's-eye.

It is, however, difficult to control the reaction when a foot darts out toward that delicate region, particularly when an unexpected scream accompanies the move. Anonymous bent his hips backward, quite without conscious intention, I'm sure, and his hands shot downward in automatic and quite unpreventable defense.

But my right-foot lunge became a leap and I charged with perfect timing. (I had practiced this particular form of attack many times, and I was delighted to see it work out so well—it takes much longer to tell than to do.) I seized the wrist of the downward-moving, knife-carrying arm, twisted it roughly, and continued its motion, reinforcing it with my own—making it move backward and upward, as hard as I could.

The knife went flying, as I knew it would, and that arm had to be dislocated at the shoulder, from the scream he gave—and he went down.

The trouble is, though, that he weighed at least sixty pounds more than I did, and while I could be quick enough and clever enough to pull his arm out of its socket, there was no way I could keep his falling mass from pulling me down with it. I had to let go quickly not to be pinned under him, and I went staggering forward, head first, into a tree.

I've got a pretty hard skull, but it won't compare to the trunk of an old, firmly rooted tree, so I saw a lot of pretty-colored lights, and went down and all but out.

I couldn't move for a while. I was almost unable to think—only slow convoluted thoughts. She had warned me—Sarah—and I hadn't listened. Had she maneuvered me into the—park—conscience twinging, so she warned me—set up—outfoxed—outplayed—and now— I would lie here and he would—get up—knife me—other hand—or she would.

"*Darius*—"

It was a scream and I heard it at last.

I could move and I forced myself to my feet, but my knees felt unhinged and I found myself clinging to the tree.

"Wha—"

I was dizzy and in pain and I had difficulty focusing.

Sarah was holding the knife in both hands. My eyes were watering and she seemed to be deep in a fog.

"What do I do, Darius?"

She was sitting on the chest of Anonymous. He was thoroughly immobilized and not because of his dislocated shoulder, either. When my vision cleared a bit, I wasn't surprised that he was, for she was holding the knife just over one of his eyes, virtually making contact. He could easily have rolled away faster than she could move, considering that she was clearly no expert in rough-and-

tumble, but his dislocated shoulder made motion difficult
for him and I could see that he hesitated to risk his
eye—and the brain behind it.

"What do I do, Darius?"

"Just hold him like that a minute," I gasped. "I'll be
there as soon as I can move. If *he* moves, just stick it in."

"That's what I said I'd do, but I don't want to."

"Do it, anyway. You can scream while you're doing it."

I managed to move and to limp over, feeling as though
I would go down at every step. It was twenty steps and
maybe twenty years before I got there.

I looked down at Anonymous and he looked sick and
sweaty in the dim light, sicker and sweatier than I felt.
His arm must have been killing him and he was staring at
a knife point at a distance too close to focus. I tried to
memorize his face, which had a blunt, somewhat twisted
nose that I would have difficulty forgetting.

"Who the hell sent you out to do this?" I asked in a
low voice. "You tell me what's going on or your friends
will call you Johnny One-Eye."

He tried to talk, but it dawned on me that Sarah was
liable to drop the knife any moment, she was shaking
so hard

I said, "Give me the knife, Sarah," and reached
downward.

But between my inability to move quickly and Sarah's
eagerness to let go, the maneuver went wrong. She didn't
wait for me to reach down so that the knife would stay
in position as it was transferred. She reached it up to me.

Anonymous moved quickly, rolling over onto his good
arm, dumping Sarah. He managed to make it to his feet
and was staggering away, with his good hand grasping
the elbow of his dislocated arm, long before I could do
anything about it.

"Let him go," I muttered. "We can't catch him."

I looked stupidly at the knife for a moment. It was
a switchblade and I made its point vanish. I dropped it
into my pocket.

She said, "Aren't we going to the police?"

"Why? What do you suppose they'll do, except go to the trouble of putting down the story and filing it?"

"But when we go to a doctor, we'll have to tell him—"

"I don't need a doctor," I said wearily. "I'm perfectly all right. Just got to get home and sleep it off." I was lying, of course. My head hurt as though it were one great big bad tooth.

"But how will you get home?" said Sarah. "Can you make it to the street? We can get a taxi."

"Don't need a taxi," I said. "I'm on home turf. Just two blocks. Help me a bit and I'll walk it. Just make sure I get to the door, then—you can go home. No danger for you—promise—" I managed a feeble imitation of a smile, I think.

"Lean on me," she said, paying no attention to what I was saying.

But I couldn't let go. I said, "I'm in no position—to endanger your virtue. Sorry about that."

She said, "Oh, shut *up*. Which direction?"

19 SARAH VOSKOVEK 9:30 P.M.

It was a strange walk home. Two blocks, then left and half a block from the park, then up twelve stories in an elevator. It seemed to last an age. My head ached abominably and it was very difficult to keep walking a straight line. I dared not look down, for when I did things began swimming. I took to staring at the streetlights, walking slowly, and breathing deeply.

Mostly I tried to look as though I weren't drunk. There's something about seeming drunk, when you're a teetotaler, that is the essence of humiliation. Besides, I didn't want to put Sarah in the position of seeming to be guiding some sot home.

I did a lot of leaning on her and I suppose it was a good thing that I weighed no more than 120 pounds at that, or she couldn't have managed.

I tried to talk, just to give a general air of self-possession, but I think I made a miserable failure at that. I hardly remember what I said, except that I'm under the impression that I tried to apologize to her for thinking she had set me up.

I remember that more because I remember her answering than because I remember saying it.

She said, "The trouble, Darius, is that you're a romantic. You keep trying to make me a villain because otherwise I don't interest you. I'm too short, I think."

"No," I said. "Just right. Just—just right."

I tried to pat her in a fatherly way, but I think I missed.

That's all I remember about any conversation. I know that when we went through the lobby, I was very grave and solemn with the doorman, much more grave and solemn than I ordinarily am.

"Ah, there, George," I said, "how are you? This is Miss Voskovek. She'll just go up with me for a moment, George. Be leaving right away."

"Yes, sir, Mr. Just," said George, grinning and nodding.

Sarah hissed in my ear, "You don't know when I'll be leaving."

"You'll have to leave right away, Sarah. It's your reputation I'm thinking about."

"You need a doctor. That's what to think about."

"No doctor," I said, and the elevator came.

There was no one in the elevator and I remember how nice it was to lean against the wall and close my eyes. Sarah kept her hand on my elbow.

She said, "Do you have your keys?"

I pulled them out of my pocket and gave them to her. She opened the door after some experimentation. I was very patient.

I walked in and said, "Okay, dear. You can go now, because I'll just go to sleep."

"No, I don't. Not yet. Good Lord, look at your clothes. I can't imagine what the doorman thought."

I tried to look down but it hurt too much. "Just a little dirt," I muttered, closing my eyes.

"And a little tear, and rip." She began pulling at my jacket.

I tried to resist, but it was a terrible effort to do so and I ended by letting her. Until she came to my pants.

"Come on, now," I said feebly. "What are you doing?"

"All off," she said. "Everything off. You'd get them off fast enough if we were going to bed together."

"Well, we're not and I don't want them off."

"I don't care what you want. I'm getting them off."

And she did, too. Everything. I remember standing there with my hands over my genitals, feeling like a maiden in a Victorian melodrama surprised by a bad baronet with rape on his mind. It was the damnedest feeling, but I don't think Sarah cared anything at all about it.

She got me into the bathroom and then made me step into the tub and sponged me down. That was the damnedest feeling, too.

I started to laugh, but I couldn't keep it up for long. It hurt.

She was drying me and said, "Lift your leg, and why are you laughing?"

I said, "Poor Giles. This is what *he* wanted. Only you wouldn't do it for him."

"Because it was *his* idea. This is *my* idea. It makes a difference."

"Sexist," I said.

"Also, that was sex, and this is nursing."

"Are you a nurse?" I asked. For a minute I think I couldn't remember who she was.

"No," she said, "but I am a mother."

"Oh? And I'm a little boy? I'm not, you know."

"Please! Where are your pajamas?"

I told her and she managed to struggle me into them after I had used my spray deodorant (I insisted) and then I was in bed and, boy, what a wonderful feeling that was. Better than sex. If a million girls, one after the other, had asked me just then, What do you want, Darius, bed with me or bed alone? I'd have said, Bed alone, one million times.

After a while, Sarah got some warm milk into me and

then she felt my head very gently, but not so gently that it didn't hurt fiendishly when she passed her fingers over a bump that felt like a billiard ball attached to my skull.

She said, "I can't tell if your skull is broken or not."

I said, "It isn't broken. If it were broken, I'd be in a coma."

"How do you know?"

"Well, it isn't broken."

"You do have a concussion. You've got to."

"Sure, but there's nothing to be done about a concussion but sleep. So let me sleep. I'll be okay in the morning."

"You might be bleeding inside. I think we should call a doctor."

"No," I said. "Doctors won't come anyway. Let me sleep. Come back tomorrow morning and if I don't answer the door, then call an ambulance."

"Oh, don't be a fool," she said, and drew up an armchair and sat down in it.

"You can't stay here all night."

"How can you stop me?"

I groaned and after that I don't remember at all what happened. I think I talked. I don't recall talking about Giles's murder, though I must have. It seems to me I talked a lot about Asimov. God only knows what I said, but I seem to remember saying that there ought to be a law against anyone having so little trouble writing.*

And then I went to sleep and that was it. There were no dreams that I can remember. Nothing! I might as well have died.

---

* I keep running into that sort of thing. It doesn't seem to occur to any of my good friends of the writing world that I suffer as much as they do, but hide it by grit, determination, and stoicism.

—ISAAC ASIMOV

Bullshit!

—DARIUS JUST

Part Four

WEDNESDAY

28 MAY 1975

1 SARAH VOSKOVEK 9:00 A.M.

I must have fallen asleep about eleven. I woke up at nearly nine. I was asleep ten hours, which is four hours more than I can usually manage.

I didn't move for a while, just stared at the ceiling, wondering what the hell everything was all about. Then I turned my head, because there was a distinct sense of someone being there and it was Sarah Voskovek in a chair, looking at me with her dark eyes big and anxious.

I started up, and then sank back with a groan because my head stabbed at me. It jogged what memory I had.

Sarah said, "Do you know who I am?"

I had both my hands on my head and said pettishly, "Of course I know who you are. You're Sarah Voskovek. And if you wait a minute, I'll sort everything out. We had dinner last night, right?"

"Yes. And afterward?"

"There was a fight in the park. Right? What happened afterward? Did you bring me home?"

"Yes."

"And you stayed—Pardon me, but I've got to go to the bathroom. Will you help me up?"

She did and then she held on to me while I made it there.

I said, "All right. You can't stay here. What do you want to do, hold it for me? Besides, that's not all that's got to be done."

She said, "What if you fall?"

"Then you'll hear a bump. Please get out."

She did, but I'm sure she stayed near the door. Talk about inhibiting factors! Try relaxing on the throne with some strange girl—some nearly strange girl, anyway—placing her ear to the crack of the door. There's something to kill romance.

I felt much better afterward and that's what I told her when I came out and she said, "How do you feel?"

I said, "I feel all right. Just this sore spot on my head,

but everything else is perfectly normal. Lots of it is coming back, but I don't remember much of the detail about coming home."

"Nothing to remember, Darius. I just got you to bed."

"And you sat up all night to watch over me?"

I thought I had said it sardonically, but she said, "If you can't have me as a villain, you want me as an angel of mercy." (I didn't at that point remember her remark the night before about me wanting her to be a villain so she'd be interesting, so I didn't quite get it then; I did later.)

"Actually," she went on, "I'm just a human being. It might have been in my head to watch over you like a mother, but I didn't. I couldn't. I fell asleep and spent most of the night asleep. I woke up only an hour before you. If you had needed a doctor in the night, I would never have known."

"But you slept in the chair."

"It's a pretty comfortable chair. And I got mostly undressed and borrowed a second pair of your pajamas. I'll pay for the cleaning."

"Don't be stupid. Do you want the bathroom?"

"I've already used it. There was not time to ask permission. Of course, I'm a little grubby now. There's no change of linen for today since I probably won't have a chance to stop off at home."

"People have been known not to change for a couple of days and live. Shouldn't you be at work? It's after nine."

"I've called the hotel and told them I'll be late. How about breakfast?"

"Sure. Anything you want that I've got."

So she made an omelet with mushrooms and ham and bamboo shoots that she found a can of. And tomato sauce on top. And coffee. And pineapple juice to start with. It was great.

It was mostly cloudy outside, which was great also. I didn't want the sun glaring at me. Not till the throbbing died down a bit.

She said, "Do you remember anything you said last night after you went to bed?"

"Did I talk?" I was astonished.

"Yes. You wanted to, and I thought perhaps it was better to let you. If you grew too incoherent, I would know to call an ambulance."

"But I didn't, then?"

"No. You switched from topic to topic rather suddenly, but within each group of remarks you made, you were rational."

I kept my eyes firmly fixed on the plate. "Did I say anything—embarrassing?"

"If you mean, did you discuss your sex life, or did you become blatantly aggressive toward myself, the answer is no, and no. You showed enviable self-control."

"Just as well. What did I talk about?"

"A little bit of many things. Your writing, your publishers, your parents, the Middle East for a while."

"Good God. Did I talk world affairs? What did I say?"

"I don't remember, really. You were most forceful, considering your condition, where Dr. Asimov was concerned."

I frowned a bit. My head had improved further now that I had some food in me. "I seem to remember that. What did I say?"

"You were rather bitter about the speed and extent of his writing. And you said that he was so secure in his intelligence that he never felt he had to bother showing it. And then you said—I'm not sure about this—"

"Go on, anyway."

"I think you said that you could learn from that to be so tall that you wouldn't have to bother looking it."

I said, "Maybe I mean I didn't have to go into the park just to show you how tall I was."

"That's what I thought, too. But you showed up pretty well, you know."

"Maybe. It wasn't coincidence, by the way. That guy *was* following us, as you had said. He would have followed me to my apartment and tried to get me there, but the park offered an opportunity too good to turn down."

"I guess I'll remember it all my life."

I rubbed my head gingerly. "It's just as well," I said, "as long as we're still alive. As far as I'm concerned, it's the final proof that Giles *was* murdered. If you're covering up a murder, you wouldn't hesitate to murder again. What other motive was there to follow me—*me*, specifically—and attack me?"

"They'll try again, dear."

"I wouldn't be surprised," I said, feeling a little grisly inside at the thought, but trying not to show it. "I'll do my best to be careful. . . . Did I talk about it, about the murder, last night?"

"Not very much. Just toward the end. Before you finally fell asleep, you know. Your voice had been growing softer and the words were beginning to run together and I was wondering if you were falling asleep or needing a doctor when you sat up and said, 'The pen, I shouldn't have done it,' or something like that. It wasn't very clear. You reached out with your hand and I took it and that seemed to relax you and you fell asleep. At first, I feared it might be a coma, but it looked for all the world like natural sleep and I decided to take the chance."

"Good. I'm glad you did. So I talked about pens. I suppose I'll never quite get over having messed up my friend on his last night alive. And I went to sleep holding your hand, did I?"

"Yes, and then, after a while, I let go." She went to the sink.

I said, "Oh, don't wash the dishes. I'll take care of that when I get back."

She washed them anyway.

I said, "You know, I've never before spent a night with a girl alone in an apartment without—going to bed with her." (Silly expression, but I shied away from the various monosyllabic terms.)

She soaped her hands, rinsed them, and dried them

on the dish towel. "And it's the first time I've ever spent
an innocent night with a boy," she said calmly. "Now we
both know what it feels like."

"I don't," I said. "I was out like a light."

"I do," she said, "and I have spent far better nights.
... I will have to use your bathroom again."

I waited, remembering that I hadn't cleaned my teeth
yet, or shaved, or done a few other things, so I went in
when she came out. And it was when I was cleaning my
teeth that the thought struck me—for the second time,
for I must have had it first the night before, when the
blow on my head had unhinged me and let me think
loosely enough, jarring me out of the same old circle
in which my thoughts had burrowed for a day and a half.

I started shouting, and with my mouth full of toothpaste, nothing much came out. Sarah must have been
at the door again, waiting for me to fall down, because
she was there beside me at once, saying in anxious tones,
"What is it, Darius? What is it?"

I had to rinse my mouth. Then I said, "What you
heard me say last night about the pens. Did I say 'pens'
plural or 'pen' singular?"

She shook her head and held out her hands helplessly.
"I couldn't swear to it. Singular, I think."

"And I said, 'I shouldn't have done it'?"

"I think so."

"Could I have said, 'It shouldn't have been there'?"

"It could be," she said doubtfully. "You were falling
asleep. You weren't exactly enunciating clearly."

"It must be," I said. "Of course." Where earlier I had
counted the flagstones and watched them, in my mind,
form a path, now other flagstones were coming together,
quite suddenly, to form a structure, one by one.

I said, "Are you ready to go, Sarah?"

She said, "Are you sure you want to wear that jacket
with those pants?"

I looked down at myself and my head only ached
bearably. "All right," I said, "I'll get my maroon one." I
made sure I had all my pocket accessories, wallet, keys,

credit cards, and so on, and then we were indeed ready to go.

Sarah said, "I think we'd better take a taxi. I don't want you overdoing and besides it looks like rain."

"Sure thing," I said, trying not to burble. "I want to get there as fast as I can. Something's beginning to make sense."

It didn't take long to get a taxi (my location is a good one for that) and during the five-minute ride, I said, "Can you do something for me?"

"Maybe. What?"

"I was told the police took a complete inventory of Giles's possessions in the room, and that Security would get a copy. Can you arrange to let me see that copy?"

She looked nonplussed. "I'd have to ask Tony Marsogliani—"

"Don't ask him. Have some underling send it to you. If Marsogliani thinks it's for me, he'll never let you see it."

She said, a little uneasily, "I'll try."

We were at a red light a block from the hotel when I remembered and said, "Oh—Thank you for helping me last night. It was a terrible imposition on you."

"You didn't force me to do it. I could have left."

"Well—thanks."

"It's all right."

I stood there looking at her and words were inadequate and I kissed her just as the taxi began to move again. There was no need to diminish the distance between our faces or estimate responses. I just put my arms about her as though it were a settled thing, and kissed her. There was no attempt to push her buttons or turn her on; no attempt to use the skill anyone gets after years of practice to make it lead to something else.

It was just a simple gesture of gratitude and affection, nothing more; and she returned it as though she were pleased, and nothing more.

No. I'm lying. It was a hell of a lot more. It was a good kiss and it lingered.

In fact, it took the taxi driver's reluctant "Hey, buddy, we're here" to pull me loose.

I said, "We'd better go, or I'll forget what I've got to do."

"Yes," she said, taking a quick breath as though to steady herself, "or I won't get that advertising campaign on the road."

I paid off the taxi driver, doubling my usual tip for no other reason than that I was in love with the whole world, and we got out. It was just beginning to sprinkle.

2   NELLIE GRISWOLD   10:15 A.M.

It was well after ten when we separated, she to take the elevator and I the escalator. We waved at each other cheerfully. It wasn't really a parting. I knew I'd see her again.

I went like a homing pigeon through the jungle of exhibits to the Hercules booth. There was a vague feeling of disintegration in the air. It was the last day of the convention and the booths would close permanently in early afternoon. The books and the placards and the gimcrackery would all be put away or discarded, and the shadow of that coming event reached forward.

Nellie wasn't there. I felt a touch of panic. Now that I was beginning to understand, I couldn't bear to have to wait to put the last pieces in place.

I said to the girl in the booth anxiously, "Where is Miss Griswold? Do you know?"

"She'll be right back," said the girl, with just enough hesitation and embarrassment to make it clear Nellie was in the powder room. That was good. They always return from the powder room. Its attractions are limited, I suppose.

I saw her from a distance, which is the advantage of looking for a person who is tall. I walked quickly toward her, hoping to keep her from being deflected.

"Nellie." I waved a hand. I had to do that, or she

wouldn't have seen me—the disadvantages of not being tall.

She said, "Darius. How do you feel? Have you had enough of this shindig yet?"

"Almost."

"As for me—quite. I'm going home tonight after the banquet and straight to bed. Then I'm not coming to work until Monday."

"Good," I said, quite willing to let her have a whole month off, if necessary, provided only she would give me the answer I wanted. I knew what the answer must be, but every notch I lowered the uncertainty, every link I didn't have to guess into existence, would make the structure so much firmer and the final gamble so much safer.

I said, "Listen, Nellie, I have to know something else about Giles Devore; you know, the autographing session." I looked up at her earnestly as I said it and it struck me for the first time that a girl could be grotesquely tall.

"I told you everything," she said.

"Just one point. Remember, he threw the red pen away when he was finished. The red pen you gave him."

"Yes, he did. I never picked it up. Do you need it? I doubt that we could possibly—"

"No, I don't need it. But when you brought it to him, he was sitting there with another pen, a pen that had gone dry. It was the second pen to have gone dry, and you were bringing him a third one."

"Yes." She had the look of one who was expecting to become confused at any minute.

"All right. Now the question is: What did he do with the second pen when you brought him the third? Did he throw it away, or put it down in front of him, or what?"

"Oh, gee, how do you remember? Well, he didn't throw it. He saw me coming—Oh, I know, he put it in his pocket."

I seized her hand and squeezed it as hard as I could. "Are you sure?"

She nodded her head vigorously, looking pleased that
I seemed to be pleased. "I remember now because he
gave me the feeling that he was afraid I would take the
pen from him and he was putting it away quickly. In
fact, I said, 'I don't want your pen, Mr. Devore. I'm
bringing you a new one.' Yes, I remember."

"Yes," I said, "his wife told me he always keeps his
dry pens. It was the throwing away of the red one that
was unusual."

I was trying to keep from prancing and Nellie said,
"Is that all you want to know?"

"Yes. It's all I need. Thank you so much." I had the
impulse to kiss her, but I thought of the upward stretch-
ing that would be required to place my lips on hers and
I thought, the hell with it.

3 SARAH VOSKOVEK 10:50 A.M.

Next, it was back to Sarah.

She'd had scarcely half an hour, but if she didn't have
the paper yet, I'd wait till she did.

I went through the door rather quickly. Ginger looked
up, startled; then recognized me, and waved me inward
with a smile.

Sarah was on the phone. She looked up and twiddled
her fingers at me, but stayed on the phone, talking rapidly,
then listening.

I was prepared to wait, but she pushed a Xeroxed list
across the desk at me.

"Already?" I mouthed, without making a sound.

She nodded and turned away so that she might continue the conversation without disturbance.

I picked up the paper with a certain quickening of
the heart beat. If it didn't work out correctly, then I
might be right even so, but less certainly, and I might
not have the nerve to try to spring the trap.

I went over the list of clothing and trivia (good God,
"one loose pill, apparently aspirin") quickly.

I didn't see it—went over it more carefully again—and again. It wasn't there.

I took a deep breath. (I must have been holding it and half asphyxiating myself.) Then I just sat there and thought.

It all worked out, but there was nothing absolutely compelling. It was all circumstantial and flimsy, and unless I could demonstrate something firm, no one would believe it. And to demonstrate something—

Sarah was off the phone and I hadn't noticed.

She said, "Darius!" and I could tell by listening backward (if you know what I mean) that it was the second time she had said it.

I looked up. "I'm sorry."

"Is that what you wanted? All I had to do was ask and they sent it right over. Is that okay?"

"More than okay. I know who killed Giles."

I was sure she would ask who, but she didn't. She said solemnly, "Are you sure you're right?"

"I'm sure, but I don't think I can make anyone else sure without something else. Listen, was Marsogliani in when you called?"

"He's in, but he's not in his office. That's why I managed to get the list so quickly. This is one of his mornings in Security headquarters in the basement."

I thought a while. Then I said, "What is your opinion of Marsogliani?"

"As a security chief?"

"Yes."

"He's been here ten years as far as I know and he's given satisfaction."

"What about honesty?"

"What do you mean, honesty?"

"Is he a criminal? Might he be involved in a drug racket?"

She stared at me as though I were crazy. "*He?* Never."

"That's just an impression, of course."

"Even so. He'd have to be the world's best actor to

be that dirty and give me the impression of being so clean."

"How long have you known him?"

"Since I've been here. Nearly seven years."

"And it is your personal and confirmed opinion that he's honest."

"Ab-so-lutely," she said, separating the syllables for emphasis.

"Then I'll have to take the chance. Look, Sarah, is Room 1511, Giles's room, still empty?"

She turned to the phone again. After a while she said, "Mr. Devore had it till today and his publisher had guaranteed it. It was no loss to leave it unrented till now, but there will be someone coming in, possibly as early as three P.M. today."

I looked at my watch. It was after eleven.

I said, "I'll have time, I think. I'll have to see Marsogliani."

"I'll try to get him up here, but when he's in the basement offices, he—"

"That's not necessary. I would rather go down and surprise him. Could you guide me down there?"

She sighed. "In the sense that I know the way, Darius, I could. But I've got to stay at the phone till the advertising campaign is settled. Please, I'll do my best to have him come up here."

"No. I don't want to get you involved. Can someone else guide me there?"

She rose and went into the outer office, then returned and said, "Ginger will take you. . . . You'll be careful, Darius?"

"Oh, I'll be careful, Sarah. What I need is luck."

Automatically, I put my hand to the top of my head. Yes, it still hurt. And I thought: I can't take another one just yet. It would very likely kill me.

She must have read my thoughts, for her face twisted and she said, "You're going to prove how tall you are again, aren't you?"

I stopped dead for a minute. "No," I said. "I know

how tall I am. I am plenty feet enough inches high. What I hope I'm going to prove is how smart I am."

And how much, I added to myself, a murderer I am.

4 ANTHONY MARSOGLIANI 11:20 A.M.

Ginger took me to the basement, then through a maze of corridors, to a glass door that was a sudden vision of light and hotel-modern furniture in the dull-ivory, pipe-ceilinged surroundings. My heart bounded when I saw Marsogliani through the door, with his vest and his half-burnt cigar. He was talking into the telephone.

I said, "Thank you, Ginger."

She smiled and left—rather hurriedly, I felt. Perhaps she expected a Homeric explosion inside the office and didn't want to be there when it took place.

The door wasn't locked (good!) and I walked in. Marsogliani looked up and I said, "It's all right. I'll wait. I'm Darius Just."

He looked slightly startled at first, and then heavily annoyed. "I know who you are," he growled, "but, as you see, I'm busy."

"I'll wait."

"I expect I'll stay busy."

I said, "All I need is half an hour. I'd rather not get mixed up with the police."

He did not react to that except to shoot me a glance from under lowered eyelids, but he didn't order me out. He said to the person on the phone. "Well, look, get back to me on that later."

He hung up, turned to me, and said, "What do you want and make it fast."

"Give me two minutes without interrupting," I said. "You've got a drug problem here. I know you have and you know you have, so don't bother covering up, but let me go on from there. I can break it. I can go to the police with this but that would mean a lot of trouble for me and, in the end, a lot of bad news for the hotel. If you help me now, you can take the credit for whatever turns up—I don't want any—and that will help the hotel."

He looked at me appraisingly and carefully disposed of his cigar, which stank abominably. "What's in it for you?"

"Giles Devore was killed because of something I didn't do—"

"That package of pens?"

"Yes. And I want to make up for it by getting the person who killed him."

Marsogliani sighed heavily and said something that was probably Italian. Then he said, "You want help? What kind of help?"

"I can lay a trap for the killer, if you help me. I'll need two people, you and your man, Michael Strong. We were all three up in Giles's room after I found the body and if we all three go up now, and if you give me fifteen minutes, no more, we'll have the killer."

"You mean, he'll walk in on us? He'll return to the scene of the crime?"

"I'm not saying it's a man," I said cautiously, "and I'm not saying it will be simple. But we three were there the day before yesterday with the dead body in the bathroom. We know what it was like then. We'll be able to understand what will happen, you see."

"No, I don't. Tell me what you have in mind, or get out."

"I can't tell you. I don't have the evidence and you won't believe me. But if I do get out, I'll go to the police. They might not believe me, either, but they'll have to check it out since drugs are involved and who knows what will turn up and how bad it will be for you and for the hotel. But give me fifteen minutes in Room 1511 and you'll have everything you want; and if I'm wrong, I'll just get out and forget the whole thing. The police won't be involved either way."

"Yes?" he said. "You'll just forget it? Listen, if you get me up there and the whole thing is a jackass screwball flop, then you're not just getting out. I'll help you out with a kick that will boost your backbone right up through the roof of your mouth."

"I'll let you do it. I'll hold still," I said. "How about it?"

There was a wait of nearly a minute, while I bet myself a despairing four to one that it wouldn't work. Then he said, "Do you want us all to go up together, or do you want Strong to join us up there?"

"All together," I said quickly, "but I want to go up by some route that won't take us through the lobby or any of the ballroom floors, so can you get Strong down here and then take us up the way you bring bodies down?"

"So no one will know we're in the room? And then the murderer will join us?"

"Just fifteen minutes is what I need."

"What will be the magic that will bring the murderer up there?"

"I've set it up," I said. "It will work. What can you lose? Fifteen minutes. In return you'll have the pleasure of hoisting me two feet with the toe of your shoe."

"By God," he said, "I'll pay fifteen minutes for that pleasure."

5   ANTHONY MARSOGLIANI   11:35 A.M.

Michael Strong was brought down by walkie-talkie. He saw me the moment he walked in and stopped in surprise. His sandy eyebrows lifted.

Marsogliani said, "Okay, Strong, we'll need your help. We're going up to 1511 and—"

"Where the guy fell in the tub?"

"Yes. This character here says if we go up and wait fifteen minutes, somebody is going to walk in and admit he killed the man. We're going to give him fifteen minutes and after that, if nothing happens, I want you to take him and get him out fast, because if you don't I intend to kill him."

"Let's go up," I said, trying not to let my voice quaver (God, suppose I'm wrong), "and it will be over by noon."

"*You'll* be over by noon," said Marsogliani, and there was no doubt of that in his voice.

Strong said nothing, but his eyes were opaque and hostile as well. I had no friends in that room, and I wasn't surprised.

We went up a freight elevator which was hand-operated. The operator greeted Marsogliani with a nod of his head and received nothing at all in return. We went up to the fifteenth floor, all of us, in silence. Marsogliani motioned me out first.

I leaned my head out to make sure there was no one in the corridor. We all got out and I whispered, "Which way?" I was disoriented.

Marsogliani led, walking quickly and surprisingly softly. We followed. There was only one place where we had to make a left turn and he motioned me forward again. There was no one there, either to left or right, and we moved on. Marsogliani let us in with his passkey.

There was the room, dead and lifeless, waiting for the next person to twist it into a faint echo of a temporary home.

Marsogliani looked at his watch. "It's eleven forty-two," he said. "I give you till eleven fifty-seven. Not a second more."

"Okay. Listen, can you have the door open so that someone can walk in without having to pick the lock."

"All right," he said. He left the door closed, but unlatched, then moved back and leaned against the bureau with his eyes on it. "Fourteen minutes," he said.

Michael Strong stood on the other side of the bed, also watching the door with a kind of fascination. And I watched with him, keeping my back to the damned bathroom.

Marsogliani said softly, "Ten minutes."

I said, even more softly, "You don't have to count."

I could feel a drop of perspiration gathering at one temple and beginning to trickle down my face. The air conditioning wasn't on, of course. I didn't want its noise drowning anything.

More minutes passed. I fumbled for a piece of paper out of the inner pocket of my jacket. It was the condensed program of the convention. I whispered to Strong, "Lend me your pen for a moment."

He said, in an ordinary speaking voice, "What?"

I motioned him to silence with an anguished gesture. "There's only five minutes left. Let me have your pen."

The tension had built to the point where all three of us were living in an unreal world, which was what I was counting on. Strong nodded, pulled out the left side of his jacket, and selected one of the three pens in his inner pocket.

"Not that one," I said urgently. "The other one."

He held out the pen he had taken. "What?"

"The other one," I whispered. "The other one."

And then as he stood there frozen in surprise, I lunged at his jacket, tore out one of the other pens, and threw myself over the bed to the other side.

The tension did its work and Strong broke apart. He let out a shriek of anger. "Give me that," he yelled. "Give me my pen."

"Why?" I shouted. "What's inside?"

He dashed around the bed and I tumbled over it again.

By now, Marsogliani had come to life with a roar. "What the hell are you doing, Just?"

"I've got a pen," I shouted, balancing myself on my toes and watching Strong sharply. "I've got his pen and I want to open it. Will you hold him?"

And Marsogliani began to see what was happening, so that when Strong dashed at me once again, he came up hard against the large man's vest. Marsogliani's arms moved quickly and, in a flash, Strong was whirled about and both his elbows were pinned behind.

"Watch out for his legs," I said.

"Stand still, Strong," said Marsogliani, "or I'll throw your arms out the window and leave the rest of you here. ... What have you got, Just?"

"A pen," I said, holding it out over the bureau, "and I'm opening it."

I held it point up, and unscrewed the body in a gesture that took the longest two seconds of my life, for if nothing happened now I was in such deep trouble that I couldn't begin to measure the consequences.

It came apart and a white powder spilled out upon the bureau.

I said unsteadily, "One will get you a hundred, Marsogliani, if that's not heroin."

It was not quite forty-seven hours since I had discovered the body.

6   ANTHONY MARSOGLIANI   11:57 A.M.

The next two hours were hectic. Strong went altogether wild and it took both of us to keep him down. His screaming, when it was coherent, removed any doubt that we had caught a link in the chain of drug transfer.

Marsogliani got out the other pens but didn't open them, and he called in other members of Security, who took Strong away and, I understand, put him "under restraint." Whether that meant handcuffs or being tied up or what, I didn't know and didn't care. It was Marsogliani's baby from here on in and that was all right with me.

He said, "How did you know?"

I told him, and he kept writing it down and staring at me as though I were crazy. He kept saying, "Was that all you had?"

Each time, I said, "It was enough for me."

"You took one hell of a chance."

"I had to. I had to build up enough tension to break him down, and I had to do it when you were around. I was told you were honest."

He didn't thank me for that. His look made it clear that he was annoyed at me for feeling that I had to ask. He said, "You'll have to talk to the police. Do you understand that?"

"I'll be in town and available whenever they want me. . . . You understand, he killed Giles Devore."

"That's as may be," grunted Marsogliani. "If that's heroin, and I agree with you that it probably is—"

"Come on, you heard him screaming to give it back or he'd be killed. Hell," I added feelingly, "he had someone try to kill me last night."

Marsogliani said, "Anything he said probably won't matter. He hasn't been warned, he has no lawyer. But if it's heroin, then he's had possession and we can go on from there."

"Okay, you got him. Hotel Security broke this thing and nabbed its own sour apple. Who knows what will be pulled down through Strong. The police will be grateful."

"Thanks," he said sourly, "but you'll still have to testify and I'd appreciate it if you would just give them the facts and speculate as little as possible."

"As long as you remember what the speculations are."

"I'm an honest man, you tell me."

The police came and it *was* heroin. I gave them enough information to explain why Strong was under suspicion. I also gave them the impression, without saying so, that I had shared my information with Marsogliani and that it was he who had laid the trap.

It was after two o'clock when they had had enough. They warned me to keep myself available, and gave me permission to go.

7 SARAH VOSKOVEK 2:30 P.M.

It was getting on toward half past two when I got down to Sarah's office.

Her first words were: "I know about it. It was Michael Strong."

I said, "Yes. Do you mind if I sit down?"

It was just a form of words. I sat down and stretched my feet out in front of me. "You've had lunch, I suppose?"

"No," she said, "I had to do something to get my mind off you and whatever it was you were doing with Tony, so I just pushed through the campaign and made the final decisions. It's finished."

"I'm glad, if it got your mind off my crisis."

"It didn't. But I had—"

"Faith in me?"

"No, I was too scared for faith. I had hope in you."

"I came through, so the hope was justified. I haven't had lunch, either. As long as you finished the project you were engaged in, how about calling it a day, and coming out with me?"

"I was wishing we could do so."

"Well, wishing will make it so."

She retired for a moment and I made use of the men's room down the hall (I could *not* have used the one in 1511), and then we walked out of the hotel into the light and air. What rain there had been that morning was over and the sun shone occasionally through the clouds. I put her into a taxi to get away from the scene more effectively than a walk would have made possible, and we went to a Scandinavian restaurant well uptown.

Since it was well past lunchtime, the restaurant was virtually empty and that was well. There was a small smorgasbord still available and we helped ourselves to it lavishly. Except for the filling of our coffee cups on two different occasions, we weren't disturbed even by a waiter.

Sarah said, "You discovered who it was this morning, didn't you? When you said something about a pen not being where it was supposed to be?"

I said, "I discovered it last night, I guess, when I was woozy and half asleep and the other half knocked out. When you told me what I had said, it came back."

"Could you explain it to me?"

"I'd love to. So far, I've told it to Marsogliani and the police but just as little as possible, and I would love to explain it exactly. It's all a matter of pens, you see, from beginning to end. There were the pens I forgot to bring up to Giles's room, the pens Strong was using to transport the heroin, the pens that went dry. If I were writing it up, I'd call it *The Case of the Three Pens*, but

Asimov will probably do the writing—I've got to get the facts to him—and he's committed to calling it *Murder at the ABA*."

She said, "Imagine carrying heroin in pens."

"Why not? Everyone carries pens; no one pays attention to that. And people are always borrowing pens. Anyone could approach Strong, borrow a pen, use it briefly, and return a different pen. And in a hotel, nothing is noticed. Who knows how many others elsewhere are doing the same thing?"

"Why three pens, by the way? You said *The Case of the Three Pens*."

I said, "That's in reference to the three pens Giles used in the autographing session. He had one pen with him to begin with, an old one. Call it Pen One. He should have had more, and he did—in the package I never delivered. And because I didn't deliver them, he went to the autographing session with Pen One and nothing else. It was an ordinary blue-black pen and it was monogrammed with his name.

"Pen One ran out of ink but, according to Teresa Valier, who was sitting next to him, he exchanged it for another pen with the person whose book he happened to be autogarphing at the time. Giles got a pen with ink, and the person in front of him got a souvenir with the author's name on it.

"So now Giles had Pen Two, and he no longer had Pen One. Pen Two also had blue-black ink but it was not monogrammed. Then Pen Two ran out of ink, and Nellie Griswold brought him Pen Three, which was red ink. When Giles accepted Pen Three, he put Pen Two in his pocket—he routinely hung on to his pens even when they were dry—so now he had both Pen Two and Pen Three. When he was finished autographing, he was so nearly out of his mind that he threw Pen Three away petulantly. When he went up to his room with you, therefore, he had only Pen Two in his possession. Is that clear?"

Sarah nodded. "Yes. But what follows from that?"

"Two hours later," I said, "when I was in Giles's room,

with Giles dead in the bathroom, there was a pen in the room. It was monogrammed and it was out of ink. It had to be Pen One. There was no sign of Pen Two. I didn't actually look for it at the time, not knowing it should have been there, but the police listing of his possessions included 'one pen, inscribed with name.' No other pen.

"The only way in which that could be is if between the time you left and I arrived, someone had come with Pen One, given it to Giles, and taken Pen Two in exchange. But the person who had Pen One was the person who had exchanged pens with Giles at the autographing session. Why should he now want to give up a valued memento in return for a pen he had already cheerfully given away and which was also out of ink?

"I'd have had no way of answering that, really, if it weren't for the little heap of powder on the bureau—which I was sure was heroin. Given that, I asked myself if the person who had exchanged pens had not inadvertently given the wrong pen to Giles. He had meant to give Giles a real functioning pen and, in the excitement of a chance to get the monogrammed pen, he had handed one over in which the ink reservoir had been clipped close so that it couldn't write for more than a few minutes and in which the internal space had been filled with heroin.

"He must have followed you two up to the room and waited for you to leave in an agony of impatience and uncertainty. After all, if, through his carelessness, anything happened to destroy the transport system, he could scarcely expect much of a life expectancy. If he got away from the police, he certainly wouldn't get away from his superiors in the racket. He came to the door so soon after you left, cutting it so fine in his anxiety, that you caught a vague glimpse of him.

"If he had been able to effect the change—and why should Giles refuse?—all might have been well for him. The trouble is that Giles had this habit of fiddling with pens and unscrewing them, especially when abstracted or distraught. He must have fiddled with Pen Two after you left, and the powder it contained had tumbled out onto the bureau.

"This couldn't have meant anything to Giles, but when the person made his entry and was ready to exchange pens, the sight of the spilled heroin must have driven him wild. He attacked poor Giles, who was completely unaware of what was going on, and, I suppose, killed him with a blow on the base of the skull. Then, thinking as quickly as he could, he got the clothes off Giles and tried to make it look like a fall in the bathtub.

"Of course, the murderer couldn't know that to strew the clothes about would be a dead giveaway to a few people, and that I was one of those few. It was a piece of incredibly bad luck for him. He took away Pen Two, but he should also have taken away Pen One and the spilled heroin. He didn't, but I'm amazed he did as much as he did. He must have been in one screaming hurry to get away, and forcing the clothes off a dead body and that dead body—a heavy one—across the room and into a bathroom must have taken time. . . . And that's it."

Sarah said, "No, it isn't. How did you know it was Michael Strong?"

"I didn't. Not at first. When the heroin I had first noticed was gone, I was convinced that Marsogliani had removed it to protect the hotel—and I didn't connect that with the murder at all.

"This morning, though, when I worked out the matter of the three pens and decided that the murder was part and parcel of the drug situation, I had to think it out again. The one who got rid of the heroin had to be the murderer, and that had to be Strong.

"It was Strong who was an admirer of Devore's and who had stood in line for the autograph. Rather cleverly, he found an opportunity to tell me this. I imagine he felt that if it had come out independently, then the mere fact that he failed to mention it might look suspicious, whereas a free discussion of the fact would be bound to make the whole thing seem innocuous, as indeed it did. He showed me the book and its autograph and I had no reason to doubt him. I even signed it myself.

"The only way in which he altered the truth was to say he was early in the line to make it seem that he had not been present at the time of the trouble with the dry pens. I had no reason to doubt that, of course.

"But once I began to focus on Strong, I remembered that the autograph had been 'Best wishes' in light ink and the signature in dark. I had attributed this to Giles's egomania, but now it seemed clear that it was at that point that Pen One had dried out and that the exchange had taken place. I actually saw half the writing with Pen One and the other half with Pen Two and that made Strong the murderer.

"It fit in with my feeling that the murder must have been the result of a man losing control, for on the occasions when I spoke with Strong privately, he seemed to me a man emotionally on edge.

"It's amazing, in fact, how the same facts change their character when seen from a new viewpoint. Strong must have remained near the room, or as near as he dared, after the murder—which was, after all, unpremeditated and undesired. He had to wonder when it would be discovered and how, and he would want to be there to establish accident from the start.

"He must have seen me go in. I heard footsteps in the corridor soon after entering and I'll bet they were his. He was into the room almost at once after I reported the death. I attributed his being upset to the fact that he was such an admirer of Giles. True, but he was also the killer of Giles.

"He worked overtime to talk me into favoring accident. He strenuously opposed the possibility of murder or of drug involvement. Naturally, I supposed he was protecting the hotel, not himself. But, of course, he was protecting himself."

Sarah said, "But why did he keep on using the pens after he had made that fatal mistake? He was still carrying heroin when he was caught."

"I don't suppose he had a choice, Sarah. He couldn't

let on that he had given the whole thing away or he was a dead man. He had to keep on as before, hoping he could cover up everything, not only from me and from the police but from his superiors as well.

"Where I made my worst mistake, unwittingly, was to seize the impulse of the moment just before the Asimov panel, when Strong and I were sitting together in the audience, to use him to check your story about the drug problem. I told him I knew about the system of drug transportation and that I knew that hotel employees were involved. It was a shot in the dark, and from his strong denial of the whole thing, I thought—sorry, Sarah —that *you* were the liar. I attributed his obvious fear and perturbation, once again, to his concern for the hotel, and that little bit of blindness nearly killed me —and you, maybe."

Sarah did not make any attempt to flatten me out for my lack of faith in her. She let it go and said, "You mean, after that he arranged to have you followed and attacked."

"I don't know what he told his bosses—that I was a private investigator who was getting too close? In any case, he was convincing enough, or his superiors were sufficiently casual about occasional liquidations, to have me marked for knifing."

Sarah muttered, "How horrible. What if they're still after you?"

"If they are, what can I do but try to be careful? I don't feel good about it, but let's hope that they're mainly interested in prevention and not in revenge. They'll be too busy trying to save themselves now, I hope, to get after me again. Besides, killing me will do them no good now.

"Anyway, the story as I told it to you is beautiful, but as Eunice Devore would say, a defense attorney would never let it get to a jury unshattered. In fact, on my logic alone, I doubt if Strong could be arrested, let alone tried and convicted. So I had to get Strong to break down in the presence of someone smart enough to see the significance and capable, besides, of taking the necessary action. That was Marsogliani, who, you assured me, was honest."

She said, "How did you know you could break him down?"

"I didn't know. I could only hope. Strong was on edge to begin with, and coming upon me alive this morning, suddenly and without warning, must have rattled him to the point of despair. When I got him up to 1511, he didn't know what he was waiting for or what I could possibly intend to do. He knew the murderer wouldn't come in, because he knew the murderer was already there. I watched the panic and tension mount in him, and I gambled that ten minutes of it would be enough to break him, if I struck suddenly."

"How clever," she said.

"How lucky," I said bitterly. "Lucky enough to prove myself a murderer. My forgetting of the pens brought on Giles's death. I had been hoping to prove that the pens had nothing to do with it."

Sarah said, "They had something to do with it, but everything in the world had something to do with it. Why did the pen have to run out just as Strong was standing before him? If it hadn't, all would still have been well. Or if Strong hadn't been impelled to offer a pen of his own. Or giving in to the impulse, if Strong had just handed him the right pen! Or if I had stayed with Devore in his room! Or if Devore hadn't fiddled with the pen he had and opened it! Or if Strong hadn't panicked! Look for responsibility and everything is at fault, including random chance and the victim himself. The only reason you so desperately want to be the villain yourself is—"

"That I am a romantic? That only people who are villains or angels are of interest to me?"

"Well?"

"Suppose I tell you that I discard all villains and angels? Suppose I tell you I'll settle for a woman I like?"

She flushed a little and said, "Well, it's over. I *hope*

it's over. . . . Will you be going back to the convention now?"

"No. I've had enough convention. The big banquet is tonight, but I won't attend. I have something much better in mind. What's on your schedule?"

"Nothing. The advertising campaign is taken care of and my son won't be back for ten days. I'll go to the office to attend to some little items and then I'm having at least a week off."

"Mind if I come back to your office with you?"

"Not at all."

"Good. I'm going to take off some time also. I think I've earned it. Why not take time off together?"

She smiled. "Now and then? Why not?"

"How about a late dinner tonight?"

"I'd love it."

"We could make up for what didn't happen last night, if you like."

"I might like."

8 SARAH VOSKOVEK 11:00 P.M.

We both liked. It was amazing how well she fit inside my enveloping arm.

She said, "This is much better than last night. How is your head?"

"Don't feel a thing," I said. (Not quite true, but true enough.)

She said, "What would have happened, Darius, if Marsogliani was in it with Strong? What if I had been wrong in my judgment of Tony's honesty?"

"Why, then," I said, "I'd be dead eleven hours by now. But I wasn't worried. I had had enough of doubting and suspicions as far as you were concerned. After last night, I was quite content to bet my life on you."

"Oh, God, if I'd known." Then she said, snuggling, "You're the tallest man I know."

"No, I'm not," I said contentedly. "I'm short. . . . But who cares?"

SPECIAL NOTICE

The 75th annual convention of the American Book-sellers Association *did* take place on the days indicated in this book, in a certain American city and in certain hotels of that city.

Some of the events did take place roughly as described. I, Isaac Asimov, *did* attend under instructions from Doubleday to write a mystery entitled *Murder at the ABA*. I *was* introduced to Cathleen Nesbit and Anita Loos (complete with pun) and to Douglas Fairbanks, Jr., as well. Fairbanks *did* speak at the Monday luncheon. Muhammad Ali, Leo Durocher, and Mrs. Namath were all at the convention at one time or another and there was indeed a panel called "Explaining the Unexplained" that included Walter Sullivan, Carl Sagan, Charles Berlitz, Uri Geller, and myself, though it was not quite at the time given in the book. On that occasion, I even made the little speech I quoted (more or less).

I also signed autographs on Tuesday (not Monday), but needless to say there were no untoward incidents on that occasion. The other person on the platform was Dan Rather, for whom the occasion was an unalloyed triumph (and whom I was delighted to meet and fawn over at the conclusion of the stint).

What's more, at least one of the incidents described as happening to Darius Just happened to me, actually. *I* came to the convention on Sunday, chasing in from out of state in order to make an appointment right on time, only to find that the appointment had been moved up for the reason actually given in the book.

Having said all this, and having written the book in such a way as to make it as realistic as possible, I am most anxious that no one think that the convention was marred by any such events as those I have described in the book, or that the hotel or hotels at which it took place were involved in any way in such things, or that any of the employees of the hotel or of the ABA, or any of the attendees of the convention, had anything to do with the incidents in this book.

I must stress that this book is a work of fiction; that the unnamed city and unnamed hotel in which the convention took place are, for the purposes of this book, creations of fantasy; that the murder and all the events connected with it are also completely imaginary; that no one who has a *speaking* part in the book—except for Isaac Asimov—has any real counterpart.

All my speaking characters are invented and if there is some resemblance, real or fancied, between any character in the book and anyone in real life, it is strictly coincidental and unintentional. In particular, Giles Devore (whom I didn't like), Darius Just (whom I liked) and Sarah Voskovek (whom I liked very much) are creatures of my imagination.

Finally, I must apologize for introducing myself into the book. It made sense (in my mind) to do this and it seemed to me that it lent authenticity to the story. I hope you'll agree that I didn't seize the opportunity to idealize myself at all. In fact, I had myself supply the comic interest and, in view of that, I hope you will forgive me.